TAMBOURINE

AF078101

Nily Naiman

Nily Naiman

All rights reserved, no part of this publication may be reproduced by any means, electronic, mechanical photocopying, documentary, film or in any other format without prior written permission of the publisher.

>   Published by
>   Chipmunkapublishing
>   PO Box 6872
>   Brentwood
>   Essex CM13 1ZT
>   United Kingdom

http://www.chipmunkapublishing.com

Copyright © Nily Naiman 2008

Chipmunkapublishing gratefully acknowledges the support of Arts Council England.

TAMBOURINE

I would like to thank my Husband, Howard Naiman for his help and patience.

Jason Pegler for publishing this book.

My son NoamNaiman for the photos and the hard work.

My son, Boaz Naiman for putting up with my repeated calls for help on spelling, on computer functions in general, and for believing in my story.

My daughter Tamar Naiman for helping with editing.

Mr. and Mrs. Gil and Nancy Hidalgo for help with the Spanish.

Miss Eunice Hidalgo for her creativity, her beautiful laughter, and help with editing.

Mrs. Evelyn Maldonado for her help with the Spanish.

And to all those who encouraged me to write the story.

TAMBOURINE

I salute the people of Spain for their courage and kindness in letting the World War II refugees from France into their country to find new life.

Nily Naiman

TAMBOURINE

Part One: Anna

(Introduction, Paris, 1927)

.

"Once upon a time, there was a pretty little Gypsy girl," Mama would start my favorite bedtime story, "far, far away in a land called Spain. The little girl was an incredible dancer. When she danced, she looked like she was floating on air. People passing by would stop and stare at the little girl, shaking their heads and wondering how anybody could dance like that.

"The little girl had beautiful wavy hair and shiny green eyes like emeralds. Everybody was struck by her beauty. More than anything in the world, the little girl wanted a tambourine, but her parents did not have the money to buy her one."
"Why, Mama?" I asked.
"They were poor," she said.
"What's 'poor'?"
"'Poor' is when you have no money to buy food or clothes," Mama explained.

I was silent. I was trying to understand how somebody could be poor. There was always plenty of food in my house, and my closet was full of clothes. Mama would have to force me to eat all the time because I never felt hungry. My aunts and my grandmas were always sewing fancy dresses for me even though I preferred to run around in pants and kick the ball with the boys. Mama would style my hair with all kinds of funny hairdos, using hairpins that hurt me. I hated that.

Looking at my closet, I decided I would give the little Gypsy girl all my stupid dresses and all the food from the kitchen. Mama smiled. "It's getting late Anna; you have to get up early for school."
"Mama, just a little bit more," I pleaded.

Mama petted my hair "Just a little bit more. One day, a good-looking prince passed through town. He was sitting in his coach, tall and handsome. All the girls were in love with him. The king was worried about his son. He brought him all the most beautiful girls in the kingdom to choose from. However, the prince was not interested in any of them. 'When I meet my true love,' he said to the king, 'only then will I get married.'

"The prince was the king's only son, and he would be the king one day. The wife he chose would be the queen. She had to be a fine, bright and beautiful girl from a noble background."
"What's 'noble'?" I asked curiously.
"Nobles have blue blood, which means that they all come from the aristocracy."

TAMBOURINE

"Madame Norine said all blood is red; there's no such thing as blue blood!"
"It is just an expression, Anna!"

Mama was starting to lose her patience; I could feel it in my bones. She closed the book. "Tomorrow we will continue. You have to go to sleep now." She kissed me on my forehead and left the room.

Paris-1942

Spring had come early to Paris that year of 1942. The fruit trees in our neighborhood were in bud, and soon the scent of flowers would fill the air. The birds would return from their far-off winter homes, and butterflies would be busily fluttering their wings around us. Also with us and growing slowly stronger was a new and not so pleasant sensation: a prevailing fear.

After the Battle of France, the National Assembly on July 10, 1940, had voted into power Marshall Petain, a World War I hero and the last president of the Council of the Third Republic. Petain suppressed the parliament and immediately turned France into a non-democratic state. The new government took its name from Vichy, the town southeast of Paris where it set up its administrative offices.

Nily Naiman

Many of the Vichy officials, including Petain himself, were reactionaries who saw France's defeat and subordination to Nazi Germany as a kind of divine retribution for the policies of France's left-wing governments during the 1930's. For them, an authoritarian government with a Catholic identity was preferable to a Republican government, even if it had to operate under the Nazi yoke. Others in the Vichy government were strong anti-Semites with open Nazi sympathies. As soon as the Vichy regime was established, it began taking measures against undesirables, such as Jews, Communists, Freemasons, Gypsies, etc. Jews were required to wear a yellow badge, and were prohibited from engaging in certain occupations. In addition, many of them had their property confiscated and turned over to the state, and were rendered destitute.

In 1942 police raids were organized against Jews in both the north and the south of the country. Many were sent to concentration camps in France and then sent on to extermination camps in Germany and Eastern Europe. Of all the nations in Europe conquered by the Nazis, France was the only one to voluntarily collaborate with them, and the only one in which raids against Jews took place on territory not occupied by Germans.

Not only minorities suffered under the Vichy regime. Shortages were common, and the government eventually had to issue food charts and tickets that could be exchanged for bread and meat. In addition,

TAMBOURINE

hundreds of thousands of French workers were involuntarily transported to Germany to support the war effort by working in essential industries. A general curfew required that at night all citizens close and shutter their windows, and not venture outside without official permission.

    I stood in front of the mirror holding the bar in the dance studio, behind the rest of the girls. Mme. Natalie poked my shoulder. "Arabesque, Anna, arabesque!"
Mme. Sophie tapped on the piano impatiently. I stretched my back and my neck, standing on my tiptoes, and turned my head to the side. For twelve years I had been dancing at Mme. Natalie's studio and had hated every minute of it. All the girls there were from wealthy homes. I went with them to the same school and would see them around me for most of the day; I had no interest in them. We all were educated to grow up to be refine ladies and wives, in spite of the fact that our school put on us girls the same academic demands as it did on the boys. Nevertheless we knew that the world did not expect any of us to make a brilliant career.

    I would go home and shake my head to let my hair fly all over my shoulders. I would put on shoes with strong wooden heels and start dancing. I tapped my feet wildly and imagined myself dancing to the music of the Gypsy guitars, castanets, and drums. I was dancing for hours imagining men around me, dark skinned and dark eyed, looking at me passionately. My body was covered with sweat, my nipples hardening, and the men clapping their hands. Faster and faster I moved my body, swaying my thighs and hips seductively. I was Carmen and all the men were crazy with desire for me. I was beautiful, I was dancing, I was flying!

A handsome young man came toward me, tapping his heels, and handed me a tambourine. I slapped it against my thigh; the chills went up and down my spine. He placed his hands on my shoulders and danced around me in perfect rhythm with my movements. He was beautiful, his dark eyes shining with desire and his body perfectly created for the dance. I gazed straight into his eyes as we slowly turned round each other. Then he kissed me. His lips were burning my lips; I held him, feeling his fire inside me.

"Anna, what are you doing?" Mama came in looking at me as if I was crazy.
"Mama," I said, "I told you to knock before you come in."
"That will be the day… that I would have to knock on my own child's door," said Mama. "Look at you, all red and sweaty, jumping around wild, what am I to do with you? When will you learn to behave like a lady? You are being talked about already; people in the synagogue are looking to see if you are a right match for their sons. You are driving me crazy!" Mama sighed.

I smiled at her. I was an only child, and all her life was about my well-being. If she would know that it was she who had planted the seeds of wildness in me

TAMBOURINE

with her Gypsy stories. If she would know that I was going every day after school to the outskirts of town, where the Gypsy wagons were parked, to watch them dance and sing. If she would know what was in my wild mind as I looked at the dark men dancing flamenco, peering at me, narrowing their eyes like wild animals. Mama would lock me up in the house and would never let me out.

The Gypsies were called the filth of Europe. They were not allowed in our schools. We were warned to stay away from them. They were dirty and had lice in their hair, and all they wanted was to steal from you and kill you. This we were told from the time we were little children. Just as we were taught to stay away from stray animals, so we were taught to stay away from Gypsies.

They were not allowed to live among the ordinary citizens, but instead were forced to live on the edges of the towns and cities. Even those who could have afforded to buy a house were forced to live in wagons. The laws against Gypsies were clear and had been in effect in France for a long time. The Gypsies were considered sub-human. But I had an attraction to them, a wild attraction that I could not control. Their music and their dance were too sensual to resist. More than anything in the world I wanted to become a true dancer, to tear up my ballet clothing and dance without restraint, like the Gypsies, to dance in a way that moves the body with an uncontrollable fire from within.

Nily Naiman

I could not hold myself. I would stand for hours on the street corner and observe them, the way they lived, spoke, sang and danced. Their musicianship fascinated me. It was unbelievable to me how each of them could master their stringed instruments. Sometimes I would find myself starting to move my feet to the music, and it would be hard to maintain control.

I would make sure to have some coins and candies in my pockets to give to the children who were getting used to my presence. One little girl in particular would wait for me to come. I would give her a coin and she would take me to the camp to see her family dance. The young men were surprised at first. I was blond and very European looking, with my expensive clothes and shoes. Little Gisele would hold my hand, sensing my nervousness, and would put me in a safe spot and then join her people dancing.

Slowly I started getting attached to Gisele. She was a smart little girl, and she immediately detected that it was the dance that I was interested in. She introduced to me her sisters and started teaching me some steps. She would teach me how to speak her language, which was a mix of Spanish dialects. She would see me coming from far away, and would come running to greet me, tapping her little feet, giving me her hand and dragging me to where her people were dancing.

The men would stand with their violins and guitars, in an extraordinary ensemble of music.

TAMBOURINE

Women and men would dance; the air would fill with passion. People would clap their hands to the rhythm faster and faster as the dancers would move to the music, sweating, tapping their heels, stronger and stronger. The girls now would raise their hands, clicking their castanets above their heads, swaying their bodies and stamping their feet faster and faster, dancing the flamenco of the *Gitano*, the Spanish Gypsies. Gisele would twirl around, her eyes gazing at the distance as if she were in another world, in another time. I would start clapping my hands together with the others, trying to compose myself, my legs itching to move to the melody,

"My love is sitting
By my wagon.
I stop and watch him,
Maybe this time he will turn around.
I would run and tell my father
To start preparing for my wedding,

"You don't like me because I am dark,
And I can't help it.
But I love you so,
More than you'll ever know.

"I love you so,
I would wait for the rest of my life
For you to turn around
And look at me standing by.

"A Gypsy girl
Wanders the streets.

Nily Naiman

If you want me to love you,
Then turn and look at me.

"If you truly love me,
Then give me your heart.
I'll sway my hips,
And give you my soul."

Gisele would give me a wise look and smile, "Come dance with me." She would pull my hands; her brothers would look at me, waiting. They would giggle among themselves, wondering if I could do their steps. I would shake my head "no" to disappointed Gisele. There was no way I would give them reason to make fun of me. As far as I was concerned, just as when I was five years old listening to Mama's stories, I would still readily rid myself of everything I had and become a Gypsy, as long as they would play the violins and the guitars and let me dance with them and sing with them.

I would be willing to sleep outside freezing in the cold, starving to death, begging for mercy from the gendarmes (police). As long as they would let me dance, I would do anything.

One day I passed by the music store and saw a tambourine in the window. In a sudden urge, remembering the story about the little Gypsy girl and the tambourine, I walked in and bought it. I would give it to Gisele, I thought; she would be happy. Gisele looked just like my Gypsy girl from Mama's story. She had dark soft hair lying on her shoulders, wild and untamed. She had emerald green eyes and danced like

TAMBOURINE

a butterfly. Babies who could barely walk were dancing. I would just stand there, my body aching from the desire to join them. If I could give up everything I had, my fancy home, my meals, my expensive clothes, I would get into the rags they were wearing and become a Gypsy in a second.

The Gypsies would cook outside in the street on an open fire in big pots. You could smell it from far away. It seemed that all the wagons were one big family, cooking in the same pots and eating from the same dishes. The children were always fed first and always washed first. The adults always had a little child on their knee or in their arms. The teenage boys would carry the babies and rock them to sleep just as the girls did. The babies and the children were the center of their lives. I would watch with envy and think that these were the most wonderful people on earth. Why did everyone hate them so much?

I loved the simplicity of the lives of the Gypsies, the down to earth attitude, the free spirits. Those people were so poor; they had nothing to wear, nothing to eat, no education, no land, they had no possessions whatsoever, but they had each other. They had their heritage, their music, their dance and somehow their beautiful independence. You have to get rid of all possessions in order to grasp the real beauty of life said a wise philosopher; he must have been thinking of the Gypsies.

Papa had already left for the clinic when I awoke that morning. Mama was listening to the BBC.

"Hitler is rounding up all the Jews in Germany and Eastern Europe now and sending them to concentration camps," she said in horror.
It all seemed so far away to me. Mama and Papa were talking about the war constantly, and I was used to being called dirty Jew. I was trained to say, "I am French, I am Christian," to people I was not sure about. My blond hair and fair skin helped.

I had a couple of Jewish friends from the synagogue, but most of my acquaintances were girls from my private school. They were rich and shallow and had no idea who I was. As long as I was wealthy and could afford to go to that school and to the ballet classes, they figured I was all right.

The horror stories about the Nazi regime kept coming to us from all sides of Europe. Jews were rounded up everywhere, and killed. There were rumors about ghettoes, the confiscation of Jewish property, and the torture and murder of Jews. We were used to being "the Jews" in my neighborhood, but the idea of the French government letting the Germans come in and take control of the country and kill us all was absurd to us. The French government was on very good terms with Hitler. Petain assumed that the Germans would leave him alone as long as he would cooperate with them.

TAMBOURINE

Andres

I could not find Gisele that day. It was early afternoon and the hot sun was beating on my head. The Gypsy camp was quiet; not many people were to be seen. I walked toward the wagons of Gisele's family, the package in my hand. I was dressed in my school uniform and my hair was collected in a ponytail.

The Gypsies were eyeing me, wondering what I was doing among them. When an outsider would hang around in their area, it usually meant trouble. Soon the French police would come and tear babies and children out of their parents' arms and would take them God knew where, claiming those kids were being abused by not living in proper homes. There would be screaming, and the mothers would roll on the ground at the policemen's feet, begging them to let the babies stay. Most of the time they would be kicked and shoved, and would never see their children again.

I stopped one of the women and asked her about little Gisele. She pointed to a wagon. I went to it and knocked. A young man whom I recognized opened the door. I had seen him dancing many times. He was taller than I. His eyes were a dark chocolate color and his hair, black as charcoal, was grown long, falling on his shoulders.

He was good looking; I could see the resemblance to Gisele. He leaned against the entrance and just stared at me silently. I blushed and lowered my head. His eyes were piercing my body. "You are

Gisele's friend," he said.
"I have this to give her." I handed him the package, turned around, and started walking away.

"What's your name?" He stopped me.
"Anna," I said.
"I am Gisele's brother," he said. "My name is Andres. They all traveled to the south for the festival. I will give her your gift."
"Thank you," I said, and turned again.
"What do you want with Gisele? Why are you coming here all the time?" he asked.
I stood with my back to him. "I don't know," I mumbled.
He touched my shoulder; I turned to him. The sun was striking our heads. He was sweating, his sweat licking on his face, it was a boiling hot day,
. "Come on, I will get you some water from the river," he said.

I walked behind him saying to myself, turn around and go home, what are you doing? But my feet kept after him unwillingly until we came to the bank of the river. I looked all around. We were alone. He could do whatever he wanted with me. I could scream and nobody would hear me. He smiled at me and bent down, collecting water in his palms and bringing it to my mouth.

His dark eyes were drawing me in. He was the most handsome young man I had ever seen. I drank right out of his hands; it was both strange and amusing. I started giggling. He bent to the river again and

TAMBOURINE

brought me some more. I took a drink, holding on to his arms, and said "Your turn."

Now I bent down and collected the fresh water in my palms, and he held on to my shoulders. I felt my head spinning; my body melted to his touch, and he drank. We smiled at each other. "I will go for a swim," he said, "it is too hot." He took off his clothes and walked into the water. I looked around nervously; nobody was there. I wanted to turn around and just walk away, but my feet would not listen to me.

He swam for a while, watching me standing there frozen in place, the sweat streaming down my face, and said, "Come on, come for a swim."
My clothes were all soaked from sweat anyway. I would go in for a minute just to refresh myself, and come out right away. I gestured to him with my hand, "Turn away! Don't look!"

He giggled and turned around. I removed my clothes and stood there naked, the sun against my fair skin. I took the ribbon off my ponytail and shook my head, letting my hair fall on my body. I looked up to see him standing in the water gazing at me. "You are as beautiful as an angel."
"And you are an idiot!" I said angrily, running into the water and splashing him with all my might. "You promised not to look!"
He laughed and dived under the water. I could feel him swimming around me, brushing against my body, and right near me, round and round me. I tried to catch him but he was fast. He was an excellent swimmer.

I walked deeper into the water and started swimming away from him. The water felt cool and fresh. I was feeling as wild as the river itself. I wished I could stay there in the water forever. I continued swimming further, and then I felt his arms around me. He was holding me tightly. "You're going too far. You'll drown."

I pushed him away. "I can swim; leave me alone." I could feel his muscles against my body. "You don't know this river. There are undercurrents. You can be sucked under the water in a second and drown."
I looked at his face; I held on to him, my hands around his neck, and felt helpless to fight my attraction to him. He took me closer to the bank; I could feel the ground at my feet.

We were together for a long time. It was silent around us. I put my head on his shoulder, and felt his fast heartbeat. His heavy breathing was mixing with mine. I closed my eyes. If I could, I would stay there in his arms forever.
He kissed me, "You must be a dream."
I looked at his dark eyes. "I have no shame," I said.
He smiled, and held me tightly in his arms, "My shameless angel," he said.

He carried me out of the water like a baby, and laid me down on the sand. We were silent for a while, and then I said, "God will punish me for what I did."
"God never punishes true lovers," he answered quietly.

TAMBOURINE

"My God does," I said.
"Everybody has the same God," he raised his head looking at me.

The sun had started to set. "Andres, let me go" I said, putting on my shirt, "my parents will kill me; I have to go right now." I collected my wet hair into a ponytail.
He was watching me and smiled. "Say you will be mine before you go."
"Walk me home and I will consider it," I said.
He put on his clothes. "You sure you want to be seen with me?" he asked.
"Why wouldn't I want to be seen with a nice man like you?" I asked,
"I am a Gypsy. You might get into trouble."
"And I am a Jew," I answered angrily. "We are all in trouble already."

"We know that we are in trouble," said Andres solemnly. My father and uncles have been talking about it for months. The police are taking the Vichy laws against Gypsies more and more seriously. We are thinking about leaving France altogether. We have family in Spain, where life would be safer for us."

I was silent. Were the rumors that had seemed so distant now becoming reality? Could my own country that I had been brought up to love and identify with actually see me as an undesirable to be gotten rid of? I was a young Frenchwoman primarily and a Jew incidentally. France was all I knew.
"I am so sad," I said. "What kind of world are we

living in, where the stupidest, narrow-minded idiots decide who is worthwhile and who is not? At least you have someplace to run away to. If I were forced to run, where would I go?"
Andres smiled. "There's room in my wagon for you."

Ah my Gypsy soul

I walked through the streets with him, catching the wondering looks on people's faces. What was a well-to-do young woman like me doing with a Gypsy? Andres was smiling at me as we were walking arm in arm. "They are all hypocrites," I said. "Each one of these fancy lady pigs would have you right now in the middle of the street if they could."
He giggled and said, "I would not touch any of them; you are the only one for me."

Andres had the movements of a young tiger. I had seen him dance, and he was incredibly good. When he danced, it seemed as though the ground was burning under his feet. He was powerful and his dance was sensual but strong. I started singing,

"They're going to round up all the Gypsies tonight

TAMBOURINE

And kick them out of town.
You are my Gypsy lover,
Hide yourself and run.

"Ah my Gypsy soul,
I am a sad woman today.
My heart is crying for my love,
They will take him far away."

He was smiling. "You sing well, and you are not even a *Gitana*."(Gypsy woman) As he walked beside me his feet touched the ground so elegantly that the ground seemed to be bowing to his footsteps.
I squeezed his arm. "Teach me to dance," I said.
He smiled, "Only if you promise to dance just for me."
"I promise," I said, and stopped in front of the house. "This is where I live."
He looked up. "I wonder how it is to live in a real home."
"I don't know how long they'll let us live in our real home. Anyway, I prefer to live with you in a wagon, as long as you teach me how to dance."
He touched my hand and asked, "Tomorrow? You will come to see me tomorrow?"
I nodded my head and walked in.

Mama was hysterical, "Where have you been? I called all your friends. Who was that Gypsy boy with you downstairs?"
"I fell into a puddle. He helped me out," I said.
Mama gave me a doubtful look. "Anna, what are you doing?"

I did not answer. Every time I lied, Mama would sense it right away.
"You will mess up your life if you continue with this wildness," she said.
Papa came in. "What happened?" he asked, and put his bag down.
"Nothing," said Mama, and rushed to the kitchen to bring the dinner.

He patted my head and asked, "What is going on, princess? You look different."
"I am in love," I whispered to him.
Papa smiled. "Somebody I know?"
I shook my head. "Better than anybody you know."

Papa's family had come from Russia. They had fled the pogroms and settled down in the south of France. Papa was the only boy out of four kids. His three sisters were always getting into trouble, and Papa learned from a very young age to protect them. My grandfather opened a general store and they all had to work there.

Papa was a bright student. He managed to get into medical school and became a popular doctor. Everybody wanted only Doctor Gross. He was pleasant, knew how to listen patiently, and was excellent in his diagnoses. Patients would fill up his clinic from wall to wall, and Janet, his nurse, would complain to Mama that he never refused any patient. He treated everyone from the aristocracy to the homeless, and of course would never charge those who were too poor to pay.

TAMBOURINE

"They're saying the Nazis are going to be here soon," I remarked. "Mr. Herbert, who is a fascist, said they will come and clean up the country."
Papa looked up at me. "From what, if I may ask?"
"From human filth," I said.
Mama shook and said, "Stop talking like this, Anna."
"He was clearly looking at me when he said that," I added.

"What human filth is he talking about?" My father was angry, "He is the one who is human filth!"
"Jews and Gypsies, what else?" I answered.
Mama gave me a warning look.
"We should stick together, the Gypsies and us," I said to Mama's horror. "We should all fight Hitler and the pig-headed fascists of this damn country. It does not belong to the Nazis or to the Vichy traitors; it is our country!."
Mama put her palm to her mouth to choke a scream, and Papa patted my shoulder. "You might become the pride of this century one of these days, princess."

I stood under the shower for a long time, letting the hot water warm my body. I wrapped my body in the towel and started dancing, tapping my feet to the sound of the guitars in my head. I will be the best flamenco dancer ever, I said to myself. I got into bed. I hugged the pillow, imagining him in my arms. God forgives the lovers, I thought. God will forgive us. I closed my eyes with a feeling of relief and hummed to myself, as happy as I had ever been. Andres would be my destiny.

*"I am jealous of the ground,
That carries your footsteps.
I am jealous of the cloth
That wraps your body.
Why did we have to meet?
I am doomed to spend my life in sorrow.*

The secrets of the flamenco

By the beginning of 1943, I could dance very well with the Gypsies. I would hurry every night after Mme. Natalie's class to where Andres was waiting for me. We would run beneath the lights of the city hand in hand to the wagons. We felt desperate because time was running out for us. Andres kept telling me that his father was determined to leave and was trying to convince the elders in the settlement that there was no alternative.

Andres wanted me to agree to join them, but how could I do that? I felt so torn. How could I leave Mama and Papa? I was about to finish school, and planned to go to university, perhaps to study medicine like Papa. Anyway, Papa said that the Vichy craziness would pass, that it could not go on indefinitely, and that

TAMBOURINE

the Nazis would never come because they had too much on their hands in the rest of Europe.

I felt so much love for Andres. We were young. In another world we could have all the time we wanted to see each other, plan our future, and let things develop as they developed. But our world was what it was, and I knew that separation was inevitable.

Andres taught me how to dance flamenco. "I can teach you basic steps; the rest must come from your heart," he said. "Flamenco is a dance that comes from within. The more fire you have in your heart, the better your dance."

The Gypsies would light their fires outside, and men would emerge with guitars and other instruments. Andres would start hitting his heels to the beat. All heads would turn to him once he started dancing. I learned how to move my fingers to the music. "The more you stretch your fingers," Andres told me, "the more elegant you look."

After twelve years of study I could dance well. I could stand straight, hold my neck high, and move my body to the music. Andres taught me how to hit my heels to the ground and move my arms to the sounds. "Move your fingers as if they were the wings of birds," he said. "Feel the beat inside your soul, and let it fly through your fingers. When you dance flamenco, you display all your sensuality; you give it all you have within you."

Nily Naiman

Gisele would strike the tambourine and dance with me. Her sisters would wrap my thighs with a Spanish skirt. I learned how to wave it at the right moments. Andres' family received me right away, without any special ceremony. His mother would brush my hair, enjoying touching my blond curls, and called me "Hija" (daughter) right away.
"*Tu le gustas a mi hijo, y sera's mi future hija*" (my son loves you, I will treat you as my daughter), she said as if it was just the most natural thing in the world.
His brothers and sisters and cousins would gather all around us. They would clap and play their instruments while we were dancing.

Andres was the firstborn. He had six brothers and sisters. Their ancestors had fled from India many generations ago and had wandered through the Middle East into Europe, being kicked out wherever they went. The British called them Gypsies because they were thought to have come from Egypt. Of those who were now living in France, not many had settled down in the area of Paris. The majority were living in the south. Many in Andres' family were across the border in Spain. Not that Gypsies were welcome there, but the Spanish had less strict rules against them.

Andres' father insisted on staying in the city. From time to time people would give him some jobs and he would be happy to do any work in order to feed his family. He was an excellent worker and would be hired by the engineers in town for their home building projects, even though the law did not allow anybody to hire Gypsies. Some of them worked in the fields, some

TAMBOURINE

in factories, for very little pay. All this had to be in hiding so that the police would not find them. That would bring disaster upon themselves and their employers.

The year 1942 was the worst for the Gypsies. Children disappeared by the hundreds and were found dead. The police would enter the Gypsies' camps and beat them or shoot them like dogs for no good reason. The Vichy government adopted the racist ideology of the Nazis and hunted minorities like animals. We Jews suffered as well. More and more government officials were pushing for laws against Jews. I personally felt the spreading, anti-Semitic cancer through the hateful looks and nasty remarks of my teachers. Many of my friends and family suffered. Jews were fired from jobs that they had held for years, expelled from schools, and no longer accepted in the universities.

Shops and businesses would be robbed in the middle of the day. People would be attacked and violated. The police would not lift a finger. Any crime against Jews became acceptable. Mama would beg Papa to leave. "Let's go to Palestine. Over there we will be able to live like human beings."
But Papa could not bear the thought of leaving his patients.

By the end of October of 1941, the government had passed the "Statute des Juifs" (law of the Jews), that excluded Jews from public life, required their dismissal from positions in the civil service, the army, commerce and industry, and barred them from participation in the professions including medicine, law and teaching. At last there was no choice. It had been more than a year since the laws were passed, and none of the officials could do anything more to help us.

Papa left his clinic and all his expensive medical equipment to the government, and went home. Mama was begging him again to leave, but Papa kept saying he would wait until the madness was over. It was just a phase, he said. When people would come back to their senses his patients would still need him. In the meantime he would take care of them at home. He set up an office in an empty bedroom, and the doorbell was ringing all hours of the day and night. Some of his patients who were government officials told him they would never trust another doctor to care for them. They made my father swear not to tell anybody that they had been in our house using his services, and in return they would not put his name in the lists of Jews that they were sending daily to the Vichy police.

In 1939, before the Nazis invaded France, the French government had opened camps such as Gur and Noe designed to receive the Spanish refugees escaping from the fascist regime of Franco. The French police guarded these camps, and in the summer of 1940 handed all the refugees over to the Nazis. They were quickly transferred to various concentration camps in Germany and were not heard from again.

I asked Mama and Papa many times what we were waiting for. It was clear that sooner or later the Nazis would come to take over supervision of the

TAMBOURINE

French police. Then we would be transferred to concentration camps. But Papa said the Nazis would never come because the French police were doing a good job for them. They had taken all that they could take from the Jews, and robbed and beat them regularly.

We had to start wearing a star saying "Juif" (Jew) on our shirts. I never wore it, in spite Mama's nagging. "Let them kill me, I will not wear a tag like a cow." And I did get away with not wearing it because of my very fair skin and blond hair. I had a Christian appearance. I did not know exactly what a Jew was supposed to look like. I assumed that the anti-Semites had their set assumptions about Jewish faces.

My appearance was very Slavic thanks to my mother's side of the family. Police never bothered me on the street. I would walk with my back straight and my head high, swaying my dancer's hips side to side, as if I were the queen of France. The police officers along with the rest of the male population would look after me longingly, and I would smile to myself at the stupidity of the human race.

Monsieur Bernard

Monsieur Bernard, my principal, came to pull me out of class one day and brought me into his office along with twelve other students. We looked at each other and realized that we were all Jews. Monsieur

Bernard was a good and gentle man. This unpleasant ordeal was hard on him. He was my father's patient and would come to our house to see him. My father had delivered all his children. His wife swore by my father. She would never use another doctor. She told her husband that the Jewish problem was not her problem. The fascist garbage did not interest her at all, as long as she could run with her sick babies to Dr. Gross any time she wanted.

Monsieur Bernard stuck his nose in the papers and coughed, clearing his throat. "I am sorry, but the police are forcing me to send you all home. Jews are not allowed in this school anymore."

It struck me hard. The ground felt unsteady beneath my feet. Now it has come, I thought, the end of everything. No more country, no more university, no more future. I'm an outcast. I'm unwanted. What do I do now?

Marie, one of the girls I knew, started crying, "Please, Monsieur Bernard, we have less than a year to finish high school. Let us finish our exams first. We will never be able to go to university if you kick us out now."

Moise, one of the boys in my class, smirked, "You will not live long enough to see a university."

Monsieur Bernard got up and shook each of our hands. He lowered his head and said, "I am ashamed. I am ashamed to be a Frenchman today. You children be strong. It will be over soon."

As we left the school I told Moise, "It will not

be over soon; it's only the beginning."
Moise gave me a pained look and said, "It's time to leave this country." He closed his fists. "I will go to the south and cross the border into Italy."
"Where did you get the idea that the Italians want the Jews? Mussolini has become Hitler's best friend," I said. "By now he has probably handed all the Jews in Italy to the Nazis on a silver platter." I sighed, "Forget it, Moise, they don't want us anywhere; it's too late to run."

    I walked to the Gypsy wagons; I would not go to my ballet class today and face another "unpleasant" kick. I would rather lie in Andres' arms, where I was always welcome. I called for him. His mother came out of the wagon, crying. "They took the boys!"
"Who took them?" I asked.
"The police," she said. "They barged into our camp at 4:00 in the morning and took all the males ten years old and up to work."

    My knees felt weak. I had to sit. Not my Andres, I thought, they better not touch my Andres. I started sobbing. I felt helpless. Very soon they will round us all up and kill us, I thought. The Nazi machine is not going to stop until they see us all dead. All French Negroes had already been deported God knew where, and the Jews and Gypsies were sure to be following right after them.

    It had started to get cold. Winter was approaching. I shivered, and thought, Andres didn't even have a decent jacket. I would go home and gather

all the sweaters and jackets that we never wore and bring them to his family.
Little Gisele came out with her tambourine and sat on my lap. "Anna," she said, "I am hungry."
I stroked her hair. "Mama didn't feed you today?" I asked.
"There is no food left," she sighed, holding her stomach.
I got up, "I will be right back," I said.

    I hurried home. To my relief Mama and Papa were not there. I packed up whatever I could find in the refrigerator and then filled up a bag full of clothes and jackets from Papa's closet. I hurried out of the house. Gisele was waiting behind the gate, her face full of tears.
"Did you follow me?" I asked, "What happened?"
"Anna, come fast," she sobbed. "Andres wants you."
I held her hand. "Help me first; there is food here." I handed her a bag. "Let's go."
"They came back all bleeding. They got beaten up badly by the police. They opened up *payee*'s scalp, beating him with a baton. All the men in the camp are hurt," she cried.

    The anger was choking me. I was furious. The French dogs had no mercy, no brains. I saw Papa getting off the bus at the street corner. He came toward me, looking older and tired. He seemed to have shrunk in the last year. His back was hunched now, he had lost a lot of weight, and his hair was all white.
"What are you doing here, Anna, why aren't you in school?" he asked and looked at me and little Gisele

surprised.
"Monsieur threw all the Jewish students out of school by order of the police," I said quietly. "Come with me Papa, I need your help."

He looked at me puzzled. "What's in the bags," he demanded. "Where are we going?"
"Come on, Papa, there's no time to lose!" I pulled his sleeve and he walked behind us, carrying his doctor's bag.

Papa.

Gisele was walking with us silently, sobbing from time to time. We entered the Gypsy camp, and my father looked at me confused. "What are we doing here, Anna? You are going to get us into trouble!" he hissed angrily.
"Papa," I said. "There are a lot of hurt people here. They cannot afford a doctor. The police worked them all day and beat them mercilessly. Some probably need stitches and urgent care; you must help them immediately!"

Papa sighed. "What is this to you, Anna? How did you get involved with Gypsies? We are all going to be arrested."
"You are a doctor," I said. "You must help these poor

people. We will all be arrested anyway; we're all considered subhuman!"

I climbed into Gisele's wagon. Her mother was crying. The boys and their father lay there motionless, only uttering an occasional cry of agony. I gave the mother the bags and said to her, "Here is some food and warm clothes. We have to bring everybody down, one by one, to my father. He is a doctor; he'll take care of them." I bent down by Andres.

His face and arms were horrifyingly bruised, and his nose was bleeding. I ran my hand gently along the side of his face. I had spent enough time in my father's clinic to know exactly what to do. "Get me some warm water," I told Gisele, "and some clean cloths."

Outside my father was working quickly and silently. There was a long line of beaten men and boys waiting to be stitched. I started working on Andres' wounds. Very soon Papa would have to send me home to get more antibiotics. Andres was weeping in my arms, and I was comforting him.

"Shh, don't talk, relax."
"You know what we were doing all day?" he stammered.
"Shh," I whispered soothingly, kissed his bruised face, and continued trying to stop the flow of blood from his nose.

"We were building a concentration transition

TAMBOURINE

camp," he sobbed. "This camp will be called Drancy. I heard the guards talking. By June of this year they are going to gather all the Jews in Paris, lock them up there, and then from there send them East to the concentration camps in Poland. We're supposed to report to work every day until Drancy Transition Camp is ready."

I felt my entrails growing cold, all the rumors were right.
"We were working all day since four o'clock in the morning, nonstop, carrying blocks, mixing cement, and chopping wood with no break, no food, and no water. If we stopped for even a second, they would beat us all over our bodies, and that was if we were lucky.
The unlucky ones were beaten on the head. Many of them lost consciousness, and some even died!"

He started choking from the pain and tears. Andres was now coughing loudly. I held him, the anger running through me.
"We cannot go back there tomorrow," he said. "We have to run away."
"If they catch you, they'll kill you," I muttered.
"They will kill us anyway, whether we go back there or not. We have to run away; we must leave Paris or it's the end of us.

"I have to go too," I said in sudden clear realization.
Andres looked at me relieved. "Do you really want to go? I would never have suggested that to you, knowing that you would not leave your parents behind."

"I don't know," I said, "but today they kicked me out of school because I am Jewish. Tomorrow they will come for all of us. It has gotten to the point where we have to flee too."

I left the wagon feeling weak. My body started rocking from side to side. Papa saw me and said, "I'm out of medicine; go home and get me some more." Andres' mother started feeding her family. "I will get more medicine for my father," I said to her. "And then I am planning to join you. We are all going to die if we stay here. I will pack up and get ready to leave with you as soon as it is dark."

"I'm not sure I want to go," she said in anguish. "It's starting to get cold, the police are everywhere, how are we going to survive"?
Rachelle, Andres' older sister, said "Mother, if we stay here, we will never survive anyway. At least let us try to find a way to live."

Andres had three sisters and four brothers. There were the two beautiful older sisters, Rachelle, twenty-four, and Nadine, twenty-two. Then came Gisele, who was eight years old. Andres was the oldest of the sons at twenty-one. He was followed by Pablo, Paco, Michel, and little Nicola who was six. All of them looked strong enough to walk and maybe to do some work.

There were stories that just in the last year 250 Gypsy children had been taken to the concentration camp at Buchenwald in Germany, and had been used as

TAMBOURINE

guinea pigs for the testing of Zyklon-B cyanide gas crystals. All the children had died. For three years we had been ignoring the rumors about mass murder of Jews and Gypsies all over Europe. It had gotten too close to home now. We had to get away no matter what.

      I helped Andres dress in one of my father's better outfits. Nobody would bother us looking like this. I let my hair fall over my shoulders. We would look like young lovers. I leaned on him and said. "If my family decides to stay in Paris, I will still run away with you, Andres."
"I was hoping you'd say that," he answered.
I rubbed my lips against his face. The night was cold. I warmed his hands with my breath. . "As long as we are together we will survive." I kissed his bruised face and snuggled deeper into his arms.

      He looked different in my father's clothes and leather jacket. The hat covered most of his hair and bruised face. I looked like an ordinary French girl. "We could cross the border with no trouble," I said. "I have some money saved. It will last us for a while, and then we can work. You pack your violin. We can play and dance for living as we go from place to place."
Andres held me tight, leaning on me, sighing from pain. "You are not going to be comfortable with all the family traveling for weeks in a wagon"
"If you are there with me I will be comfortable enough" I answered.

Mama

We entered the house. Mama ran to me and hugged me. "I was so frightened," she said, "Where have you been?"
"Mama, this is my friend Andres," I said, pointing to Andres who was standing there appearing confused. He smiled and said, "You have a nice home, Mrs. Gross."

Mama looked at him in horror, his dark features, his bruised face. "What are you doing with him?" She squeezed my arm.
"Andres is the man I love, Mama." I put my hand in his hand. He linked his fingers around mine firmly to assure me.

Mama sighed and sat down. "Where is Papa?"
"He is at the Gypsy camp taking care of wounded people there," I said. "I came to pick up more medicine for him."

Andres told her the story of what he had gone through. Mama shook her head. "I told Papa we should have left a long time ago; it is too late now."
"It's not too late, Mama," I said. "I am planning to leave tonight. I am not going to fall into their hands. Andres and I are going to try and cross the border into Spain. You and Papa should come with us," I said.
"You can't just go!" She raised her voice. "You can't

TAMBOURINE

just decide what to do without our agreement."

Andres squeezed my fingers. "I have decided, Mama," I said. "They kicked all us Jews out of school today. It is the end, and nobody here is listening to logic. I am not going into the Nazis' teeth. I want to live, I want to survive, I will not stay here and wait for them to come and kill me."

"How can you leave your family like this?" Mama was crying. She had lost all her rationality. I put my arms around her. "Mama, I love you. We want to save ourselves. It's the right thing to do. Come with us. We don't have to separate from each other."

Mama looked at me and sighed, "When did you get the idea that you are suddenly grown up enough to make decisions for the family?"
"I turned eighteen six months ago, Mama," I smiled.
Mama wiped her tears and thought. "I cannot leave grandfather and grandmother alone here, Anna, and I am not strong enough for such a trip. I will stay here with Papa. I am not sure you are right."
Andres said, "As long as I am alive Anna will be fine; I promise you."

Mama had never spoken to a Gypsy man before in her life, and she fully believed all that she had always taught me about them. "Where did you come from? What business do you have with my Anna?" she asked.

"I love Anna, more than life," said Andres softly.

"Love her? What do you kids know about love? And Anna, do you have any idea what kind of hardships you'll be facing, running from place to place as refugees?"

"Mama, what is a greater hardship than just sitting here waiting for the Nazis to kill us? Andres has a strong and loving family. We will all protect each other. Come with us. If you stay here it will be your death sentence."

"No, Anna," she said and hugged me. "I do understand. I should let you go; maybe you are right, maybe it is not too late. I will stay here with Papa. With God's help we will see each other after the danger is over. You go on your way. I will never forgive myself if I will force you to stay and something awful happens to you.

She helped me pack up medicines and handed them to Andres. I gathered more warm clothing and food. "Mama, take care of yourself," I said, feeling my heart shattered to pieces.

She kissed me. "God be with you, children."

I hugged her, tears flooding my face. It had suddenly hit me clearly that I would never see her again. Mama was always in control, always on top of me and Papa, of the household business, of my affairs, my life. Mama was an authority always, and now she seemed so weak, so frail, as if she had shrunk.

"Go!" she pushed me. "Go to Papa. Make sure you take some of the medicines with you for the trip." She shoved me a package. "You have enough money

TAMBOURINE

here for a while. Be careful; the police are everywhere."

We left the house and started walking silently. Suddenly a gust of wind blew across the street, rustling the branches of the trees. I shivered, and tied my hat. Andres was walking beside me, his head lowered, holding the packages.

"Andres," I said.
He looked at me in sadness.
"What's the matter?" I asked, "Why are you down?"
He shook his head. "I hate to take you away from the life that you had, that house, your parents, everything. I have nothing to offer you," he said.
I dropped the packages on the floor. "You are everything for me! You have the world to offer me. I am not taking another step unless you tell me that you understand that."

When we arrived at the camp, I walked over to my father and said, "Papa, I am leaving tonight."
"I know," he said, as he was stitching a boy's head. "Andres' father told me that you would be leaving with his family." The Gypsies had brought their horses out of the stables and tied them to the wagons. There were at least ten wagons ready to leave. Andres held my hand. He turned to my father and said, "Please bless us. I love your daughter. When all this is over I will marry her."

Papa was tired. He must have stitched fifty heads that night. He shook Andres' hand. "Take care

of her. She is my only child. If we survive this ordeal, I would like to see you two wed properly."
I hugged my father with tears in my eyes. "Take care, Papa," I said, my heart sinking.

Andres' mother handed Papa a glass of water and tried to convince him to eat something, but Papa had to go. I watched his frail image leaving the camp. Andres put his arms around my back and kissed my neck. "Come with me," he said, "we have his blessing."

We went to the wagon in the back of the camp. He laid me down gently on the hay. I had so much I wanted to say, but all I could mumble was "I know I have made the right decision" I closed my eyes letting my body and soul drift with his to another world.

Gisele

When night fell and Andres' father came for us, we were lying in each other's arms half asleep. "The wagons are ready," he said, "we must leave now!"
I kissed Andres. "It's time to go."
He pulled me back to his chest. "Not yet."
"Come, we must leave now, we will have plenty of time to be together from now on. "
He got up unwillingly and we dressed ourselves.

We climbed into the family wagon; it was time

TAMBOURINE

to move. "Don't rush! One wagon at a time!" shouted Andres' father, "we don't want to draw attention." The wagons started rolling. We would have to get as far as we could from the camp, so that when the police would come early in the morning to round up the men for work, they would be unable to chase us.

The women in the wagon were curled under their blankets dozing. Little Gisele was sound asleep holding the tambourine in her hand. I covered her well with the blanket and kissed her forehead. She was moving, mumbling out of sleep. I wrapped myself in my coat and lay down, dosing off. From time to time I would open my eyes to see Andres in the coach seat beside his father, looking over his shoulder at me. "I am fine, son, you'd better take a short nap," his father said. Andres turned into the wagon and lay beside me. I cuddled against him, listening to the slapping of the reins, the galloping of the horses, there was never more pleasant music than that.

For several days we were riding through the forest uninterrupted at night and stopping to rest during the day. Andres and his father would take turns at the reins. I would help the women with the cooking and washing and taking care of the children.

One morning when I woke up Andres was not near me. Gisele was sleeping peacefully, her head touching mine. The wagon was not moving. I got up and looked outside. It was early. The women were by the fire, cooking. We were in a forest of pine trees, the wagons parked in a circle. The horses were resting, drinking by the river. I rubbed my eyes and got down from the wagon, went over to the fire, and washed my face with warm water.

Nadine handed me water and bread. "Where is Andres?" I asked.
"He went with my father to survey the area," she said and then put her arms around me. "I'm so happy you came with us. My father had a big argument with the camp's eldest, and they insisted on staying. Only few families decided to leave."

"Why?" I asked. "They will be killed, if not by the Nazis, then by the French police."
"They call themselves Gypsies" she smirked, "but when it's time to move they all back up."
I drank my water and ate my bread slowly. The forest seemed peaceful. Andres and his father were coming back on their horses. I walked toward Andres and hugged him. His father said, "You two need to be wed; you can't continue to live in sin."

Andres laughed, "Is that what people are saying, father?"
"This is what I am saying," his father answered, "Tomorrow night at our next stop you two will get married."
I looked at Andres. He smiled at me and then put his arm around me. He dragged me to the wagon and pulled me into his arms. "I am a Gypsy in love," he said. "I am a crazy Gypsy, crazy in love with you."

TAMBOURINE

The blast of a shotgun startled us. We froze in fear. Andres got up. "Don't move," he whispered, "they might be looking for Jews." He grabbed his violin and the guitar and went out.
 I tried to look outside through the open crack in the doorway, but could only make out Gisele's little shoulders, shaking in the distance. It was quiet except for the occasional cry of one of the babies. "Who is in charge here?" I heard a loud voice asking.

"I am the head of the camp," answered Andre's father.
"What are you doing here, all of you in the forest?" demanded the voice.
"We are a traveling Gypsy musical group; we are heading to town to perform," the father answered.
"Gypsies," said the voice, "they are just filthy Gypsies. You should be all burn with the Jews," he spit on the ground and shot his rifle into the air again.

I opened the door a bit more; there were four policemen on horses. I choked back a scream. Then I saw little Gisele get up and hit her tambourine. The men looked at her as if they were bewitched. Andres started strumming his guitar and a second later Paco picked up the violin. Gisele was striking her tambourine against her thighs and was dancing flamenco, holding the side of her skirt and waving it with the music with her free hand.

The police were watching the girl's slender hips swaying. The Gypsies started moving to the music, the men clapping rapidly and the women dancing to the rhythm, whirling rapidly and singing,

"Ale' ale 'oh
Ale' ale' oh
Vengo Gitano
Vengo Gitano
Ale 'ale;' ale 'oh
Ale' ale' ale' oh
Le 'e' le' le' ... "

The policemen too began clapping to the music. They could not resist its power. They were smiling

now, clearly in a better state of mind. Then as the music died down Gisele bowed to them and smiled one of her most beautiful smiles. One of the policemen looked at his friends and then threw his cigarette to the ground. "That little girl just saved you. Don't let me catch you in this forest again. Get your stuff together and get out of here," he said, and they kicked the horses and rode off.

I got down from the wagon and caught Gisele in my arms. "You are the bravest girl I have ever seen," I said, and kissed her. She clung to me. "Why do they hate us so much, Anna?"
"Maybe because they are jealous," I said. "They are jealous of your beauty, your talent, your free, beautiful spirit. The truth is everyone would like to be a Gypsy, but no one admits it."
Gisele nodded her head, thinking about what I said.

"Get in the wagons," said Andres father. "We

are going right now! From now on before we stop we have to make sure there are no police patrols anywhere."
I squeezed Andres' hand and he smiled to me and murmured, "We will finish what we have started tonight," putting his guitar back in its case.

We walked to the wagon. The women were hugging Gisele and patting on her on the shoulders. "One day," I said, "you will be a famous flamenco dancer; you will be the most famous *Gitana*. People will come from all over the world to see you dance." Gisele held her tambourine and smiled, "This is my dream, Anna," she said.

Once upon a time there was a little Gypsy girl

The wagons rolled. I knelt behind Andres, my arms around his back. His father held the reins. "The farther we get from the city, the fewer police there will be," he said. "We must make good timing today. We have to ride until night and cannot stop any more." Andres held my hands, his fingers linked with mine His father smiled and said, "You still getting married tomorrow?"
"Father, we will get married tomorrow even if the entire French police force comes to attack us."
His father laughed and slapped his shoulder. "It's fine,

son, you will get your wedding."

We rode for a week without incident. The women would prepare the meals inside the wagons, and we were napping most of the time. As we traveled south it seemed to get colder. "The winter is going to come early this year," said Andres' mother.
I crawled under a blanket and Gisele joined me. "Tell me a story, Anna," she said.

"Once upon a time there was a little Gypsy girl," I started.
Little Nicola came and snuggled with us under the blanket.
I held the two kids. "The little girl was an incredible dancer. When she danced it looked like she was floating on air."
"Was she a *Gitana*?" asked Nicola.
"She was the most beautiful *Gitana*; she had wavy black hair and green eyes just like emeralds."
"She looked like me?" asked Gisele.
"Just like you," I said, and pinched her nose.

"People would stop to look at the little girl dancing and wonder how anybody could dance so beautifully. They would freeze in their spots and look at the little girl and say, 'this is not a dance; this is magic.'"
"Like *Tio* (uncle) Jacques, he can do magic," said Nicola.
"With cards and also with coins," said Gisele.
"All *Gitanos* can tell fortunes," she added, "that's magic."

TAMBOURINE

I kissed both their hands "You are magic," I giggled.

"More then anything in the world the little girl wanted a tambourine, but her parents were too poor to buy her one," I continued.
"What's 'poor'?" asked Nicola.
"Like us," said Gisele.
"But you have the tambourine Anna bought you," said Nicola.
"Yes, but we don't have a big house and a lot of food," answered Gisele impatiently.
"Are we poor, Anna?" Nicola asked me.
"You are very rich," I said. "Look around you. Who else in the world has such a big family that loves you and cares for you? You can play music, you can dance, and you are a proud Gypsy."

Nicola's eyes started to close. He put his little hands on my stomach; Gisele put her head on my chest. It seemed that the noise and movement of the wagon would go on forever. I closed my eyes. "More, Anna, tell me more."
"Sleep a little now," I said, "I will tell you more another time."

When we woke up the wagons were still going. I looked at my watch. We had been riding more than twelve hours. It was seven in the evening, and already dark outside. Andres was holding the reins by himself.
"Where is your father?" I asked.
"He is sleeping inside. We have been taking turns sleeping."
I tied my coat around me; the shawl was covering half

of my face, shielding it from the bitter cold. I sat by him, gazing at the dark. "Are all the wagons behind us?" I asked.
"I hope so," he yawned. "They are supposed to be following each other's signal lanterns."

"Let me hold the reins," I said, "You are tired."
"Now when you are near me, I am not tired any more," he said.
"Did you eat?" I asked.
"A little," he smiled, "how much stale bread can you eat?"
"The horses are very tired. We should stop for the night," I said.
"I am looking for a good spot," he said, "I will stop soon."
I put my arm around his shoulder and rubbed my face in his cheek. The night was clear, the sky filled with stars.

We entered a forest. Andres slowed down and brought the horses to a stop. "There must be a river here; this will be a good place for the night," he said. The others circled around. We counted ten wagons. Everybody was there. We could see lights far ahead. "It must be a village," I said. "We might be able to buy meat from them."

The men and women were untying the tired horses and preparing water and hay for them.
"Somebody has to go check the area, to see if it's a friendly village." said Andre's uncle.
"I will go," I said. "I look like ordinary French girl;

they might be collaborators." I took my shawl off my head and shook my blond hair to make it fall over my shoulders.

"The girl is right," he said, "let her go with three of the men to guard her." He gave Andres some money. Buy some meat," he said. "If all is quiet we shall celebrate your wedding tonight, my boy."

Andres handed me a knife. "Use it if you have to."
"Why?" I asked, looking at the thing in my hand, feeling the cold metal shivering my spine.
"You never know," he said. "Hide it in your skirt."
I pushed it under the skirt against my thigh and got on the horse. We started silently toward the lights. Andres was riding next to me in front and his cousins Pablo and Antonio were behind us.

Meat

The woods were quiet. We were on the side of a road, proceeding parallel to it. "I am crossing; I am going in," I said.
Andres handed me a whistle. "Blow it if you are in trouble. We will hear you and come right away."
I put the whistle around my neck and rode into the village slowly, taking stock of everything around me. It was a cold night. People would have finished the day and would be sitting by their fireplaces at this time. I was thinking about the fancy fireplace we had in Paris. Mama would bring hot cocoa on a night like this, and we would all sit in our pajamas by the fire listening to

the radio playing American music.

I tied my shawl around my head and got off the horse. I was standing in front of a house that was clearly a farmhouse. I tied the horse and knocked on the door. An older man opened, and asked "Yes?" I removed my shawl and shook my head. "We are merchants passing by, looking to buy some meat. Do you have any?"
"Pierre," he yelled. A young man came to the door and took a surprised look at me. The old man said, "She wants to buy meat."

The man rubbed his chin and narrowed his eyes. "Who are you?"
"I am from Paris. I am with a group of merchants. We need some meat."
"Paris," he mumbled looking at me and then down my figure, "How much meat do you need?"
"Enough to feed about fifty people" I said.
"Fifty of you are there?" he looked out.
"They are all waiting for me on the road." I started getting nervous. "You want to sell me meat or what?" I asked, patting the knife on my thigh.

The two men looked at each other. I could hear noises of kids in the house, and a woman yelling angrily. They had a whole family in there, I thought. It calmed me down.
"We will slaughter a cow and cut it for you," said the young man. "You can wait here in the house."

I went inside. It was a simple house. Children

TAMBOURINE

were running around and there was an older woman knitting by the fireplace. A younger one was in the kitchen. I smiled to her and said, "Nice home you have."
"You want coffee?" She asked.
"I would love to," I said.
She handed me a cup. "It's cold out there. Normally not too many people pass through our village at this time of year."
"Is it a big village?" I asked. "Is there a school, stores, police, post office?"
"No," she shook her head, "from here to Dijon is about half an hour's ride; over there you can find all the services."

    I drank the coffee; it tasted good. The kids came running to the kitchen and the woman said to them, "Look at you, filthy as Gypsies! What will our guest think? Go wash your hands and face!"
"I did not know Gypsies are filthy," I said, against all the rules of survival Andres had lectured me before we left.
The woman looked at me wondering. I smiled, "Any Gypsies who worked for us in Paris were pretty clean."
The woman shook her head. "Well, we had some near Dijon and they were filthy."
"Where are they now?" I asked.
"Thank God," she said. "The police came one night and cleaned them all out."
"And what did they do with them?" I asked.

    "Well, our Vichy government has rules now, right? No Gypsies running around in France any more.

Thank God for President Petain. He is getting rid of all the human trash in our country, the Jews, the Gypsies, and the Negroes. This country will become a safer place to raise our children." She took a deep breath, looking very proud of herself after enlightening me.

    I kept watching the door. Andres would get worried and ride right into the teeth of these villagers. "I have to go; it's getting too late," I said. "Your husband is taking too long."
"My husband will be back with your meat soon. Don't worry," she said.
"He is taking too long. We have to reach Paris by morning," I said to make her think we were going the opposite way in case she got any ideas.

    As I walked outside she ran to look for her husband. "They are coming now," she shouted to me. They were carrying the packages in sacks. I tied them to the horse and paid them. "I must hurry. We have to get to Paris," I said.
"You going north?" the young man asked.
"Yes," I answered, "We will find a place on our way and cook your meat. Thank you." I paid him, and went on my way. When I got to the road I could see Andres smiling in relief.
"Why so long?" he asked, "I was worried sick."
I looked over my shoulder. "Let's go," I said, "I will tell you later."

TAMBOURINE

The wedding

We rode silently back to camp. The men all came surrounding me. "What happened?" Andres' father asked.
The men unloaded the meat and brought it to the women to start cooking. "It's safe here for tonight, but we have to change direction." I said. "They are hunting for Gypsies here. The woman told me the Vichy police came and took all the Gypsies out of this area. God knows what has been done to them."

"What do you suggest?" he asked me.
"I think we are getting too close to the Swiss border. We should go more inland. The closer we are to Switzerland, the more Vichy police there will be hunting for Gypsies and Jews. If we go deeper into the forests, we have more chance of meeting resistance fighters who might help us."

The men talked with each other and started examining the maps. Andres and I strolled off hand in hand, trying to sneak away from everyone. The women ran and surrounded us giggling. "Where do you think you are going? We are preparing a feast for you," said Rachelle. "You better come with us." She pulled me behind her.

The young men came and dragged Andres away. The women took me to one of the wagons and removed my clothes. "My god, Anna," Nadine gasped. "You are so light," she said, looking amazed at my fair skinned body.

The women all took a step backward looking at me. I was trying to hide my breasts with my hands, and Gisele said, "Anna is not just a woman, she is an angel; that is what Andres says."
The women giggled and brought hot water and soap and started washing my body and my hair.

"You know," said Sara, one of the cousins, "I was in love with Andres for years until you came and stole him from me."
"I am sorry," I said.
"Many girls were in love with Andres in the camp," said Nadine. "You were not the only one."
"Don't pay your mind to her; he never gave her a second look."
"Sara I am sorry," I said again.

"Don't worry," she smiled. "I have my eyes on somebody else already."
"You see?" said Nadine sponging me as hard as she could, "she is stupid."
"And you are an old maid; you and Rachelle are too old to get married," snapped Sara.

Gisele rushed to defend her sisters, "They had millions of marriage offers. Did you have any?"
Sara did not answer. She was brushing my hair silently and started sobbing.
"What you crying for, stupid girl?" asked Nadine.
"I am scared. I am afraid we will never see our old camp again; we will never see Paris again."
Nadine countered, "Who wants to go back to Paris

TAMBOURINE

anyway? You will see better camps in the south that are full of *Gitanos* just waiting for us Parisians to come and save them from their loneliness."

I could smell the meat cooking on the fire outside; I was craving hot food. The smell got into the girls' nostrils too. "I am hungry," said Gisele. "Stop the talking. Let's finish and go to eat."

They dressed me in a long, wide skirt with colorful flowers, and tied bows to my braids. Gisele also decorated her tambourine with bows. Outside the tables held an abundance of cooked food. The people formed a circle around Andres and me. Andres was standing tall and handsome in a black suit, his hair combed to the side.

Gisele was my choice to be my bridesmaid since it was she who had introduced me to the family. Pablo was Andres' best man. We exchanged vows and people stood in line to shake our hands. Pico and Pablo started playing the violin and the guitar. "Dance," they ordered, and a bottle of wine was passed around. I pulled Andres to the table and served him meat and rice, and then filled my plate. As we ate, the men were stamping their feet and the women started clapping and dancing for us.

"In a world of turmoil,
In the grim world of hate
You and I
Would tie the knot.
Le' le' le'

*Ale' oh
Ale' ale' oh."*

I squeezed his hand. "Andres let's go." We got up and the assemblage applauded us. Andres' mother came, kissed us, and said, "I could not have dreamed of a more beautiful bride than you."

The girls brought me to a wagon that had been prepared for our wedding. The girls removed my clothes and rubbed my body again with perfumes and oils. Then they covered my naked body with rose petals and leaves.
"You are going to have your wedding night with tree leaves," Nadine laughed. "We couldn't find many roses."
I threw the petals at the girls, and Rachelle and Nadine caught some and put them in their breasts. "We are next," smiled Rachelle, and they left the wagon laughing.

In the light of the kerosene lamp I could see the sheets ready for us. On the hay the pillows and blankets were new. "Look under your pillow," he said.
The package contained a small jewelry box. I opened it to find a gold wedding band in a braided shape. I kissed Andres. "It's beautiful" I said.

He put it on my finger and then kissed my fingers one by one. I removed my gold necklace with the Star of David and put it around his neck. "That is all I have to give you," I said sadly.
"I will never take it off, my love," he said, and then lay

TAMBOURINE

beside me on the blankets.
Andres kissed me. "My wife, you are my wife now," he said in disbelief.
I pulled him into my arms and we became one.

When morning came we woke up in each other's arms, "Don't go," he held me tight. "If you love me, don't move."
I rested in his arms kissing his hand, "I am the luckiest man on this planet." He said.
I untied myself from his arms, put on my Gypsy skirt, and brushed my hair.
"You look like gold, *Gitana*," he said in a satisfied voice.
I made a turn holding the edges of my skirt and stamped my foot in a flamenco move.
"Come dance with me," I said

He got dressed and then gave me a bullfighter look, and started stamping his feet and clapping his hands. I turned around him, raising my chin, moving my fingers to the sound of his heels. Then he caught me in his arms and held me close.

There was a knock on the door. "We have to move, kids, you have had enough," we heard Andres' father calling. We walked outside. Andres' father shook our hands and patted Andres on his shoulder. "A Gypsy is not a real Gypsy unless he is married to a pretty girl," he said.
Andres smiled and said, "The prettiest of all."

Nily Naiman

A fancy Parisian

We went over to our wagon and prepared the horses. We would follow a new trail now deeper into the woods and the fields, riding south through Bourges to Limoges into Montanan. Then we would make the turn to Montpellier and Arles. From Arles we would try to cross the border into Spain. The people of Spain were known as good people. They would probably receive us. The Franco government's affinity with Hitler had allowed Spain to take a neutral position in the war. They were being left alone by the Germans, at least for the time being.

As I climbed the wagon, the women all congratulated me. Andres' mother and Rachelle gave me silver bracelets for my wrists and ankles and Nadine handed me a pair of castanets. I kissed them. I loved my presents. Andres' mother handed me water and bread and said, "My son chose well. May I live to be healthy, to see my first grandchild coming to this world."

The wagon started moving. "We are heading in the direction of Tours. We will ride most of the day and stop only to rest the horses," Andres said. "Tell the women to get some rest." I put my arms around him and kissed him.
He held my hands, pulling them to his mouth, rubbing his cheek on my arm.
"You are a happy Gypsy" his father said.

TAMBOURINE

"I am," Andres nodded.

I entered the wagon and lay down. I was the happiest woman in the world. I closed my eyes and fell into a deep sleep, not even feeling the little ones Nicola and Gisele snuggling against me under the blanket.

We were on the road for several weeks. The winter arrived with all its might. It was December, our food supplies had been seriously reduced, and some of the children had gotten sick as the cold, bitter winds blew mercilessly through our wagons.

As we got deeper inland, we had to be more careful. The Germans, as we heard from villagers on the way, were pouring into France after heavy losses on the North African front. The French police, the German troops, and the SS were in a frantic search for the remaining Jews and Gypsies. Ten wagons would draw too much attention. We decided to split up into two groups. Five wagons would wait behind for three days and then follow. We were among the five that were left behind; it was a blessing for the exhausted horses.

As usual I was sent to survey the area. I was very quick by then to be able to tell a friendly village from a hostile one. I came to realize that the French population generally was divided as to pro-Vichy and anti-Vichy sentiments. The farther south we traveled, the stronger were the anti-Vichy feelings, whether the people hated Jews and Gypsies or not.

This worked well for us. Ever since the Germans had broken the treaty and come into France there were more and more people willing to help us. I would say that I was a merchant traveling north with my workers and people did not doubt me, thanks to my appearance and the educated manner in which I would speak to them. The men would wait for me at the entrance to the village. I always had my whistle and my knife with me, and would come back to them with information and meat.

At one village I rode in hoping to buy enough meat and grain for three days. Andres blew me a kiss while I entered the gates. It was a neat little place. Wooden fences surrounded the small homes, and smoke billowed up from the chimneys. It was early morning; the village was waking up. People were feeding their animals in their yards. From one of the homes came a young woman holding a baby in her arms. I stopped my horse and asked, "Have you got some chickens or meat to sell?"
She pointed toward her house. "Go talk to my husband, I have to go to work."

I tied the horse to the fence and knocked on the door. A young heavyset man opened it and looked at me, surveying my body up and down. "Your wife said I might be able to buy some meat from you," I said.
"Who are you?" he narrowed his eyes.

"I am a passing merchant from Paris. I have to buy some food for my workers," I said.

TAMBOURINE

"Fancy lady from Paris, ha?" he said rubbing his face.
"How much meat do you need?"
"I will take six chickens and grain or rice if you have," I said.
"How you going to carry it?"
"My horse is outside."

"Where are you coming from?"
"Limoges."
"Lots of Germans now in Limoges, ha?" he said.
"Lots of Germans everywhere," I said, starting to feel nervous.
"Good for business," he said.
I nodded my head, "The food monsieur?"

"Twenty-five francs I give you six chickens and a sack of rice" he said.
"For this price I can get ten chickens and three bags of rice from your neighbors! *Merci* (thanks), goodbye." I turned to go.
"*D'accord* (fine), wait!" he called out to me. "I give you seven chickens, two sacks of rice, and one sack of potatoes."
"Fine, make it quick or my men will get nervous."
"What men? I don't see any men," he said looking around.
"They are there, don't worry."
The man came out and said, "Wait here, I will go prepare the food for you."

I walked into the house and turned on the radio that was on the table to try to pick up news. It was harder to get the news the farther we journeyed from

Paris. The local stations just broadcast music, as if there were no war, and no refugees like us trying to escape like hunted animals.

I walked around the living room and the kitchen. It was a simple home. On the table were two Sabbath candleholders, a menorah and a silver wine cup. I was surprised; that couple did not look Jewish at all. I sat down. I missed Mama and Papa. God knew what had become of them. The rumors were that most of the Jews in Paris had been rounded up and sent to camps. Papa has too many connections, I said to myself. Somebody would hide them if things got too serious.

The man came in with the sacks, noticing me looking at the candles. "Pretty, ha?"
"Pretty" I said.
"They rounded up all the Jews in the village. I was quick to take some souvenirs," he giggled.
"Who rounded them up?" I asked.
"The SS and the Vichy police" he said.
"Where did they send them," I asked.
"To Auschwitz," he said. "That's a place where they know how to deal with Jewish scum," he smiled.
I got up feeling nauseous "Tie the sacks onto my horse" I said.

The man came toward me. "What's the rush?"
"I told you," I said putting my hand in my pocket to feel the knife, "If I am not back in five minutes, my workers will come looking for me, and they have rifles."

TAMBOURINE

     I was nervous as the man now licked his lips under his moustache looking at my figure. "I never had a fancy lady from Paris," he said.
I stepped back, the cold fear flooding my spine. "Don't touch me," I warned him.
He had his hands on my shoulders now, "Come to me pretty Parisian," he said silkily. "I will show you a real man."

     He pushed me down; he was strong. I fell, my head banging the floor hard. Everything started turning around. He took off his pants and lifted up my skirt. His hands were on my breasts, trying to tear my blouse. His breath was stinking. He was trying to kiss me now, attempting to open my mouth by force. I closed my lips tight, fighting, turning my head to try to get away from his mouth. I was holding my legs tightly closed too, as much as I could, while he was trying to separate them with his knee.

     Finally he lost patience. He slapped me and growled, "Open them up, bitch!" and separated my legs as wide as he could. I could hear my bones cracking; it felt as though my legs were coming out of their sockets. He pushed himself inside me; I felt a sharp pain. I started screaming. He shut my mouth with his palm; it was stinking from chicken meat. His other hand was tearing my blouse.

     I reached for my knife, and holding it strongly in my hand stabbed him in the back. The man yelled and jumped up, gasping in surprise and pain. I quickly lifted myself up and continued to stab him in his stomach. He was howling from pain, the blood streaming all over. He was still alive, lying in a puddle of blood. I opened the door and blew the whistle as hard as I could.

The man was moaning from pain. "Have mercy," he mumbled. I got my clothes on and tied my hair with my bow. "I will perform surgery on you," I said. "It will make you feel better!" I bent down and slashed his testicles one at a time, and chopped off his penis in one cut.

He was fainting now as Andres and the other men came in. They were standing stunned, looking at the dying man in the river of blood, and then at me wiping my knife peacefully on a tablemat.
"Sweet Jesus," mumbled Andres' uncle.
"I performed surgery on him," I said softly. "He was sick."

Pablo looked at me as if he were looking at a ghost. "Holy Madonna," he mumbled.
Andres took my hand. "Let's get out of here, fast" he said, his eyes opened wide with fear.
"Here are the bags of food," I said "Take them. They are free."
The men took the bags and left the house in silence.
"Come on," Andres pulled me.

I turned and went back to the kitchen, packed up the menorah, the wine cup, and candle holders, and then grabbed the radio, while Andres was staring at me in shock. Then I spit on the man, and we left the house.

No one said a word as we rode back to camp. I dismounted and then started vomiting and sobbing loudly. The family was surrounded me, trying to hold me, but I could not stop vomiting. I could see Andres crying, his hands covering his face, and then I lost consciousness.

Rosa

I woke up in Andres arms and touched his swollen eyes. "Why are you crying?" I asked him. "You are not going anywhere alone again!"
"He tried to rape me," I said matter-of-factly. "The man tried to rape me."
Andres held me against his chest and rocked me. "My god, Anna."

Only then did I notice that we were still outside, the whole family surrounding us. We have to get out of here right now," I said. "The police will look for us now. I murdered the bastard. From what he was saying, the place is full of police and SS men".
The women had begun cooking. "We will eat and leave," said Andres' father.
"I need to color my hair black," I told Rachelle. Too many people saw me in the village.
"I have no way to color it," she grabbed me, "but I will make a Gypsy out of you."

Nily Naiman

I kissed Andres and went with her to the wagon. She completely covered my hair with a colorful shawl, put some blush on my cheeks, and handed me big hoop earrings. Then she handed me a mirror. "Look," she said, "you are a real *Gitana* now."
I looked at myself in disbelief. "My god," I mumbled, "even my own mother won't recognize me now."

Andres was feeding the horses, his back to me. "Andres," I called him.
He turned around and looked at me in shock, and then caught me in his arms. "I will not let anybody harm you again." he said. "You are a very brave woman, Anna; you are an amazing creature. Every day I discover something new in you, another fascinating side to you. I don't know how I became so lucky, winning you to be mine."

I washed the dishes with the women and we got on the wagon. The sun was setting. The horses started pulling. I lay down on my blanket and closed my eyes. Suddenly it all hit me. My whole body began shaking violently. My head felt ready to explode from pressure, and sharp pain was stabbing through my neck, my back, and every part of me.

It had all happened so quickly. I felt again the stink of the man and his weight on my body. My panic had been so intense that I couldn't even think. What instinct had led me to grab the knife and stab him to save myself? What kind of savage was I to have calmly mutilated him and murdered him after I had

TAMBOURINE

already disabled him? Was I any better than that disgusting brute? He was only a rapist. I was a murderer.

Intellectually I had to admit to myself now that I was strong enough to take care of myself. The bastard had gotten what he deserved. I would do it all over again if I could. But this firm conviction brought no comfort to my mind. I was confused. If Papa were here he would be able to help me sort things out. I felt lonely and violated.

I touched the cold metal of the knife in my pocket. It somehow gave me reassurance that it would not be easy for anybody to attack me again. Days passed before I could come to terms with what had happened.

Gisele and Nicola came to lie beside me. "I like you better with your blond hair uncovered," Gisele said, touching my head.
"I want to look like a Gypsy," I smiled. "No blond Gypsies out there."
"Mother said if you and Andres have a baby he might be blond; and he will be a Gypsy" said Nicola.
"Shall we continue the story?" I asked.
The kids nodded their heads.
"The prince was watching her dancing," Nicola said.

"The prince was struck by the little girl's dancing and by her beauty. He called her over and asked her, 'What is your name, pretty girl?'
'Rosa,' said the girl."

"*Como abuella,*" (like grandmother) said Nicola.
"*Como abuella,*" I nodded my head. "The prince handed her a coin and asked, 'Would you come to the palace with me?'
The little girl said, 'I cannot leave my family behind.'
'If you come to the palace with me, you can ask for anything you want,' said the prince.
'All I want', said Rosa 'is a tambourine.'
"Then you will get the nicest tambourine in the whole wide world,' said the prince. 'I will await your answer in the palace.' The prince raised his hand and the coach left."

The wagon stopped with a jerk. I heard Andres and his father calming the horses down from the sudden stop. I got up and looked outside. "What happened?" I asked Andres.
"The wagons," he pointed ahead "all five wagons."
I jumped off. All five wagons that had left us that morning were there. The rest of the family came running. The wagons were empty. We were frightened.
"I am going to look around," said Andres.
"I am coming with you," I said.
He looked at my stubborn face and was silent. Andres' father and uncle joined us. We started walking through the woods holding the oil lamps in our hands. Andres linked his fingers around mine, cutting the branches with his sword to make way for everybody.

We got to an open field, and I stumbled and fell over something soft. Andres pulled me up and turned the light of the lamp on the object. He put his arm

TAMBOURINE

around me and made me step back. We were staring, frozen with horror. All the family's horses from the five wagons that had gone ahead of us were lying dead on the ground. I held on to Andres putting my face in his chest.

"They shot them," he mumbled, "They shot the horses."

Andres' father was crying now. His uncle let the dog sniff the grounds. I felt cold chills in my back. "They are all there," I said to Andres, "all thirty two of them."

Andres' uncle started digging. At the sight of the first arm he jumped back, and then slapped his own face again and again. "Bastards," he kept sobbing, "bastards."

Andres fell to his knees, howling in sorrow." he kept crying.
After all we had gone through; I knew it would be wrong to try to console him. The grief had to be allowed to express itself.
I was wiping my tears. He was at a breaking point, and I had to bring him back from it. Knowing Andres, I realized that only a need for action would distract him. "I am going to get all the men," I said, "We need to give them a proper burial."
Andres got up. "I will go with you; you are not going anywhere alone!"
"Get all the shovels you can get," said his uncle.

We started walking. "Andres," I said, "We can no longer travel like this. We have to strip all the wagons of the canvases and decorations and religious symbols, so we can look like ordinary peasants."
He put his arm around my shoulder, "I don't know if I would be able to survive all this without you." His eyes were tearing.

I stopped. "We must survive, Andres. We must survive and build a family together."
"We will," he said. "I am determined; we will! After what I saw now I owe it to my dead family! All those good people, women, children, slaughtered like this in cold blood." He was hitting his chest with his fists, crying.

I was silent. The night was so bright and beautiful; it was hard to believe that so much horror had happened on a night like this.
"How do we tell them?" he asked.
"Don't," I said, "let's bury them first. We have to get out of here before daylight. We can't start any mourning processions now."
We collected all the men and all the shovels we could find.
"What is happening?" Paco asked me.
"Go," I pushed him, "Go with the men; go fast!" Then I went to Rachelle and told her we must strip the wagons. She did not ask any questions; but got all the women working.

By the time the men came back, the wagons were stripped and looking more like farmers' wagons.

TAMBOURINE

"No Gypsy clothes," I said to Rachelle. "Tuck away all the long skirts and dress up like farmers."
Rachelle had learned not to argue with me. We had heard from villagers on the way that the week after we left Paris all Gypsies there were rounded up and sent to concentration camps. She realized that we had to do whatever was necessary in order to survive. "Get scissors and cut all the men's hair, no long hair," I said, and went to change my clothes.

Without hesitating I put on farmer's pants and tied my hair in a shawl. I grabbed a pair of scissors and went with Rachelle to cut the men's hair. A stream of energy was running through me. I was determined to live. I would not wind up in a mass grave. I would live to see myself happy, and I would live to see myself free.

Medicines

We continued traveling. Our supply of medicines was getting low. The wagons were exposed now to the bitter cold air, and many in our party were becoming ill. We had five family wagons, all of them filled with aunts and uncles and cousins of Andres. The babies were wrapped with blankets but were constantly sick. I would count the medicines again and again and give them out only in extreme cases, but we would have to stock up very soon. We would have to find a hospital or pharmacy that would agree to sell us some medicine.

Along the way I asked local villagers where I could buy some, and they all directed me to the hospital. It was late December when we got to Bergerac. The town was crawling with SS. We kept saying that were peasants coming to look for work, and nobody bothered us. People would sell us food willingly; we were paying well and we were no threat to them.

Christmas was coming in a few days and that made people more generous. "I will go to town and try to buy some medicine," I told Andres.
"You are not going anywhere anymore; I thought we agreed on that," he said.
"I am going to the hospital," I smiled. "Nobody will try to hurt me in a hospital."
"Anna, you are not going alone," he said.
"Then I will take Rachelle and Nadine with me," I said. "I have to get some more medicines. Too many people are sick and it is only the beginning of the winter." Andres nodded his head. "You have to take knives, all of you."

I went to get the girls. It would be too dangerous to go into town with a man during the day. There were usually not too many men walking about. They were either working or serving in the Vichy police. Sometimes we would see a couple walking around in the evening. I felt that during the day three young girls walking in town would not be irregular.

TAMBOURINE

Rachelle, Nadine, and I put simple shawls on our heads and we were walking with back packs and baskets in our hands into the town. It was a cold day, but bright and sunny. We were strolling in a casual way talking to each other as any young women would do.

It was clearly a town under occupation. I was struck with the change that war can bring to a simple, typical community. The streets were quiet. There were no children outside shouting or kicking a ball, and no sign of business activity. We saw from the corner of our eyes the Germans trucks passing by. The German soldiers would whistle to us from time to time, and we would smile and wave to them, not to raise their suspicions. People on the street were walking with their heads down, glancing about uncertainly. No one paid attention to us. We looked just like common villagers.

"When we get to the hospital," I said to the girls, "don't lose your minds if I have to take drastic measures to get the medicine. Just work with me."
Nadine gave me a look. "You are not planning on another surgery, are you?"
I shrugged my shoulders.
Rachelle gave me a quick glance. "Don't do anything stupid. Andres is going to kill us if anything happens to you. The place is crawling with SS. We will be lucky to get out of here alive as it is."

It was a big hospital and a busy one. Nurses were running around with trays of medicines. There were a lot of German soldiers; some of them were in hospital gowns. I assumed they were contracting all kinds of diseases in North Africa and were being brought here to be treated.

"If they are all sick with bacteria, then they are getting treated with antibiotics, and that's what we need. We must follow the nurses and see where they are getting the medicine. We will split up. You sit here and pretend to wait for a doctor. I will follow the nurses," I said to the girls decisively.
Rachelle looked at Nadine apprehensively. "We promised Andres we won't let you do anything alone," she said.
"I will be fine," I said, "Andres is worse than my mother."
I turned around to go before the argument could start.

A nurse about my age was walking in a rush, with an empty tray in her hand. I started following her. We went through a very long hallway. I had been to the hospital in Paris many times with my father. He would take me to visit his patients there and to help out when his nurse would be missing. I knew she was on her way to the medical supply room.

As she was pushing on the door handle going in, I stopped her and said, "Excuse me, I was just hired as a nurse and they told me to come here to get uniforms." She looked at me surprised.
"They usually give you everything down in the office," she said.
"They are overwhelmed with work down there," I said "They told me to find a nurse who would help me."

TAMBOURINE

She looked nervously at her watch. I gave her a reassuring smile and said confidently, "My name is Carolyn, what's your name?" opening my bright blue eyes wide, knowing that they usually gave me an angelic look.
"I am Janet," she said. "Come with me. Where are you going to work?"
"They are going to start me in emergency. I hope they will move me to a better department later," I said casually.
She gave me the uniform and I thanked her. "See you," she said, "maybe we can have coffee later."

Dressed in nurse's uniform, I walked back down the hall to the medical supply room and pushed on the handle. The door opened readily. I looked around. There were shelves on top of shelves full of medicines. All I was thinking about was the little kids waiting in the forest, burning with fever. I found the antibiotics and started filling up my backpack. I worked fast and filled it to the top and then put it on my back.

The door opened just then and a man dressed in doctor's uniform came in. My stomach turned cold. He was a tall man, broad shoulders, typical German. He smiled at me. I straightened my nurse's cap and smiled back, trying to keep calm.
"Good afternoon," he said in German,
"Not speaking German," I said, shaking my head and smiling to him pleasantly.
He shook my hand. "Gunter, my name is Gunter," he said

Nily Naiman

"Janet," I said and looked at my watch. "I have to go," I said and started moving to the door.
"Halt," he said, and held my arm "You and I go out later for a drink, pretty girl?"
I touched my knife. I might have to use it if he didn't let go. I showed him my wedding ring. "I am married," I said.

He raised his hand and showed me his ring "Me too."
I turned again pulling my hand away. He stopped me and pinned me to the wall. I could see his face turning red, and could smell the schnapps from his breath. I figured I should not make trouble if I wanted to come out of there alive with the medicines. Sooner or later somebody would come into the room. He could not do much to me in a time frame of two or three minutes.

I looked in his eyes, "Mein Herr, I will meet you at five outside by the gate, ok?"
I gave him my most charming smile. He was happy, and loosened his grip on me.
"A fast kiss on the way?" he asked.
I closed my eyes as he was kissing me, feeling disgusted. His hands went to my breasts when the door opened again.
A nurse came in; he let go of me. I looked at the nurse, blushed, and hurried out.
"Finve" (Five), he called after me.
I turned and smiled "Finve," I echoed.

I rushed to the lobby and went through the hospital doors. Rachelle and Nadine were standing

TAMBOURINE

outside by the gate. I tapped Rachelle's shoulder as I was passing by her. She gave me a surprised look and then poked Nadine with her elbow.
I started walking fast, knowing that they were following me. I would have to change my nurse's uniform fast in case someone got suspicious and started looking for me.

German trucks were beeping to me as I walked quickly down the street. I would smile and wave to them. The scum, I was thinking, they have no idea what they are and what they are doing to the world. They looked so carefree and confident, as if they were going on a school trip. I found a thick bush and changed my clothes fast. The nurse's uniform might help me in the future, I was thinking. I waited for Rachelle and Nadine to catch up with me.

"Mission accomplished; I have medicine to last us for the whole winter."
Nadine jabbed me with her elbow. "Now tell us the story."
"Nothing to tell; it was easy."
"Come on; you're hiding something. It couldn't have been that easy."
"Nothing worth talking about," I answered.
Rachelle sighed and asked, "Where do you get those steel nerves of yours?"
I laughed and shoved her. "If not for my steel nerves would I ever be your sister-in-law?"

She was laughing as we were watching the police cars running down the street. "Hide the bag," I told Nadine, "put it in your basket." I tied my scarf over my hair; they would look for a nurse in uniform with a backpack. I threw a piece of cloth on the basket to cover the bag and kept on walking, looking careless, laughing and talking. The police vehicles kept passing us and finally we reached the forest. We were safe.

The Monastery in Toulouse

It had been a harsh winter. The roads were icy and the snow was heavy after Christmas and into January of 1944. We would hide during the day and travel at night. We thought if we could get to Toulouse in February we would be in good shape. The SS were everywhere now. The news we were getting was very bad. All Jews and Gypsies in France were being sent to death camps. From time to time we would meet partisans and resistance fighters, who would help us out and give us news. Apparently, the Vichy police now worked hand in hand with Hitler to clean up France. For the life of me I did not understand the purpose of this alliance but all I knew was that my family was no longer safe.

Michel got very sick and none of the medicines helped. We were worried. He did not stop coughing and sometimes he would have blood in his mucus. We were sitting by him in shifts, wetting his lips and keeping cold towels on his forehead. I would lie by his side begging, praying, "God please make the boy better!" I would sing to him and tell him my Gypsy story again and again, not even knowing if he could hear me.

I tried all the antibiotics and would put steam over his face and cover his chest with ointments, but it seemed he was getting worse. Andres' mother was sick too. She had a stomach virus that lasted for weeks, with diarrhea and fever. The only thing she could eat now was plain bread and water, and she lost a lot of weight. Two of Andres' little cousins were also in bad shape with vomiting and high fever.

I was knowledgeable in medicine and medical care, as I had learned from my father, watching him all through my growing up, treating his patients. I took care of the sick people the entire trip; they all looked to me for answers. I would tell Andres again and again, "I don't know what to do any more. If they die it will be my fault." I was becoming hopeless about them. Andres would stroke my hair. "Nobody has the right to expect anything from you; they know you are doing everything you can."

They were wasting away every day. I told Rachelle and Nadine that the only way to save their lives was to get them to a warm, clean place, where they could rest and get proper medical care. In the end we gathered the family together.

"There is a monastery on the way to Toulouse" I said. "We have to bring the sick there and leave them there. They cannot continue the trip with us."

The men and women looked at each other in horror; Gypsies stick together, they roam the earth together, they never separate from the families. They have no possessions, no land; their reason for surviving is their families. Their babies, their parents, their siblings, their cousins are their oxygen. Take away their family members, take away their lives. The women started crying. "You cannot take away our babies and the rest of our family," one of Andres' aunts said to me sharply, as if I were the devil himself.
I looked down at the ground wishing for it to open its mouth and swallow me.

Pablo got angry. "How dare you talk to her like this, Aunt Carlota? If not for her you would be dead a long time ago! Do you really think she wants to separate us? She is trying to save our lives!"
"Stop, Pablo," his father tapped his shoulder, "calm down! Do not talk like this to your aunt!"
Pablo's dark eyes were shooting fire. I touched his hand, "Pablo, don't."
He leaned toward me. "They are all so stupid, they make me sick!"

Andres got up, "If they go on with us they will die, it is the reality. If the monastery will take them, you can stay there as well. There is nothing else we can do right now. I am not letting my mother and brother die because of your hysteria."

TAMBOURINE

I turned my finger around in my hair as I always did when I was nervous. The women were huddling together in terror looking at me for answers and then looking at the men. "The girl is right," said Andres' father, "We are going to do what she says, we have to try to save their lives." The women started crying. Pablo and Antonio got up and left, disgusted. I pressed my face into Andres' chest and sobbed.

I wanted to be miles away from there, with Andres. I saw in my mind a field full of sunflowers, and we were running to each other carefree and laughing happily. I hit the tambourine and we danced, the most passionate dance ever, and fell into each other's arms to worship our love among the sunflowers.

I clenched my fists. Where was God? How could he sit up there and see this hell and do nothing? We would move now and ask the villagers for directions to the monastery. We expected it to take about two days to reach it. We pushed our horses all night. We had to hurry. The sick people had gotten worse.

When we arrived at the monastery at last, late at night, the horses were in terrible condition; we could see the foam dripping from their mouths. If we could not give them proper care, we would lose them. We found a little park nearby where we would have to rest for a day. The iron gate of the monastery was locked. I was knocking and knocking for a long time, my fists hurting, until a crack in the gate was opened and a middle-aged nun stuck her head out.

"What do you want?" she asked, looking to all sides fearfully.
"I need help," I said and took of my scarf to shake my blond hair.
"I cannot help you," she said and started closing the gate.
With my boot I blocked the gate from closing. "Get away," she started breathing hard and angrily.
"You are a nun. You are supposed to serve Christ. You are supposed to help the needy," I said firmly, raising my voice.
She opened the gate a little more. "Jews?" she asked.
"Gypsies, Christ loving Gypsies" I said.
"How many?" she asked.
"Six," I said. "They are very sick. They have to stay with you. We can't travel with them any more."
"Until when will they stay?" she asked nervously.
"Until they are well and it's safe, until the war is over," I said, looking her right in the eye.

"You are crazy!" she said. "We have the SS coming over every day to check on us. You have no idea what you are talking about." She started closing the gate.
I blocked the gate with my foot again.
"You will take these people or they will die," I said.
"Move your foot. I have a gun; I will shoot you," she snapped.
"I have a gun too; you don't scare me," I replied.
She pointed her gun at me "Move your foot or I will

TAMBOURINE

shoot!"
"Go right ahead and shoot me. Christ is watching." I raised my voice looking right in her eye.

I looked at her face, reaching for my knife; I could slash her nun's nasty throat in one second if I wanted to.
"Christ is watching you, nun," I said again. "Don't you have any mercy in your heart? Don't you have any shame, any fear of God"? I stared at her, knowing the force of my bright blue eyes.

She sighed and opened the gate. "I cannot be responsible for their well being if the Nazis find them," she said.
I smiled, "Christ will guard over them and over you, good lady," thinking I was ready to kiss her behind too if she would just turn around.

I whistled to Andres and the men brought the sick in. I kissed Michel and Andres' mother. "Promise you'll take care of Gisele," she said.
"I promise mother, I will care for her as if she is my own! We will come find you after the war."

Andres and his sisters were crying, saying goodbye to her. His father was wiping his tears. He had never parted from her in all the years they were married. Gisele was crying, hugging Nicola and begging Andres to keep him with us. "He is not sick," she sobbed, "Why can't he come with us?"
"He is too small, Gisele, he will be safe here with the nuns. I promise we will come and get him. The war

will end very soon."
Andres hugged her. "Say goodbye! We have to go now!"

We were waiting for the men at the gate as they were carrying the sick. Nine in all stayed with the nuns. Nicola and two of Andres' aunts would not be able to make the trip anymore; it was too hard on them. The nun gave me an angry look. "You said six," she muttered.

"It's not a big difference," I smiled, "nine, six, for Christ it's all the same. And by the way they all have jewelry sewn in their clothes if it's money you are worried about. They have enough jewels and money to care for their needs for a long time, sister."
She gave me a nasty look and closed the gate.

I smiled to myself as I was walking back to the wagon. I had learned to love the life on the road, the rattling wagon wheels, the crack of the whips, the horses' footsteps cracking the ice beneath them. I was becoming a true Gypsy.

We settled down for the night in the park, and lit a low fire to cook some rice and soup. The men fed the horses. I was mixing the lentils in the soup, Gisele still sobbing on my shoulder. "I want mother, I want Nicola and Michel," she cried.
"They will be safe now, Gisele, they would die staying with us. The war will be over soon and we're all going to be together again. Go get the bowls. We will serve the food now, my big brave girl," I kissed her.

TAMBOURINE

"We will never see them again, Anna," said Pablo. "But you were smart to let them stay there."
I touched his hair. Pablo was the most handsome of the boys in the family, his face carved as if by a sculptor. He moved like a panther. Pablo was slightly older than I was. The girls in the compound loved him. There were stories about two Gypsy girls who committed suicide because he rejected them.

Andres used to call him Black Panther. "Your hair is too long," I said, "Who was supposed to cut it?"
"It's my hair," he said and shook his long pony tail backwards.
"Pablo, I am just trying to save our lives here," I said, frustrated.
"I am not cutting my hair, sister-in-law. I am a Gypsy," he straightened his back and gave me a defiant look.

"Pablo," I said, "Pablo, don't hate me."
Pablo looked deeply into my eyes and was silent for a while. Then he smiled and said, "I am sorry Anna, I did not mean to be nasty, I don't hate you, I will never hate you."
"You really wanted a Gypsy girl to marry your brother, right?" I asked, the tears flooding my eyes out of a sudden wave of self pity.
He put his arms around me.

"I don't care about that," he said quietly. "You are the one my brother loves, and he is the luckiest man on earth."

I held on to him, calming down. "Thank you, Pablo," I sighed, and kissed his cheek.
He let go of me. "Just leave my hair alone, Chiquita," he smiled and went away.

Pablo somehow always managed to make me feel helpless, needing reassurance, uncertain somehow. He had an aura about him of confidence and strength. Pablo was the family favorite; he was good looking, defiant, and he knew how to get what he wanted. All his life he was a proud Gypsy, never once thought about another world other then the Gypsy world. It was the family, the horses, the music, the dance, that made him happy. Pablo worshiped the black Madonna, he lit candles and prayed for her every day.

The concept of killing

We were sitting and eating silently, the horses standing at rest. Everyone was too tired and upset to talk. I put my head on Andres shoulder. "We did the right thing," I said, unsure.

"We did, Anna, don't worry about them, they will be fine. When we took my mother and the rest of them in, we met some very nice nuns. They fell in love right away with Nicola, and seemed caring. I wouldn't be surprised if they were hiding Jews in their basements."

I got up to collect the bowls, when Pablo stood

TAMBOURINE

and said, "Quiet, I hear vehicles."
We all jumped up. We listened in absolute silence. There was a sound of engines in the distance. The fire was still burning. It was too late to try to hide or run away.

    I held Gisele's hand. Andres was pale, holding my shoulder. The lights came crashing into the park. The horses started moving nervously. I touched the knife in my pocket and felt better. Whoever it was, we had enough knives among us all to defend ourselves.
    The lights blinded our eyes as the three army jeeps tore up the bushes and parked right in front of us.
"SS," whispered Pablo in horror.
We all stepped backward. The men got out of the jeeps. There were six of them in SS uniforms, and they were walking slowly, surrounding us like hunted animals. I took off my shawl and shook my head, my blond curls swinging in the air, and stepped forward.

    Andres saw that I was going to say something. He stopped me firmly and went forward himself.
"Bitte, mein Herr, is there a problem?
The man looked at him as if at a sack of garbage standing in his way, and then hit him with his gun as hard as he could. Andres gave a painful scream and rocked side to side, and then fell to the ground, blood gushing from his head.
I ran toward him. "Andres," I yelled in horror.
Two of the men stopped me, holding me by my arms. I was struggling, but they were laughing.

    Pablo was moving behind me. I could sense his

hand on the knife in his pocket, his warm quick breath on my neck. I closed my eyes. "My god don't, Pablo, don't" I thought.
The older German, who seemed like a commander, was walking around with a metal stick in his hand and then said, "Who is in charge here?"

We looked at each other. None of our people could speak German, but I had learned some in school. I stepped forward "I am."
The commandant scrutinized me, measuring my figure. He came close to me. "Let her go!" he snapped at the two soldiers, and then raised my chin.
"What is a pretty looking Aryan like you doing with this filth?"

"They are good people Herr Commandant," I said.
"Good people don't light fires in a public park; nobody ever told you that Gypsies are bad? Why are you hanging around with subhumans? " he said.
"I am sorry, mein Herr, that won't happen again," I said, my whole body shivering

The man removed his finger from my chin, and walked around looking carefully at all the faces with his flashlight. Then he took a look at the wagons and turned to me. "Gypsy scum," he said. "What are you doing with Gypsy scum?"

"They work for my father," I said, "We are going to the north to gather merchandise."
"It is forbidden to employ Gypsies. Does your father

TAMBOURINE

know that?"
"I am sorry Herr Commandant," I said in confidence. "It's hard to find good help since the war began."

The man looked at me and rubbed his hands together, and then said to his soldiers, "Pick up the scum," pointing his stick at Andres. The soldiers lifted Andres. He was hanging on them like a puppet, still unconscious. "*Waser*" commanded the man. One of the soldiers handed him a bottle of water, and he spilled it on Andres' face.

I could feel Gisele waking up from her paralyzing fear behind me, and starting to sob. Andres' face was a mess, the blood and the water dripping from him. He was coughing as he tried to stand up. The officer opened his shirt and raised the Star of David necklace with the edge of his stick.
"Juden garbage," he snapped, "where did you get it, Sinti filth?"

Andres mumbled something. The man turned to me.
"What is he saying, Lolita?"
"He stole it a long time ago, from some dirty Jew," I said calmly, gathering all my strength to look.
The soldiers looked at each other and then burst out laughing. They were slapping each other's shoulders, rolling from laughter.

I examined them closely. They all had rifles. There was no way we could get them with our knives. I started thinking that if I could get the rifle out of one

of their hands, I could possibly save our lives.
Gisele started moving behind me. I could hear the tambourine ringing in her hand. She started hitting it on her thighs, and moved forward toward the soldiers, stamping her feet and lifting her hands. The men stopped laughing and watched her curiously. Gisele was now hitting her tambourine with more confidence and making her flamenco steps around the men, moving her thighs and her whole body, looking at them straight in the eyes and turning around them, lightly brushing against them.

Pablo touched my hand. I could see the flash of the kill in his eyes. He was shaking his long hair backward, his face taut from the strain.
"Don't," I whispered. "Pablo, please calm down." I held his hand, linking my fingers around his. I could him breathing hard, his eyes closing for a moment on his tormented face.
"Don't move," I whispered, "you will get us all killed."

He squeezed his fingers around mine tightly. I felt a sharp pain. Andres was still bleeding, his father holding him desperately. "God, oh God, in heaven have mercy," I mumbled.
The commander muttered, "The little bitch can dance," and then started clapping his hands to the beat of the tambourine. Gisele was dancing like the devil had gotten into her. She seemed to be in a different place.

The soldiers were watching her enthralled. I pushed Rachelle and Nadine and started dancing too. I

TAMBOURINE

was stamping my feet to the beat of the tambourine, dancing around the men together with Gisele, clicking the castanets in my fingers, whirling around the men seductively. We were clapping our hands and singing,

"*Yo me' oh,*
Yo me' oh,
Ley' ley' ley' ley'.
Mira mira la Gitana,
Ley ley ley ley,
Ley ley ley ley,

    Rachelle and Nadine started dancing too. Sara pulled out her castanets and started moving her body toward one of the soldiers. We were all scared to death, attempting to save our lives by bringing those beasts some happiness, some sense of logic, trying the only way we knew to remind them that we were just people, innocent people who never harmed anyone and had no idea why we were being hunted. We were all offering them a present, a gift of music and dance, a clean reminder that there was goodness and pure joy in the world. They were clapping their hands. "*Tantz*" the commander yelled. "*Tantz, Sinties,*" and started dancing heavily himself.

    Andres' father pulled out the violin and began playing a melody, and all the soldiers were moving around the girls, dancing and jumping. I moved my body in circles as enticingly as I was able, pointing Pablo and Paco toward the rifles the soldiers had left on the ground. Pablo nodded his head to me. I looked at Andres' uncle's eyes; he nodded to me also.

Suddenly one of the soldiers grabbed Sara and asked the commander, "May I have the Gypsy whore, Herr Commandant? I did not have a woman for a whole month now." The commander took a flask of whiskey out of his pocket and sipped slowly, then laughed, "Go ahead, Rudolf."

He continued to dance and then sat watching us still moving. "Bring me the French beauty. I will have her in the jeep."

I could see from the corner of my eye one of the soldiers picking up little Gisele who was yelling for help now, and going into the woods with her. Another soldier grabbed Rachelle and lifted up her skirt and made her bend over, while he was pulling down his pants getting ready to rape her.

Nadine's blouse was torn. She was shaking, her eyes wide in terror. The drunken SS man she was struggling with kept gulping alcohol from his bottle and tearing more and more of her clothes saying, "Stop fighting, *Sinti* scum, you should be proud to be with a German soldier."

Two of the SS seized me and brought me to the commander. He was reclining on the seat of the Jeep, sucking on his bottle. He scrutinized me quietly for a while, and then said "Take of your clothes."

Smiling at him and doing my best to appear calm, I slowly removed my blouse. He raised his baton and touched my breasts. The cold metal chilled my

TAMBOURINE

flesh. "The bra," he growled.
I took it off. He stared appreciatively at my breasts for some time, and then sat up and said, "You are a very beautiful girl."

He opened his fly and took out his penis. "Come let me feel your French lips. If you do a good job, I will let you live," he said, and grabbed my hair, forcing me to bend down, my lips on his penis. I felt the nausea coming up my throat. I took him in my mouth and reached for my knife and held it firmly.

The commandant started moaning, moving deeper and deeper in my throat. I bit him as hard as I could, hearing his loud scream of pain, feeling the blood and urine pouring into my mouth, and then raised my head and slit his throat. He snorted loudly and then stiffened.

As I got out of the Jeep and spit on the floor, loud gunshots rang out. I turned around to see two soldiers falling to the ground while in the midst of raping Rachelle and Nadine. Andres' uncle and Pablo had shot them in the back.

Nadine was screaming, trying to get the dead soldier off her, and then Andres' father shot another one, who was getting ready to rape Andres' little ten year old cousin. Andres and Pablo were running toward me. "The rifles," I said, "Gisele! Go get Gisele!"

They ran toward the bushes. The soldiers had

heard the shots, but had assumed it was their friends shooting us, and did not bother to come and check what was happening. I could hear the shots from where I was standing, the chills going up and down my body.

The soldier who had taken Sara appeared suddenly. Andres' uncle pointed the rifle at him. He looked about and saw his friends dead on the ground. He fell on his knees and cried "*Nein, Schieben sie mich nicht, den ich lhnen geld*!" (Don't shoot me, I'll give you money!).

Andres' uncle held the rifle against the trembling SS soldier's head and looked at him curiously. It was as if the old Gypsy had been struck with light. I don't think he had ever before held a gun.

The whole concept of killing your enemy was new and strange to him. Andre's uncle was a gentle man; he had a good nature and had never hurt a soul in his life. He always kept to himself and cared for his family as best he could. He had suffered a lifetime of abuse as a Gypsy, having been kicked around and treated like scum ever since he was a little boy. No one had ever told him that he could fight for his life or for his honor.

Here he was standing with the rifle in his hand, having already shot one Nazi, thinking shall I kill this bastard or let him live? How strange is the feeling you have when you are the master of someone else's life.

"Shoot," I said, "Jesus Christ shoot, man!" but he remained motionless, as if he hypnotized by the

TAMBOURINE

sight of the crying German. I grabbed the rifle from his hands. The German started getting up toward me. I could see a flash of metal in his hand. He had a knife. I pointed at his heart and shot. He rocked a little and then collapsed. I kept shooting repeatedly, until Andre's father tapped on my shoulder. "Enough, *Hija,*" (daughter) he said, "He is dead now."

I rocked from side to side, an overwhelming nausea shook my body, the taste of urine and blood was in my mouth and my guts. I bent down on my knees and vomited streams and streams of frustration until my whole body seemed to be emptied out.

Andres and Paco came back with Gisele. She was naked and quivering, a glassy look in her eyes. I ran and held her in my arms. I looked up at Andres; he was nodding his head to me, his eyes tearing. I kissed the girl and said, "Come Gisele, you are safe now."

I went to the wagon with her and took some water and a washcloth and cleaned her body. She was lying on the hay silently, listening to the women screaming and crying. They had found Sara back in the woods, dead. Her naked body had been stabbed so many times they could hardly recognize her.

I dressed Gisele with warm clothes and laid her down. The men were untying the horses. They would no longer have their rest; we had to get away fast. Andres picked up the rifles and threw them in the cart.

"Strip the bastards," said Andres' father. "We

might need their uniforms one day."
The men threw the clothes in the cart and rolled the bodies into a ditch by the field.

We started moving. I could hear the strong slap of the whip. Gisele was in my arms. Her eyes were closed. I touched her forehead; she was burning with fever. Her little body was still shaking. Her breaths were short and choked, and she was moaning out of sleep, her dry lips moving, forming silent words that I could not understand.

I started crying loudly, almost screaming. The pain hit me so badly; I felt I was being torn apart. Rachelle was curled into the corner of the wagon in a fetal position, her head in her arms. Nadine was still shrieking, clawing and slapping her own face. I took some water and helped her lie down too. "Sh…it's over, Nadine, be strong," I mumbled, and washed her face and her body, wiping the pig's semen from her legs. "Go to sleep now," I said, and covered her with the blankets.

Rachelle, who was usually very composed and tough, pushed me away, not letting me touch her. I lay beside Gisele, cursing the heaven and the earth. Pablo was on the other side of her, calming her, petting her hair and kissing her face, sobbing from time to time out of frustration.

I touched his tears, wiping them with my fingers slowly. He opened the palm of my hand and kissed it. My hand was in his hand. "Anna," he said.

TAMBOURINE

I did not answer.
 He squeezed my hand. "Anna."
"Sh…sh…," I whispered, "she has to sleep now."
I felt his tears falling on my palm. I was trying to guess how much more pain God intended to bring upon us.

Partisans

We never spoke of that day again among ourselves. We were grateful for Sara's mother not being with us. She had decided to stay with Andres's mother and aunt in the monastery; we would not have been able to bear her sorrow, seeing her daughter the way she was found. We had no choice but to bury Sara in the woods. The forest had claimed another life from us. It would be strange and painful to go on without Sara's laughter and liveliness.

Gisele stopped talking altogether. She would just not speak at all. She would sleep restlessly, tossing and turning, crying, sometimes screaming in her sleep. I would tell her how brave and strong she was, how this was the second time she had saved our lives with her tambourine, how if not for her delaying those Germans with her brilliant performance they would have slaughtered us on the spot. But she would just sob and remain silent. I felt completely helpless not knowing how to comfort her, how to make the horror go away.

Pablo and I would keep an eye on her all the time, not letting her out of our sight. We slept together with her in the middle. We fed her, talked to her, and told her stories. Pablo would sing and dance for her and we would beg her to smile, to say a word; but little Gisele was lost in her misery.

The men hurried the horses. Soon the Nazis would find their friends dead, and by the wheel marks on the ground would know to look for our wagons. The horses were huffing and puffing. I could see that they could not hold on for long. Andres' uncles were driving them deeper into the woods, trying to find a harder trail for the Germans to follow. We continued to ride hoping and praying that the horses would hold on.

After many long days we were riding deeper and deeper into a forest, kicking up the ground around us. The air was bitter cold. I covered the girls with all the blankets I could find. I looked again at our horses. "A few more minutes and they will collapse dead," I said to Pablo, and then heard Andres yell, "Whoa, stop!"
A group of men was standing in the distance with rifles directed toward us.

My knife was in my hand. I was angry enough this time to stab the entire group by myself. I would fight until I died, but I was not going to let any of us get hurt any more.

TAMBOURINE

The group approached us pointing their rifles. They were not in uniforms, but looked more like peasants. Then one of them yelled in clear French, "They are not Nazis! They are Gypsies!"

I dropped my hand from my knife feeling relief. We got down from the wagons with our hands in the air. "Relax!" said the leader, a heavy, pleasant faced man, "We are not enemies; we are partisans!" For the first time since we had left Paris we were looking at friendly faces. We simply stood and stared in disbelief. "You are safe, people," the man smiled, "We are all partisans here."

Rachelle fainted on the spot.
Andres put his arm around me; the women started wailing, the kids clinging to them. Andres' father woke up from his frozen gaze and touched the man. "Are you really a partisan?"
The man nodded; the two men hugged each other.
"God bless you," Andre's father was mumbling.
Andres calmed down and released my shoulders a bit.

"Partisans," I whispered to him, "real partisans!"
 I had almost given up ever being able to have faith in anyone.
"Tonight, Gypsies," the man slapped Andres' father's back, "we will celebrate! I did not think I would ever live to see another Gypsy again in this country!"
He stopped by me and said, "You don't look like a Sinti; what are you doing with the Gypsies"?

"I am Jewish!" I almost screamed; it was so good to tell the truth finally. "This is my husband Andres."
"That's Anna!" Pablo said pointing at me, "She is my sister-in- law!" he blurted out. "My sister-in-law!" he repeated as if in disbelief.
I looked at him surprised and touched his hand.

The man shook his head. "Now I have seen it all. Café!" he yelled to his friends, "Bring café and bread for the poor people!"
"You come with me, Gypsy." He put his arm around Andres' father's shoulder and popped open a bottle of wine. "You will come with me and tell me your story, from the beginning to the end."

We sat down on wooden benches still in shock and watched some young women cooking over the open fire. The pleasant scent of freedom and coffee was in the air. I leaned on Andres. He put his arms around me. I closed my eyes. "I promise I will make you happy; I will do everything I can to bring you to where we will have peace," he said.

The women brought the food. We were dipping the bread in the coffee and devouring it ravenously, not having realized how hungry we were. I watched Gisele eating at last, and Rachelle engaged in conversation with a young partisan. I tapped Andres' shoulder. "Watch," I said, "Rachel will not continue the trip with us."
Andres laughed. "You are always right in your

predictions. You are worse then an old Gitana fortune teller, I am done doubting you."

One of the young women invited us to take a shower; the partisans had set food cans with holes and hung them on the trees. We went happily one by one as we were pouring warm water in the cans, scrubbing ourselves with soap, washing our hair and our bodies, and finally getting into clean clothes.

I scrubbed Gisele from head to toe. "There, my child," I said, "You are clean now," and dressed her up with her Gypsy skirt and a clean blouse. She gave me a lively look for the first time since she was raped, and then started to cry. I held her, listening to her weeping, stroking her hair, kissing her face. "Go on Gisele," I said, "cry, child."

She was hitting my chest with her fists, crying out loud. "Your revenge on the bastard will be your will to be strong, to live to see yourself happy. You will dance, you will sing, and the Nazi will rot in the ground for his sins."
She calmed down and hugged me. "Mother," she formed with her lips.
"We will go fetch Mother, Michel and Nicola soon; you will see," I said.

We walked hand in hand back to the fire. Plates were set on the benches. The women had started serving food. Andres' father came back with the commander, both their faces covered with tears. The man came to me and extended his hand. "Let me shake your hand, Anna," he said. "It's an honor to meet such brave woman. Your father-in-law told me all about you."

Andres' father was wiping his tears, smiling to me embarrassed. "I am nothing," I said, "This is the real hero," pointing at Gisele.
The man bent down and took Gisele's hand. "Maybe you should stay with us, little girl; we need true fighters here."
Gisele looked at him and then smiled her beautiful smile.
"She smiled!" Andres whispered in disbelief.
"She will be all right now," I said and hugged him. "She is back."

A baby

We stayed with the partisans for three weeks. The horses needed the rest. The men built tents for us, which proved to be surprisingly warm; I finally had my corner alone with Andres. We would lie down in the tent together for hours at a time, making love to each other, discovering each other's passion all over again.

We would walk hand in hand in the woods kissing and laughing like a carefree young couple. We would gather berries and bring them to the camp to make jam. It was the most wonderful time; we almost forgot that there was a war out there. Our world was the partisans, the woods, and our tent.

TAMBOURINE

At night we would get the guitars and the violins, and dance, lighting the whole camp with passion. Our sensual music was driving the young men and women crazy. You could hear the moaning of the lovers all over the woods. Andres' handsome cousins and brothers were grabbed by the female partisans.

Pablo, Antonio, Henri and Chico were gone for nights with the girls. Chico and Pablo were the most popular ones; with fights breaking out over them among the girls. Louis, the commander, was complaining to us constantly that ever since we arrived, nobody was focused on the missions. "Those Gypsies of yours are ruining my fighters," he complained to Andres' father. "If you don't control those hotheads I will have babies delivered here, not bombs!"

Rachelle and the young partisan were inseparable. Now that she was totally attached to him, the memory of what had happened with the German soldier was fading away. She was ready to tie her life to his. Alain was Louis' son; he too forgot why he was in the woods. All that was in his mind was Rachelle. They were talking endlessly into the night and finally they moved together into their own tent.

Nadine started a connection with a handsome young Jewish partisan by the name of Jacob. They would walk together hand in hand and she would come back flushed. She was clearly healing from the horror that she had gone through.

"Funny thing, the soul," she said to me, "It can be shattered to pieces in a split second, but if you find purpose you can gather all the pieces and put them back together in a matter of days."
"We've lost Nadine too," I smiled to Andres;" The resistance is taking your sisters away from us one by one."

Andres rolled on his back, his hands under his head, looking at the stars. "I wish I could stay here forever with you," he said. "Just live in the woods, pick berries, and make love to the most beautiful woman on earth."

"We have to go," I said, "We have to find a safe place and settle down. There is no sense in our staying here; that was not the purpose of our journey. I don't want to be a resistance fighter. I just want to live my life with you in peace."

Andres sighed, "You are right. We have to go; we always have to go," he held me tighter, breathing in the fragrance of my hair.
"El destino de los gitanos es estar de lugar en lugar"
(The Gypsies' fate is to wander from place to place)

"Let's promise something to each other," I said.
"Don't say It, Anna," he mumbled.
"If one of us dies, the other one must continue," I said softly.
"Don't say it; please stop," he started tearing.
"If you truly love me you will find another woman, build a family, and be happy. It's the only way I would

TAMBOURINE

rest in peace."

    Andres turned to me, his nose rubbing my nose. I could feel his tears wetting my face. With a stifled cry he came to me. "Anna," he kept sighing.
"Promise," I whispered desperately.
"I love you," he said.
"Promise, Andres," I moaned.
He was lying on my body crying. I tangled my finger around his curls. "Promise," I said.
"I promise," he answered. "Your turn" he rested his head on my chest.
"What?"
"You have to promise too!"

    I was silent; it was as if I were about to put a death sentence upon myself.
"Anna?" he raised his head and looked at me.
"I promise!" I finally was able to say, feeling the cold fear spreading all over my body.

    Not too many of us would continue the journey. Nadine and Rachelle decided to stay with their new loves and some of Andres' cousins determined to stay and fight along with the partisans. We made a decision to leave three wagons and six horses with them; we would draw less attention traveling with only two wagons.

    Spring was on the way. The air was getting warmer and the ground was softer under foot. It was definitely time to move. The French radio stations were talking about resistance and violence against the

Nily Naiman

Vichy government. The Americans were preparing a new government. "Very soon the great American forces will land in Normandy," said Louis. "The Germans will regret ever starting this war."

Their regret would come too late, I was thinking, by the time their regret would come I would have no family left, no land, no home; we would all be wounded and broken beyond repair.

Louis had developed a very special friendship with Andres' father. They would talk for hours. Since his son was the one who had fallen for our Rachelle, he felt like family with us, always making sure we had plenty to eat, giving presents to the kids, giving us again and again reassurances that we were cared for. "When you get to Arles," he said, "look for my sister Juliet; she will help you."

Andres' father said goodbye to the commander, swearing to meet him after the war. Louis promised to take care of Rachelle and Nadine. I was hugging them and crying, realizing how much I had gotten attached to them. "Be happy," I said, "Show the entire world you are strong. Make a lot of children; I need cousins for my baby."

Nadine started jumping up and down, "Baby! My god! You're going to have a baby!"
I shushed them. "Andres does not know yet."
"What don't I know?" Andres came by, smiling at our excitement.
"Nothing," I said, and blushed.

TAMBOURINE

Gisele pulled his sleeve and pointed at my stomach, and then made a rocking motion with her arms.
Andres looked at me and paled. "A baby," he mumbled, "our baby, is it really true?"
"We are going to have a baby; I wanted to be sure before I told you."

He took me in his arms and lifted me into the air. "A baby," he was yelling now, "my baby!" Everybody ran to us as he was swinging me in the air, "My wife is going to have a baby," he was yelling to everyone.
I was laughing aloud; the flood of happiness was so strong I got caught in it too. There was a lot of back slapping and hugging, bottles of wine were opened, the violins and the guitars were brought out of their cases, and we were playing and dancing until evening came.

We were making our way out of the forest, clearing off the path until we reached the road. We were hoping to reach Tarbes before dawn so we could make camp and rest the horses. I was lying down in the wagon holding Gisele in my arms, looking at her sleeping. We were eight now in the wagon. I could hear the horses' heavy breathing in front, and in the back from the other wagon. Uncle Marcel was behind us with the other eight. The paraffin lamp was swinging on top of the roof to give us light.

"Tell me the rest of the story," Gisele motioned.

"I thought you were asleep," I said.
"Tell me," she pulled my sleeve.
"We promised Nicola we would wait for him, and then we would finish the story," I said and pinched her little nose.
Her eyes grew dark as if covered by a cloud. "We will never see Nicola again," she signed to me.

The pain pierced my heart. What an innocent nine year old child has to go through in this world, where was God? Was there a god? I clenched my fists in anger.
"I promise I will tell you only if I feel that we really will never see him again" I said. "Now you have something to look forward to. We must see Nicola again so you can hear the rest of the story."

She rested silently in my arms and then pointed at my stomach with a sudden smile. "The baby can hear it too," she motioned.
"The baby too," I repeated, and held her close to me. I would not let anybody harm this child anymore. I swore to myself I would first kill her and myself before I let any vicious dog touch her again.

Muret

We arrived at the outskirts of Muret at dawn; the horses were too tired to continue. We stopped in a forest. Andres, his father, and his uncles went to sleep. We started a low fire; the partisans had supplied us with

TAMBOURINE

enough food to last us for at least a week, which gave us some peace of mind. We started cutting the meat and cooking the potatoes. We felt safe in the pine forest.

Gisele took a basket to look for mushrooms with the other children. "Don't go too far," I warned her, "If you don't see the smoke from the fire anymore, you know you went too far."

She left with the kids; I was sitting with the women singing with them.

"I came from the wagons
In the skirts of town
Where people have no future
Where people have no life.
I belong nowhere,
I just wander alone.
Nobody wants me,
Nobody trusts me.
My heart is crying for you.
You are blind to my love."

Paco brought out his flute and Pablo his guitar and they started playing to the song. I got up and began stamping my feet and swaying my body.

"I belong nowhere,
I just wander alone.
Nobody wants me,
Nobody trusts me."

Nily Naiman

The other young women were joining me one by one clapping their hands, tears coming from their eyes.

"My heart is crying for you,
You are blind to my love.
Let me light your soul on fire,
Let me burn your body with my touch."

My hand was on my stomach as I was dancing; the baby was growing in me. The baby will have land. He will have a home. I was dancing as I had never danced before.

"I was born for you

In the mercy of the law

In the mercy of your love"

Pablo got up, handed the guitar to one of his cousins, and started dancing toward me, seeing my tears rolling down my cheeks as I was doing the flamenco. He was stamping his feet fast, turning around me and brushing against my body.

Pablo was as good a dancer as Andres and maybe better. At our parties, all the young women wanted to dance with him. He had an incredible sense of rhythm, and he was very handsome. In the partisans' camp we knew he broke some hearts. He would disappear with the young women partisans for hours.

TAMBOURINE

He was all about being a Gypsy. "That is who I am; I might as well do it right," he would say. He perfected his playing of the guitar and the violin to a point where one would think he had learned his skills in a conservatory with the best teachers in the world. His dancing was so elegant the eyes would freeze in amazement upon his body. From the audience all you would hear would be gasping.

Eight children Pilar had brought to the world, "Eight free spirits," she would say, "They were a mix of my stubborn and good looking family, and my husband's talented, artistic, intelligent genes. She would look contentedly at her children and then say, "Pablo is my cherry on the cake; he is the most perfect of all of them. This is a person without a flaw, and he is my masterpiece."

She would cook for the whole family, but put aside a special dish for Pablo. "The Black Madonna herself comes every day to bless his plate," she would smile to me. "Pablo will always be protected by the Madonna. Even she cannot resist him. She is a woman after all, isn't she?"

He was giving me a burning look, turning his face toward me as we were moving around each other. We both raised our hands toward each other and started wiggling our fingers in a silent conversation like two birds, stretching our fingers as much as we could, touching each other's wings lightly. "Pablo," I sighed, my eyes fixated on his, "Pablo, ho god Pablo."

Nily Naiman

"I was born for you

In the desert of love

In the desert of emotions."

I started to feel dizzy; it must be my pregnancy, I was thinking, and I stooped and went to sit down. Another young cousin took my place. We were clapping to the music as they were dancing, and then one of the mothers said, "*Los niños!*"
I got up feeling the familiar, cold, icy fear in my stomach. The children! My god the children! We were so wrapped up in our dance we had forgotten all about them.

    I started running into the woods. All I was thinking about was Gisele, God, not Gisele. Paco and Pablo joined me running franticly, yelling "Gisele." My heart was pounding. I would die if something happened to her. I would slit my own throat.

    We were running crazy all over the woods; there was no sign of them. I sat down on the ground, the lump in my throat choking me. My whole body was shivering with fear. Antonio and Paco sat by me.
"We will find them." said Antonio.
"They were taken by the Nazis," I sobbed.

    "The Nazis would come looking for us too; it doesn't make sense," he answered.
I leaned on him. Antonio was always calm and

TAMBOURINE

composed. I could be in the worst situation and he would find a way to relax me. He sat me down gently on the ground and patted my stomach, "Stop panicking. Think about that baby that is growing in you; I promise you we will find the children."
I put my face in my palms, feeling the desperation filling my heart. "I am going to wake Andres up," I said.

As I started walking, I heard Pablo yelling, "I found them!"
I ran toward his voice, Paco and Antonio behind me. There was Pablo pulling Gisele out of a ditch in the middle of the forest.
"Give me a hand," he said.
We were pulling the kids out one by one. I hugged Gisele and cried from happiness. Then I turned to Pablo, "You brought me back to life," I said.

"You know how I found them?" he asked smiling. "It was your blessed tambourine that you gave Gisele. She kept hitting it to try and get attention. If not for that I would never have found them in this wide old ditch. The kids were too weak; they stopped calling for help."
I put my arm around Gisele's shoulders "No more mushrooms, young lady," I said.
She looked at me, and showed me her basket full of mushrooms, "I am hungry" she signed.

We got back to the camp; the mothers ran to their kids. We all agreed, "No more mushrooms." We washed them and sat to eat. I was sitting on the ground near Gisele, making sure to fill up her plate, leaning with my back to Pablo's back, eating my potatoes and meat.

"I decided I would slit my own throat if you would not have found her, I want you to know," I said to Pablo quietly.
"You would never end your own life! You are too strong! Too smart!"
"I don't know where you are getting all these fancy ideas about me; I am just a stupid, weak woman!"
"No you are not! I admire you! Ever since I met you I have been fascinated by your strength and your intelligence. You are very special!"
I was silent. I could feel my heart racing. "Pablo," I sighed.

"When we get to Spain," he said, "I will join the Spanish army."
"Why?" I asked, "Why would you do such a stupid thing? You are a talented musician and an incredible dancer. That is the direction you should take."

He was silent. I could feel the warmth of his back rubbing against me; I could sense his desperation. How could I have been blind to all this? We had been traveling for almost a year now. How was I so stupid not to notice him all this time hurting so much over me?

"It's just a crush, Pablo."
"A crush does not last a whole year," he answered bitterly.

TAMBOURINE

"Any woman that lays her eyes on you falls in love with you instantly; you can have anyone you want with the snap of a finger," I said.
He put his plate down silently and got up with pain in his eyes and walked away. I looked at him climbing the wagon; the women started collecting the dishes singing,

"*It hurts so badly,*
My soul,
My heart cried so much,
My soul is on fire,
I am telling you all,
I cannot bear my love any more."

    I filled up two plates of food and went to the wagon; I put the plates down looking at Andres sleeping peacefully, his beautiful hands on his chest. He did have the most beautiful hands. I loved his long fingers, his wide, warm palms. I touched his lashes and He mumbled something and turned to the other side. I kissed his hand, feeling confused and lost. "My god," I whispered to his palm, "God help us."

    Andres' father coughed and sat up rubbing his eyes. "What time is it?" he asked.
"It is noon already." I served him the plate with a piece of bread.
He took it in his hand and started eating silently, and then smiled at me. "If Pilar were here with us, knowing you are pregnant would make her the happiest woman alive. Can you imagine her reaction to her first

grandchild?" His eyes filled with tears.

"She will be all right there with the nuns," I assured him. "They will take good care of her and the kids. You will see; she will hold my child in her arms very soon."

"She will, father," Andres sat down and yawned; "Mother is strong, she will be there waiting for us, Anna is right."

I served him some water to wash his face and his mouth, and then served him the food. Andres' father got out of the wagon and I sat by Andres.
"What happened?" he asked.
"Why do you think something happened?" I looked at him.
"I know you," he was pushing the potatoes in his mouth.
"We lost Gisele and the kids," I said, and told him the story.

He nodded his head. "Pablo is as stubborn as a mule, but from all my entire family he is the most reliable and smart one, He always comes to the rescue at the right time."

I was quiet; he put the plate down and held me in his arms laying me gently on the hay. "You are unhappy," he said. "What's wrong?"
I curled in his arms, "Nothing, just hold me."
"I will hold you forever."
We could hear the women singing,

TAMBOURINE

"In the desert of emotions
In the desert of passion,
Our bodies
Came together…"

Andres was passing his hand on my body, kissing me on my neck, on my face. The women kept singing,

"It's you I love,
It's only you I crave…"

He took me gently. "Come to me," I whispered, "Love me."

"Lo li, lo li lo li lo li lo li lo liiiii.
My heart,

Crying begging for your arms.
Lo li lo liiiii lo li lo lii lo li lo liiiii…"

The guitar sounds were clear and beautiful now. The singing felt like angels' voices. I was one with my husband the pain was gone at least for a while.

Arles

Early the next morning I went into town with Pablo, Andres, and his father to look for Juliet, the partisan commander Louis' sister. Our horses were in bad shape, foaming and feverish. I was pouring some of our antibiotics into their mouths, but the amounts that I had to spare for them were not nearly enough. We were going to let them rest an extra day. We were not very far from the border. From the maps it seemed that we could get to Lourdes in two days and hide in the mountains there.

The village of Arles seemed to be promising in terms of the population. It was a little Catholic village with churches and a peaceful way of life. I remembered going there with my family for my summer vacations. Mother liked the place because of the beautiful mountain scenery and art life, and father liked it because of their excellent wine and cheese. If we would hike up the mountains, we would see the border with Spain down below and wave to people on the other side.

Arles was established by the Greeks in the 6th century BC. The Romans took the town in 123 BC and built it into a great, important city with a canal link to the Mediterranean Sea. Julius Caesar rewarded the town as a Roman colony for the Roman legion since it sided with him against Pompey. The history of the Romans was marked in every corner of Arles, the bridges, the shape of the buildings and churches.

Papa was always so excited to come there. He would tell me stories about the Roman Empire as we would explore the town. There were statues and gardens everywhere. The most famous artists used to

TAMBOURINE

come and paint the beautiful churches and sights. Papa would point to the statues. He knew all the stories of all the saints, especially Saint Hilary who became the Archbishop of Arles.

Arles was the favorite city of Emperor Constantine, who built baths there and whose son was born there. It was the capital of the west in 408 when Constantine the third was the emperor.

Arles became a favorite destination for the painter Vincent Van Gogh who first arrived in 1888. He fell in love with the landscapes and made more than 300 paintings and drawings during his time there. Paul Gauguin and Pablo Picasso visited him in Arles, and they too fell in love with the place, the bull fighting and the views.

Van Gogh left after he cut off his ear over a woman and the locals circulated a petition that he be placed in a mental hospital. "I think it was adorable for him to cut off his ear for a lady," I would say to Papa. "The people of Arles missed out on a genius!" Papa would giggle and say, "Some day if a guy would cut off his ear and send it to you in the mail, I wonder what you would do."

Arles is home for the three saints, Mary Magdalene, Marry Salome and Mary Jacob, who are believed to have been the first women to witness the empty tomb of Jesus after the resurrection. All three of them sailed from Alexandria, Egypt and reached the coast of France at Sainte Marie-de-la Mer.

Nily Naiman

It is a pilgrimage destination for the Gypsies who gather for the religious festival in honor of Saint Sara, who was Mary Magdalene's daughter. Since she was dark skinned she was called Sara-la-Kali, which means Sara the Black.

We followed the directions Louis had written out for us. It was a big village with a beautiful view of the water. It was quiet as we walked down the main street. Not many people were out, even though it was a Sunday morning when people should be going to church. We stood before a neat little house with a brown-shingled roof.

There was no answer when I knocked. I knocked again much louder. The shutters were closed. "They don't answer," I said to the men. "They cannot be sleeping through all this knocking."
An old woman came out of the neighboring house and looked at us suspiciously. I walked over to her, and smiled. "Do you know where Juliet is"?

"Who are you?" she asked nervously.
"I am her friend," I answered.
She looked around and said in a hushed tone, "They were all arrested and sent away."
I felt the cold fear crawling up my belly. "What happened?"

"They were hiding Jews in the house. The SS found out about it and took them all away," she said.
"Do you know where?" I asked.

TAMBOURINE

"I don't want to know!" she muttered, and went back into her house slamming the door.
"Come, let's get out of here," Andres said.
The town did not seem very pleasant any more; they could all be collaborators.

"We have to get out of here quickly," Andres' father urged.
"The horses cannot take the trip now, father," said Pablo. "We will have to walk. We are not too far from the border. We will pack what we can on our backs and walk. It will take us about seven days to reach the border."
We looked at each other silently; we would have to abandon all our belongings and shoot the poor horses dead.

We had made it with those horses for almost a year. They had become our best friends, our most precious possessions. The thought of shooting and killing them just devastated us. We started walking back. More people were out now in their Sunday clothes. Some vehicles passed. "Don't look at them," said Andres' father, "Just walk confidently and straight."

I hung on to Andres' arm adjusting my hair and straightening my back. He put his arm around me. "We are just a French couple in love," he said, letting Pablo and his father walk ahead of us.
"I did not see SS vehicles" I said. We knew the Vichy government was dying, and they might be desperate to show off, as these were their last days.

"We will soon be free in Seville." Andres smiled at me and started singing quietly, to calm me down.

*"There in Spain,
There once was a girl,
Living in a small wagon.
Give me a heel,
So I can stamp my feet*

*As she passes by,
And then she might notice me."*

*"There once was a girl,
Living in a small village,
No Gypsy could resist her."*

I smiled. I loved when Andres sang to me. It would boil my blood just as when he would caress me. I looked at his dark eyes and beautiful face, and felt Pablo's eyes piercing my figure from behind. "What do I do?" I thought. I could feel the young man was suffering. His heart was torn, walking behind us, seeing us like this again in each other's arms.

"You think we will be in Seville one day?" I asked.
"We will," he said. "We must get there. That's where my mother and brothers will meet us after the war, and then we will go and settle down in Andalucía, where we have lots of relatives."
"I don't know enough Spanish," I said.
"You will learn. You are smart. By now you know

enough to get along."

We entered the forest and I went to the wagon to start packing. I took Gisele with me and explained to her that we had no choice anymore but to walk. The women were crying and howling. "They are crying for the horses," I said.
Gisele looked at me with tears in her eyes.

"It's better. The horses are very sick." I hugged her. "Soon we will get to Andalucía where all the *Gitano* live. You will dance and sing all day, and you will be the happiest girl alive." I bent my finger around hers. "This will be our sign and our solemn vow to each other from now on, and we must make it to Spain no matter what."

She wiped her tears and smiled.
"Agree?" I asked.
She nodded her head.
We heard the four shotguns one after another. I held her in my arms, the pain tearing me to pieces. The women were quiet now. I finished loading my backpack and put it on.

Gisele tied her tambourine to her waist. I helped Andres and Paco with their backpacks. The sun was setting. The women held on to the kids, and touched the Black Madonna necklaces on their chests. We took a last look at the dead horses and our wagons, and started walking.

Nily Naiman

I often wonder why the Gypsy cries so much

I was holding Gisele's hand, walking behind Andres and his father. We left the forest and found an alternative road to walk along the town heading south. It was a quiet Sunday evening. We were thankful for the clear spring weather. The fresh mountain air hit our nostrils. We could feel Spain in our blood. It was close, as close as life. I touched my stomach and felt encouraged. No matter what happens I must give this baby life, free life!

Pablo was walking behind me. I looked over my shoulder and smiled to him; he gave me a dark look and lowered his head.
"Don't," I whispered to him, "Don't do this, Pablo."

He shook his head and was silent. Gisele took his hand, pulling him forward to her other side.
"*Canta para mi Pablo,*" (sing.for me Pablo) I said.
"I don't feel like singing," he answered.
Gisele pulled his sleeve, "Sing," she signed.
"Come on Pablo, when you sing everybody starts feeling better," I said.

"You ignore me because I'm just a gypsy,

TAMBOURINE

And say nothing at all.
I am the one who loves you
And you're driving me desperate."

"I go to the fountain to drink,
The taste of the water is the taste of the salt.
My tears are mixing,
With the fresh water in my mouth."

His voice broke and he started sobbing. I put my arm around him. "Pablo," I sighed, "your pain is burning me."
Andres looked back at us surprised. "What's the matter?" he asked.
"Nothing," I said, "he is upset about the horses."

Gisele gave a fast look between her two brothers and then looked at me and shook her head. I could guess what she was thinking. Gisele was nine years old but much wiser than her years. She was a little girl who had seen and experienced too much misery in her short life not to understand that we had troubles here. I started singing,

"When I will have a little boy
I am going to buy a tambourine,
For him to tap on,
And keep him happy.

"I often wonder,
Why does the Gypsies

Cry so much.
You are in such pain,
But so am I.
So stamp your feet,
And so will I."

      A little smile appeared on Pablo's face and Gisele smiled too.
"I am an idiot," he said.
"No you are not; you are the best man alive. I will love you forever."
He smiled; the light came back to his dark, shiny eyes.
I sighed and looked at Andres and touched my stomach.
Gisele pulled my sleeve, "Sing the song again," she signed.
I looked at Pablo, "Sing with me," I said.
He smiled again, and held my hand.

"When I will have a little boy,
I am going to buy him a tambourine,
For him to tap on,
And keep him happy…"

      All the other people joined in singing together.
"Gypsies need music to keep them going," Andres once told me. "A Gypsy without music is a dead Gypsy."

"I often wonder,
Why does the Gypsies,
Cry so much.
You are in such pain,
But so am I.
So stamp your feet,

TAMBOURINE

And so will I."

We continued singing to ourselves. "Dreams take on musical forms," I said to Pablo.
He gave me a piercing look. "Dreams are a torment."

All night we walked. When the sun began to rise, the women and children sat on the ground refusing to move. Light rain had started, and it had gotten cold. We were near a village and I had enough money, I was thinking. I would go look for shelter. There had to be a barn where we could rest for the day. I started walking off the road.

"Where do you think you are going?" Andres held my arm and stopped me.
"We need shelter; I am going to look for one."
"You are not going alone anywhere," he said, getting angry.
"Let me go, Andres, I have a knife."
"No!" he said, "No more surgery."
"No more surgery. I promise."

Gisele got up signing to her brothers, "I will go with her."
"You need a man," Andres said, looking around for the least Gypsy appearing among us.
"I will go," said Pablo.
"No, you look more Gypsy than any Gypsy I ever met," I laughed.
"Antonio," said Andres, "You go." Antonio had light skin and his hair was cut short. He could be mistaken for a young Frenchman. "Bring them back in one

piece," Andres said to him.

I took the shawl off my hair and brushed it and spread it long around my shoulders. I put some blush on my cheeks and lipstick on my lips.
"You are the most beautiful woman on earth," Andres sighed and took me in his arms. "I beg you Anna, you must come back. Don't start trouble there."
"Have I ever?" I asked.

Our lips met. He kissed me, holding me tightly in his arms. "If I find shelter," I whispered, "you will love me tonight."
"Again and again," he whispered, his lips rubbing against my ear. "I will worship you tonight."

Over his shoulder I saw Pablo's piercing look; my head was spinning. I held Andres as if all my strength was pouring out of my body. How I wished I could be with him far away from all this, the confusion, the pain, the tragedies that had been hunting us one after another. What would it be like just lying in his arms, carefree, going to visit Mama and Papa on a Saturday afternoon? I pulled myself out of his arms, "Don't worry about me, you have to learn to trust my good judgment" I said.

Andres nodded his head and pressed his lips together. He would not speak his mind. It was useless. I gave Gisele my hand and we walked away.

TAMBOURINE

Antonio

It seemed like another one of the very Catholic villages. I could see a large church in the background. The mountains were still covered with snow on the very top. People were obviously well-off in this village. The homes looked nicer than any we had seen since Paris, and the streets were kept neat and clean. There were little stores and bars all around. I could see from the way people were dressed that they were doing well.

I could also see that they looked down on us with our simple clothes. Antonio had a hat covering his dark hair, Gisele was dressed with her old skirt and a simple old coat, and I had wrapped myself in my expensive coat that looked like a rag by now after a year on the roads.

"I look terrible!" I said.
"You look beautiful!" Antonio put his arm around me.
"What makes you so incredibly wonderful, Antonio? You are like a dose of medicine always!"
"I was born like this *Chiquita,*" he smiled, "My mother always said that I was the one that was brought to her literally by the storks. She did not have any birth pains when she delivered me."
"I hope I will have a birth like that," I touched my stomach. "I want a baby just like you!" he squeezed my arm; Gisele held his hand and then held mine too.

Most homes had little farms in back with animals of one kind or another. I was looking for a ranch where horses were raised so they would have stables big enough to hold all of us. We were walking for a long time. I started getting tired and was thinking about going back when Antonio said, "Look, Anna, here are horses."

It was quite a large, impressive home. I wondered if these people really needed our money. Risking their lives for us for a bit of money did not seem to be a realistic possibility here.

"We are not in the best place right now," I said to Antonio, "These people look too comfortable."
"We have to try; we don't have many choices," he said. "The children will get sick again in the rain. We are out of medicines."

We went to the house and opened the gate; there was a farmer outside fixing the fences. "*Monsieur,*" I said "*pardon*, we are looking for a place to stay and rest for the day."
He gave us a look and said "There are inns up the road."
"We are way too many for an inn," I said, "If monsieur will be kind enough to let us stay in the stables, I will pay you well."
He put his hammer down; he was interested now.
"How many," he asked.
"Many," I answered, moving my blond hair around to assure him I was French, opening my blue eyes and

looking right into his.

He was a young man; I could see him drawn to my eyes. "How many?" he asked.
"Sixteen," I said.
"I have a big stable," he said. "You will not cause trouble. I will let you use it for the day, but I will call the police if there is any trouble."
"No trouble, monsieur," I smiled. "We just need some sleep."

"Your husband?" He pointed at Antonio.
"My brother-in-law," I said.
"And your husband?" he asked.
"He is here too," I said.
"Let me go talk to my wife," he said.

He entered the house. Antonio was uncomfortable. I could sense it. "When the woman comes out," I said to Gisele, "Start crying, say you are hungry and tired."
"She doesn't talk," said Antonio.
"She talks in her own way," I said.
Antonio sighed, "Let's go Anna, they taking too long. I don't think it is going to work. We are tired; we will rest in the woods."

Antonio was Andres' favorite cousin; they were best friends. When Andres needed advice he would go to Antonio first. He was very clear and realistic. "Antonio sees the world only in black and white colors," Andres used to tell me. "When he looks at a picture, he sees only the main details, the highlights.

His brain is not tuned in to the rest of the story. When I need advice I go to Antonio and get it fast and short and to the point.

    I turned around; I felt very tired too. We were walking toward the gate as the man came out with a young woman.
"Wait," he called us.
We went back to him. "We are very tired, monsieur," I said.
The woman looked like a nice person. She smiled to Gisele, "What's your, name pretty girl?" She asked.
Gisele opened wide her green eyes, and formed "Gisele."
"She can't speak," Antonio said.
The woman looked at him. "You are from Paris?" She asked.
"Yes we are," he said.
"We are heading south to find work," I said quickly.

    Gisele pulled my sleeve and started crying.
"Why is she crying?" asked the lady.
"She is hungry and tired," I said.
The woman looked at her husband and nodded her head, "Fifty francs," he said.
"With some food and coffee," I answered.
He looked at his wife. She nodded her head. "You come cook with me," she said. "I am not able to cook for so many people by myself."

    I signaled to Antonio to go and fetch the people and went in with the woman. It was a nice big house. Gisele was wandering around in shock. She had never

TAMBOURINE

been in a real house in her life, and this one looked like a palace to her. The woman brought some clean clothes for her. "This used to be my daughter's," she said sadly. "She was about her age. She died six months ago; she was very ill."

"I am sorry Madame," I said, touching my stomach in horror.
The lady looked at me and then put her hand on my stomach, "You are pregnant."
I nodded my head silently.
"God help you and your child," she said, her eyes tearing.

She took Gisele into the shower, and showed her how to work it, and then came back to me. "She behaves like she never saw a house before."
"She is a Gypsy" I said.
"A Gypsy?" the woman asked surprised. "There are no more Gypsies in France. They all were arrested by the Vichy police and were sent to the Nazi death camps."

"We ran away," I said. "A whole year we've been on the run.
"My god," she said, "what is a girl like you doing with the Gypsies"?
"I am married to her brother; I am married to a Gypsy."
She shook her head. "This is an amazing story; tell me all about it," she said, bringing out meat and rice. I washed my hands and started cooking with her. She was the friendliest, nicest woman. I told her all about my meeting with Andres. She would shake her hands from time to time. "How romantic," she would sigh.

Gisele came out looking beautiful in her new clothes, and sat down on the sofa.
"She is beautiful, why isn't she speaking?" the woman asked.
I told her about the rape and she started crying. "Those animals," she said, "They destroyed us together with the damn Vichy; let them all burn in hell."
I started breathing easy; I had judged her right. This was all I needed to be sure she could be trusted.

"Leave the child with me until after the war. I will take good care of her; she will be my Denise," the woman said in a sudden outburst.
I looked at her surprised, "No, Madame, that cannot be," I shook my head.
"Why not, you can come and get her after the war is over. Why should she drag along with you in this danger? I will be like a mother to her."
"Gisele is like a wildflower. You tear her up from her family, her music, her life, she will die," I said softly.

The woman seemed disappointed. I started thinking maybe I was being egoistic. Maybe I just wanted Gisele for myself. Maybe I was taking away from the girl the opportunity of her life. I looked at her sitting on the sofa, her head leaning back, her hand on her tambourine. She looked so tired.

"What news do you hear"? I asked.
"The Americans are coming," she said, "The Vichy are falling apart. Soon the judgment day will come for all the collaborators."

TAMBOURINE

I continued to work silently.
The husband came in. "She fell asleep, the child," he said.
"Take the poor girl to sleep in Denise's bed." She wiped her tears.

He looked at her surprised. "Denise's bed?" he asked.
She nodded, "Go do it; make sure to cover her."
"Thank you Madame, God will repay you for your kindness," I said.
"Call me Marie," she said.
"Anna." I shook her hand. "Her father and brothers are coming. You could talk to them. My opinion might be wrong. They might agree to leave the child with you."

"You look tired," she said. "Let me give you some clean clothes. You go to the shower. The food is cooking; I will finish the rest."
My head was spinning a little, I was so tired. I stood under the warm water. I could not believe my good luck. It had been a year since I had taken a real shower. I washed my hair and soaped myself. It felt like I was born all over again.

Then I stood before the mirror. I had not noticed how my stomach had grown. I looked more than half way into my pregnancy. The baby would be born in the early summer. Marie gave me a lovely, flowered dress. I looked in the mirror hardly recognizing myself. I brushed my hair and came out. She ran to me. "You look lovely," she said, "Now your stomach shows."

Her husband entered. "They are all here," he said, "I have put them in the stable."
We carried the food out and Marie started serving. I could see she was taken by the family.
"This is my husband, Andres."
She shook his hand and sighed. "Now I see why you fell in love with him, such a nice, handsome fellow."
I introduced her to everybody and she went to the children, making sure they ate, bringing them little toys to play with. Pablo and Paco went with her to bring hot water and soap for a bath for everyone.

"You and your husband will have the guest room in our house," she said. "You will sleep like human beings for one day."
I kissed her. "You are the best person in the world. God bless you," I said. "This evening when everyone wakes up, before we leave we will sing and dance for you; we will make you and your husband happy".
She looked at her husband and smiled. "We would like that very much."

The man showed Andres the way to the shower and gave him clean clothes. I lay down on the bed and stretched my body. It's a funny thing, I thought to myself, how you learn to appreciate the little things in life, like a shower and bed, when you do not have them for a while. Andres came in and closed the door. He lay down by me.
"Come here, my trouble maker," he said, and took me in his arms.

TAMBOURINE

"You smell good," I sniffed his chest.
"Nice people, nice shower," he smiled.
"I wish the whole family could have a decent shower and bed too," I said.
"They will, when we get to Spain," he kissed my neck.
"The lady, she wants to take Gisele," I said.
"She talked to father," Andres answered. "He told her what you told her; we do not part with our kids until the day we die."
I gave a sigh of relief. "I feel better now. I thought maybe I was wrong to say no."
"You are never wrong," he mumbled.

I am jealous of the water

I woke up from a deep sleep. I could hear the woman talking behind the door. Andres was sound asleep in my arms. I looked out the window. It was evening. The bed was so comfortable. I stretched my arms. It would be a crime to leave this bed and start walking all night. I kissed Andres gently on his nose, on his mouth, on his eyes. I loved looking at him asleep. He was so comfortable and in peace. This was how we should be sleeping every night, in each other's arms, our bodies full of passion, our hearts content, without a worry in the world.

I got up and got dressed; the woman was sitting with Gisele in the living room. I went over and hugged the little one, and took the money out of my pocket, and gave it to her. She shook her head. "No, no money. After what you people have gone through, it's my duty as Frenchwoman to have you in my house."
I hugged her and sobbed. "Thank you. God will bring you many more healthy children, I will pray for you all my life."

She smiled a sad smile. "My pay will be that after the war you come visit me with your good looking husband, your healthy baby, and Gisele."
"I will, I promise."
Andres came out of the guest room and put his arm around Gisele, "How did you sleep, little hermana?" he smiled at her.
She smiled back and nodded her head.
"When we get to Spain you will have your own room and your own comfortable bed" he hugged her.

Marie handed us coffee and cake, "I sent my husband with coffee and milk and sandwiches for everybody. They all just woke up now."
"We will never forget your generosity," said Andres.
"You are really going to walk with all those kids to Spain?" she asked. "There are not too many SS around here any more and the Vichy police are falling apart. You should take the train."

Andres asked, "Is the railway close?"
"It's fifteen minutes from here. It will take you all the

way to the border," she answered.
"What do you think?" Andres asked me.
"I don't like it," I said. "We should not be seen by anyone until it's completely safe."
"Let's talk to the others. They are all very exhausted. We have to let them decide," he said.

I was silent. My heart told me it was wrong, but I did not say anything. He was right; they were all run down and sick of hiding. It was not that dangerous any more. I should let them take a chance. I would not take the blaming looks, the criticism. Who ever appointed me to decide these people's fate? Who was I to tell them what to do and what not to do?

After our journey started, I had somehow come to have the last say in the group. The final decisions fell on me, and it was I who always took the comments, whether they were good or not. I told Pablo and Andres many times that I was getting all the hate, all the blame, no matter what I did.

In the Gypsy world, men make the decisions; women's job is to just do what they are told. In this situation the men quickly realized how easy it was to shake the responsibility of decision-making off their shoulders and happily transfer it to me. "Well that's because you are very smart," Andres would comfort me.
"Yes, and I am also a damn outsider; how easy it is to hate an outsider."
Pablo would raise his voice, getting all fired up.
"Outsider?" I will show them an outsider!"

Nily Naiman

We went out to the stable; it seemed that Marie's husband had made friends with the men in the family. They were sitting together drinking coffee and sharing cigarettes. They were laughing and slapping each others' shoulders, and seemed very comfortable with each other.

Andres talked to the men, and they agreed to take the train as I thought they would. "You worry too much," he put his arms around me.
"There is no worrying too much in this situation," I said.
"She is right" Pablo said, "We are making the wrong decision. We should walk in the woods and not expose ourselves to the world."
"The majority decided to take the train." Andres said.
"The majority is lazy and irresponsible!" Pablo said angrily, looking at me.

I was quiet. Andres had his arms around me. Against my back I could hear his heart beating faster, and could feel his breath coming heavier on my neck. Pablo was becoming very angry; he was giving me his piercing look. The two of them had not gotten along since we left the camp in Paris.

Pablo gave an angered look at Andres and said, "You can take the train; I will walk."
"Then go start walking now, you stupid Gypsy."
Andres let go of me, and stood in Pablo's face. I could hear the bullfighter's steps, and gave Gisele a fast look.

TAMBOURINE

She started tapping her tambourine, and I began stamping my feet, waving to the women to start moving. I was swaying my hips and dancing, hitting the floor as hard as I could. I danced around the two men who were staring at each other as if they had never been brothers. I was clapping my hands rapidly, stretching out my fingers in the best flamenco I had ever done.

The two never even looked at me; they were standing there ready to kill each other. Paco started playing the guitar, and Andres' father and uncle pushed the two away from each other. "Dance," they ordered. "Dance now."
Andres looked at me, his face tight and his eyes shooting fire, and started dancing around me, stamping his feet angrily, moving his arms sharply as a bull fighter.

Everyone got up and started dancing. I started singing, looking at Pablo who had calmed down a bit and sat down looking back at me. Marie and her husband got up and danced with us trying to copy our footsteps. Andres' face relaxed; he was turning around me clapping.
"Andres," I said, and he smiled at me now. I turned close to his face, "Don't ever hurt Pablo."

"I am not blind, Anna, he is overstepping his limits."
"He is your brother; don't forget that," I said in his ear.
"And you are my wife," he said sharply.

I was surprised. Apparently not everybody was blind like I was. "Stop, Andres, you know its all nonsense," I said. "It's your imagination."

Andres smiled bitterly, "Anna, this is not nonsense; he has been crazy ever since I brought you to our camp in Paris. You are my wife; you think I don't know what's in his head?"
"There is nothing in his head." I patted his hand. "It's your imagination. Please, Andres, stop this stupidity between the two of you. Think about all the family we've lost. God knows how many of us will be left when all this is over. Don't do this. You are his older brother; you know better."

Andres' father was talking and arguing with Pablo. I closed my eyes. I felt dizzy again.

*"I was born to be with her
I was born to die for her..."*

Gisele was hitting the tambourine as hard as she could, dance as if she were in a trance around Antonio.

*"I am jealous of the water,
That reflects your face.
I am jealous of the cloth,
That wraps your body."*

*"See this girl,
The one in the white dress will marry,
To my brother,
She will break my heart; she'll be my sister-in-law."*

TAMBOURINE

Gisele was moving her fingers and her arms. Her whole body stretched in the best flamenco performance I had ever seen her do. The others stopped dancing to watch her, clapping their hands to the music, bewitched by the elegance of her dance.

"You're in such pain,
But so am I,
So stamp your feet,
And so will I..."

She danced toward Pablo and grabbed his hand, pulling him up. He started clapping, moving his long ponytail to his back with a sharp snap, arching his spine and raising his head as high as he could. I could see the veins in his neck as he was stamping his feet hard and moving his arms.

"Ale' ale' ho,
Ale' ale' ho,'
Li li lo lo lo,
Li li li lo lo lo... "

Gisele whirled him to me, and Andres and the others circled around the three of us. Then she stopped and grabbed Andres' and Pablo's hands and put them one on the other. Then she grabbed my two hands and made me hold both their hands together. Only the three of us knew what she meant. The two of them could have me. She had found the perfect solution to the problem.

I was standing there holding their hands looking from one to another, both still stamping their feet. I smiled; they were both very similar in looks and in character, stubborn and proud, smart as foxes and good looking like gods.
"It's time to move," I said, "We have to go, it's getting dark. We will try and catch the nine o'clock train to Lourdes."
They were calm now, the two of them.

Gisele smiled at me. I held her in my arms. "Get your stuff together. We have to go, you little smart owl," I said.
Marie hugged me. "Keep the clothes, all of you," she said. "You will look more like townspeople." She gave the girls her daughter's clothing and her husband dressed up the men with whatever he could find in his closet.

"God bless you." I fell in her arms "I will see you after the war. It's my solemn promise to you."
"I will never forget you," she said and smiled a clever smile. "I would grab both guys."
I shook my head and laughed. "You come to us to Andalucía, I will grow pomegranates and olives in my back yard, and we will sit in the sun with the baby and drink sweet wine with home made cheese."

We left their house. I was leaning on Andres, holding Gisele's hand, walking into the night. The clouds were still covering the sky, hiding the moon. It was pitch black. Pablo walked behind me. I could

TAMBOURINE

almost feel his warm breath on my neck. His footsteps behind me seemed insecure. "I have a bad feeling," I said.

Andres kissed me. "Stop; you worry too much."
"I was always right before; you always listened to me before," I said. "Andres, let's just walk."
"They all decided to take the train," he said.

"They are wrong," I said, "I can't take a chance on losing you. Let them go; we will walk."

"I can't abandon my family," he looked at me surprised, while I started crying.
He stopped and held me, "Don't Anna, you are breaking my heart. Don't cry."
I bent down and pulled the SS uniforms out of my bag. "At least wear that," I handed it to him.
"No, Anna, stop," he said
Pablo came to me "I will wear one, and took it from my hand.
"Me too," said Paco. I handed him another.

"You too," I said to Andres, "It will make me happy. Don't you want to make me happy?"
He shook his head. "The only thing I want is to make you happy, but this doesn't make sense. You can't pass us for Germans; it's stupid."

"And anyway" said Antonio, "what are a bunch of Germans doing with Gypsy women and children? But I will put this on because I learned a long time ago to do exactly what you want us to do," and he grabbed

a uniform for himself.
I was quiet. I looked at Andres and then touched his face. "You are the most stubborn man alive," I said and smiled sadly.
"Don't be angry at me" he mumbled holding me tight.

"I forgive you, even if you are the only one that won't listen to me," I said, my heart was crying for him.

The three men came out with the SS uniforms. Pablo collected all his hair under his cap. He really looked very much like an SS man with his confident air, his straight back, and his dark face and hair covered well with the SS cap.
Paco looked good too. His uniform was a bit big, but he would pass as an SS with no troubles. Antonio had light features and looked like he was born to wear the uniform.

Antonio was Andres' age and was a handsome young man. Back in Paris he was engaged to a beautiful girl, but her parents decided not to leave. They swore to each other to meet after the war and get married, but he too had plenty of girls in the three weeks we spent with the partisans. The memory of his fiancé had faded away and he knew that fate did not want them together. Antonio was a quiet man. We never knew what he was really thinking or feeling, but he was much attached to Andres because they had grown up together. Whenever Andres was in trouble, Antonio was right there.

Gisele pulled my hand. I started walking. She

pulled my hand again. She could feel me like a thermometer; she sensed my fear, my discomfort.
"Listen Gisele," I said, "Once we board that train just look at me and do as I say."
She nodded her head.
"The most important thing is to stay alive no matter what. Is this clear?"
She nodded her head again, squeezing my hand. I remained silent for the rest of the way.

Cry Anna

The station looked empty. Our train was scheduled to come at nine o'clock. It was five minutes before nine. We put our packages down. There were only a few people waiting there. They looked at us suspiciously. Pablo and Antonio noticed that and went with their backs straight, circling the people. They were both squinting to each other and smiling. Holding on to their rifles, they started brushing against the frightened villagers. Pablo would point his rifle at the crowd as if he wanted to check it. People would duck and Pablo and Antonio would laugh.

"They are all probably collaborators and Jew and Gypsy haters anyway," said Antonio to me, noticing my eyes open in horror. "Let us have some fun, *hermana (sister)*".
Antonio took one of Andres' cousins in his arms, as if she were his lover, and hugged her, giving threatening looks to the people. Paco put his arm around Gisele. I

could see that the disguises were a success. I bought the tickets for everybody.

The clerk looked at me in surprise. "Sixteen?" he asked.
"We are going to a family wedding."
I walked around the ramp, moving my hips side to side, my hair blowing in the wind. The dress that Marie had given me made me look like an ordinary French girl. I could see the men's looks following me. I brushed against Pablo. "If there are problems, I say you are my husband."
"I can't speak German very well," he said.
"I can. Just continue to look relaxed; it will be fine."

The train arrived. We prepared the tickets and got on. My heart sank. The train was full of SS soldiers. We walked down the narrow passage trying to look for seats. Antonio, Pablo and Paco were saluting "Heil Hitler" to the soldiers, and found seats among them, not being noticed at all. I could feel the looks of the soldiers at my figure; I was holding Gisele's hand and found two seats.

I could see Andres' and his father's backs, ahead of us at the end of the car, sitting together. I put my arm around Gisele. "Don't be afraid; just act natural," I said. I took a brush out of my pack and started brushing her hair slowly, looking totally calm.
"Hubsches Madchen" (Pretty girl) said one of the soldiers sitting by me.
"Danke," (Thank you) I smiled pleasantly.
"Hans," he offered me a cigarette.

TAMBOURINE

"Danke, mein Herr. Rauche ich nicht," (I don't smoke) I smiled again.
"You speak good German," he said.

    I looked at him. He was a dark haired young man, and did not look like a monster at all. He did not even look Aryan. He could be anything, Spanish, French, just a guy. I wondered to myself what the devil made these people murder? What made them give in to all the brain washing and propaganda that the Hitler regime inflicted upon them?

    "Wo Sie gehend sind? "(Where are you going) he asked.
I could see from the corner of my eye Pablo starting to get uncomfortable seeing me talking to the soldier,
"Ich gehe zu Lourdes mit meinem botfriend und meiner nichte," (I am going to Lourdes with my husband and my niece) I said.
"*Ho, Hubensie einen friend? Die ist schlechte nachrichten*"
(Ho, you have a husband, that is bad news) he sighed.
"Who ist er?" (Where is he) he looked to the sides.
"Dort der SS soldat" (Over there, the SS soldier) I smiled.
"Glucklicher kerl." (Lucky guy) he sighed again.
"I am going to introduce him to my family; they never met him." I smiled and finished braiding Gisele's hair calmly.

    Suddenly we heard a scream in the back.
"Papiere!"
All our aunts and the children were sitting there. I

could feel the chill coming to my bones.
"*Papiere!*" I heard the scream again.
Now we could hear the cries of our aunts; we looked over our shoulders. I held Gisele's hand tightly in mine.
"Don't move," I whispered.

"*Sinti, Sinti Roma shmuutz*" (filth) I heard the yelling.
I could hear the screaming the cries of the children and the women. Andres turned and looked at me, his face pale. I could see his father's body rocking.

I should have forced him to wear the Nazi uniform, I said to myself, as if it would matter now. I put my hand on my stomach, I was so angry at him. Why did he have to be the only one that would not listen to me? He would always tell me that he trusted my gut feelings, and here he refused to listen.

Now a lot of the SS soldiers got up, going toward the back, slinging their rifles across their shoulders they did so. A few of them started running through the train looking at each face methodically. I could see two of them stopping by Andres and his father.
"*Papiere!*" they were yelling.

I could feel my cold sweat mixing with Gisele's. I looked again at Pablo in the back. I could see his face pale, his fist closed hard, Antonio holding him down, not letting him move.
"That is a phenomenon," said the soldier who was

TAMBOURINE

sitting by us.
"I thought we rounded up all Jew and Gypsy *Abschaum* (scum). They were all supposed to be dead by now," he shook his head as if trying to solve a riddle.

The soldiers now were hollering all over the train. One of them caught Andres' father by his collar,
"*Stehem sie oben schmutz*" (stand up filth) !
Andres' father was saying something; one of the soldiers gave him a heavy slap across his cheek.
"*Schlieben sie abshaum*" (shut up scum) he was yelling.
Gisele started moving restlessly, the tears coming down her cheeks. I held her face into my chest.

I looked at Pablo and signed to him with my hand to calm down. His face was like a death mask. Andres was pulled out of his seat too, and was dragged with his father to the back, signing to me "Go! Get off!" I knew I would never forget his expression. It was a mass of feelings of pain, regret, fear and humiliation.

His father looked right into my eyes, trying to sign me something that was unclear to me, pointing his face toward Giselle. I turned my head after them trying to catch another glimpse of Andres but he was dragged quickly away to another car.

A hollow wail arose among the woman in the back; I was trembling all over my body, holding Gisele in my arms. The children were screaming, the soldiers were yelling "Obeen *geschlossen, lassen sie jene zicklien oben schlieben*!"(Shut up! make those kids shut

up!) And then we heard shooting.
There must have been hundreds of shots sounding in the back. I blocked Gisele's ears with my hands.
"Andres," I mumbled, "Andres, oh God in heaven."

The soldier smiled at me. "No more Gypsies. That was probably the last of them."
I stared at him in shock. Gisele bent her finger around mine as if she wanted to remind me that we were still going to Spain.
"I apologize, miss, that you had to see it. Our boys get easily excitable," he said pleasantly.
I swallowed my spit "Did they kill them all?" I asked my throat dry.

He looked back. It was quiet. "Yes, mein Frau, they sprayed them all dead, they are throwing the bodies now into the train furnace. There will not be any sign that were ever here."
My whole body ached as if I had been beaten by rods. I saw Gisele's wilted mouth shaking and crying desperately.
I mopped the sweat off my face, feeling the icy chills in the pit of my stomach.

"*Wasser*"? The man handed me a bottle of water,
"*Danke shein*" I mumbled and took a drink.
"Gisele drink," I handed her the bottle.
She took a drink still crying. "Tell the pretty little girl not to cry. We are cleaning your country for her," said the soldier.
I handed him the bottle.

TAMBOURINE

"Keep it; we have plenty," he said.

Gisele clung to me. My head was spinning. I rested my head on hers. Andres was dead; my love, my husband, my soul mate, the love of my life was dead. In a split second a lifetime of happiness, of passion, of hopes and dreams was thrown to the fire burning like a piece of unwanted paper.

I wanted to scream, to cry, but I was frozen, not able to do anything with my rage, with my incredible rage. I was screaming inside my head. I could feel the airflow starting to get thinner and thinner into my body. There was a baby inside me. Andres' baby will not have a father; his father went up in flames. His father, the most incredible man on the face of this planet went to his death because he was a Gypsy, because he was a proud Gypsy.

I looked over my shoulder; my eyes met Pablo's. I could see the angel of death lingering in his look. "Pablo," I whispered, my god, Pablo."
He nodded his head to me and then closed his eyes. Antonio and Paco were holding him. Antonio signed to me, "We are getting off soon."
I started getting Gisele's things together and collecting my bags.

We said goodbye to the soldier and started making our way to the door. I could see from the corner of my eye the three men walking to the opposite door. My knees were weak; I had to hold on to the seats along the way. Then I stood by the door as the train slowed down, and I held Gisele's hand. The soldiers were whistling a German tune, as if nothing had ever happened on the train. I gathered all my strength to smile. At last the train stopped and we got off.

It was April of 1944. As we got off we heard the news on the train radio. The Vichy government was crumbling. I was walking down the street holding Gisele's hand, still feeling Andres' lips on my lips, his arm around my shoulders, the odor of his body in my body, his fingers playing me like they played his guitar, his heavy breath on my face. "It's you, it's you I love." I shook my head trying to find the scream in there, the tears, the courage to kill myself. I touched my stomach. The baby was still there.

The men were walking behind me silently. The roads were full of Germans, laughing wildly, their arms around the French girls. It seemed as if the whole world had turned German. Antonio would walk a bit ahead of the others, saluting Heil Hitler constantly to the Germans.

He was wearing the commander's uniform; we did not realize it until we saw the reaction on the soldiers faces. He got into the act right away, slanting his light eyes to the solders when they saluted to him, showing his power, the rifle hanging casually on his soldiers.

He came by me and put his arm around me. "Walk as if you are my girlfriend," he said.

TAMBOURINE

I leaned on him. "Antonio," I mumbled, "tell me it was a bad dream."
Antonio shook his head and did not answer.
"Antonio," I whined, "tell me Andres was not shot."

He squeezed my arm and held my other hand, "The baby, it's the baby that matters now Anna."
"I will not have this baby without Andres," I whined again.
He looked at me and linked his fingers around mine. "You will!"
I looked at his determined face.
"You will survive and have the baby for all of our sakes!"
I looked around, and saw a church in the distance.
"Take me to the church," I said, "I need a break."

Gisele was still sobbing from time to time, holding my other hand. I could feel the shivering in her body. My knees felt very weak. I held on to Antonio as much as I could, squeezing my fingers around his with all my might. I could hear him moan with pain, which made me feel better; I had to feel that there was still a sense of pain in all this madness.

"The instruments, the jewelry, everything is lost," I said, not to the point.
"Our lives are not lost," Antonio answered me.
"Lives," I said bitterly, "worthless lives."
"Lives," he said, "your baby, our little Gisele, our music, our ability to love, to dance, our Gypsy blood, our families that are waiting to meet us in Spain, nobody can take that away from us."

Nily Naiman

I closed my eyes, the tears finally starting. "Antonio," I gasped. He put his arm around me. "Cry, Anna," he said, "you can cry now."

I was sobbing into his chest as we entered the dark church. It was lighted only by a few candles, and nobody was there. The door was closed behind us; Antonio sat Gisele and me on a bench, and sat between us. Paco and Pablo were sitting behind us, still silent, not able to say a word. The scream came out of my mouth, a painful wail from the depths of my soul. Then Gisele gave a shriek, "Mother! Father!"
We all held our breaths. She was talking; her voice had returned!

She kept wailing, "Mother, Father!" like a sheep being slaughtered. I could not stop crying loudly, my hands on my face. The men were crying too. We were huddling together, throwing our arms around each other, weeping, muttering; we could finally mourn. Our pain spilled out like gushing water. I did not know any more who was screaming and who was pounding his fists on me.

Then we sat exhausted silently for a minute. Pablo put his hand on my stomach, as if trying to communicate with the baby inside me. Antonio then said, "It's the five of us now, one for all and all for one; we can't let anything beat us any more."

"Pardon, mein Herr," we heard a voice behind us. Pablo jumped up pointing his rifle. I reached for my knife right away. A priest was standing there by the

TAMBOURINE

door. Antonio and Paco pointed their guns and moved together as one unit toward him. The man raised his arms. "Don't shoot," he begged.
"Who are you" Antonio asked.
"You speak French?" The man's face lit up.
"Talk," Pablo commended.

"I am the priest of this church. I heard voices from my house; I live upstairs," he said.
The men were stressed. I could feel that they might take it in the wrong direction. "We need shelter," I said, "We are not Germans."
"Who are you," he asked stepping forward.
Pablo put his gun to his chest pushing him back, "If you make a mistake I will shoot you like a dog!" he said sharply.

"I am Jewish" I said. "These people are Gypsies, Christ loving Gypsies."
The priest turned white as the wall. "You are in great danger here. Our village is full of SS men," he said.
"Lots of collaborators?" I asked.
The priest sighed, "Lots of them; the sinners will suffer after it's all over."

"We need shelter," I repeated, "We intend to pass the border to Spain. We will pay if you will hide us for few days until we can get out of here."
"I have a basement," he said, "but you will have to share it with others."
"Who are the others?" Antonio asked.
"Two families of Jews," the priest said. "I have been hiding them for a year now."

Nily Naiman

My heart lighted up." Germans don't come to search here?"
"No," he said, "I have been in good relationship with the commandant ever since they set up their headquarters here."
Pablo lowered his rifle, and Paco and Antonio did the same.
"We will stay for a while; we need you to transport us across the border."
The man nodded his head.
"No mistakes or everybody dies," Pablo said.
"Don't worry young man. I am with you, not against you," the priest put his arm around his shoulder.
Pablo was uncomfortable; he got away from him and was silent. I could see him gripping his rifle tightly. I took my hand off my knife and we followed the priest down to the basement.

It was a large room. There were some mattresses on the floor, a round table and a wood stove. I could see a desk and a few chairs beneath statues of the saints, and framed religious paintings. "Where are the people?" I asked.
"They know to hide when they hear footsteps." He turned a handle behind the desk, and the wall swiveled to reveal another room.

I held Antonio's hand and walked in. People were sitting on the floor, huddling over each other. A few of the older men were very Jewish looking with long beards and yarmulkes on their heads. There was a girl who seemed to be Gisele's age, and some other

TAMBOURINE

young men and women. They were looking at us in horror, their hands raised. They were saying their prayers.

Antonio moved a bit toward them. They all shrunk and moved backward, looking at his SS uniform and his rifle.
He squeezed my fingers, and then I said, "Shalom."
The people looked at me in shock.
Antonio put his rifle down, "Don't be afraid; we are not Germans," I said. "I am Jewish."
One of the women started crying and the rest started breathing relieved.

"Thank God," said an old man. "I thought it was the end."
Two of the young woman came and hugged me, and then cuddled Gisele. "Thank God," they kept saying.
I put my packages down, and sat on one of the chairs. I felt exhausted.
"You are pregnant," one of the women said. "My god, you really are pregnant."

I closed my eyes; everything was turning.
Pablo and Paco came from the bathroom wearing their real clothing.
"Should we keep the uniforms?" asked Paco.
"Tell the priest to burn them," said Antonio coming back from the bathroom. "We can't push our luck any more."

They all looked at me. I nodded my head in agreement. Paco went to the priest with all of the SS

uniforms.
"Burn them now!" he said.
"Pablo," I said.
His pretty face was so drawn and tired, my heart was breaking. "Pablito come near me," I said.
He knelt in front of me, his head bent down to the floor. I stroked his long hair slowly. "Ha, Pablo," I sighed.
I raised his tormented face in my hands. "None of it is your fault, Pablo," I said quietly, "None of it is any of our faults."

The tears started flooding out of his eyes.
"Anna, Anna," he mumbled.
"Andres is watching us now from heaven; you need to be strong for Gisele and me. Antonio was right, we must survive." I wiped his tears with my fingers gently. He nodded his head and kissed my hand.
"Pablo, arrange a corner for me away from everybody; I must rest," I said.

He got up and dragged a mattress to the other room, where the families were hiding, and placed it there covering it with blankets. He helped me out of the chair. "Come," he said, and laid me down. I stretched my aching body and closed my eyes. I felt a hundred years old.
"Don't leave me, Pablo. Don't go."

Pablo sat down near me. I held his hand tightly, as if I was afraid he would run away,
"I can feel the baby in me turning round and round," I said exhausted, and pulled his hand to my stomach.
He kissed my hands again and again sobbing, "I killed

TAMBOURINE

Andres," he said. "I prayed for his death ever since we left Paris."
I was silent.

"I was jealous; I was an idiot," he cried. "And you really think that God listens to idiots? Nothing that happened was caused by any of us. It just happened because the world is evil, because it's a stupid world," I said angrily.
"I need your forgiveness; I can't continue to live without it".
"Tell Antonio to make sure Gisele eats," I said, and turned my back on him.

I could hear him sighing and wiping his tears. My heart was breaking for him. I knew what he was going through. He started going out.
"Pablo."
"What?"
"If you need to go out of this room, tell Antonio to stay with me; don't leave me alone."
"I will talk to Antonio, and bring a mattress for him too."
"Pablito," I closed my eyes.
"Yes, Anna."
"I forgive you; we will never talk of it again."
I could sense the air rushing back to his lungs.

It was quiet now. My face was burning to my touch. I must have a high fever, I thought. I should get up and go to my bag to take medicine. I felt so weak I could not even move. "Pablo," I whispered, "Pablo, help me!" I closed my eyes and fell asleep.

Pablo and Antonio

    I was walking in the woods holding my baby by the hand. The baby looked at me through Andres' dark eyes. He had long black curls and dark brown eyes just like dark chocolate. We were picking berries and putting them in a basket. It was a nice day. The birds were chirping. "Mama," the baby pulled my sleeve, "tell me a story."
"I will tell you an old story I heard from my Mama years ago, when I was a little girl,
'Once upon a time there was a little gypsy girl,' I started the story. 'The little girl was a wonderful dancer. Everybody would stop to look at her dancing in the street and wonder, how can anybody dance like this?'"

    The baby's hand parted from mine. I stumbled and got up. I was standing in an enormous field of dead bodies, thousands and thousands of bodies all tangled in each other, their mouths open and a bullet hole in each of their foreheads.

    The baby was gone. I started screaming Andres! Andres! I was running around, searching, stumbling over bodies of people I knew. Mama was

TAMBOURINE

there lying dead, looking right at me. There was Papa and Grandma and Grandpa, all my uncles and aunts and cousins, my friends from school, my rabbi and all the members of my synagogue.

And then there were all the members of Andres' family, his father, his mother, his sisters, and Andres himself looking at me. He did not look dead. I ran to him yelling "Andres, Andres!" He did not move. I shook him hard and then blood came pouring out of his mouth, a river of blood covering me all over. "Andres!" I was screaming, "No, Andres!" Then there was Antonio, coming toward me with the baby in his arms. "Antonio" I was crying, spreading my arms toward him, "Antonio."

I woke up still crying for Antonio, and then I felt strong arms around me, holding me.
 "Antonio," I cried, "Help me, Antonio."
"I am here Anna, I am here," I heard his voice whispering to me.
I was shaking in his arms. He was lying beside me, trying to calm me.

The room was dark. I hung on to him, clinging to his body. "Antonio," I cried, "don't go Antonio."
"I am right here Anna." He held me tightly.
 I was sobbing, moaning my pain into his neck, pounding my fists on his chest. "Andres! I want my Andres!"
He was silent, letting me hit him repeatedly.
"Andres," I sobbed, "my Andres," until I calmed down.
"Don't leave me, Antonio! Please don't leave me." I

cried.
"I am not leaving, Anna, I am here." He held me against his chest. I turned around in his arms and fell asleep again.

After waking I lay there in the room for some time. My eyes got used to the darkness. Gisele was sleeping by my side peacefully. What was dream and what was reality? I tried to sit up; my head was pounding. I could feel my fever going sky high. I crawled to the door unable to walk. "Antonio," I cried, "Help, Pablo, Antonio," and then I lost consciousness.

Seven days

For seven days I slept on and off, not able to distinguish between days and nights. A doctor came once to check on me. Antonio was shooting medicine and water into my mouth from a syringe. I would wake up, my mind fuzzy, one time in Antonio's arms, one time in Pablo's. I would shake and cry and beg whoever it was, "Andres, don't leave me, Andres! Please don't leave me!" I would scream for Antonio, and then I would cry for Pablo, "Help me, help me! My baby is dying!"

I remember Pablo washing my body, the warm water, the smell of the soap, his tears on my chest, "Live, please live!" his warm breath on my face, he was kissing me, "Anna forgive me; I love you Anna."

TAMBOURINE

I touched his lips, mumbling his name; his face was now Andres' face. "Andres, Andres take me with you, Andres don't go!"

Then it was Antonio, putting the medicine in my mouth, saying prayers to Saint Sara, "I am here, I am here Anna." Gisele holding my hand, Andres whispering in my ear, "You are my angel; if I wake up from this dream I will kill myself."

On the eighth morning my fever broke. I opened my eyes; my body was covered with sweat. There was a weak light coming from a crack in the wall into the room. Pablo was asleep by my side, his hand on my stomach, as if trying to shelter the baby in there. Antonio was on my other side, his hand holding my hand. Gisele and Paco were sound asleep by the door. I moved a little, trying to stretch my body.

Antonio opened his eyes and looked at me. "Antonio" I whispered.
He held my hand to his mouth and kissed it. Then he rose up and touched my forehead. "Praise the Lord," he whispered, "Your fever finally broke."
I caught his hand and held it, pushing it hard to my forehead, and closed my eyes. "Antonio," I said "thank you."

He kissed me. "Thank Saint Sara," he said.
"Water," I whispered.
He got up and brought me a glass of water. I pulled myself to a sitting position and Pablo woke. He looked at me and smiled for a second, and then sat up next to

me. He touched my face
"No more fever," he said, looking at Antonio.

I smiled to him a little and then touched his hair. "You saved my life," I whispered, "You saved my baby."
Pablo smiled. I had not seen him smile for a long time. His face lit up as if it was shining. He suddenly looked so much like Andres that for a second it was Andres smiling to me from his face.

My heart was bursting as I held his hand. "Pablo, your smile burns me, your soul burns me."
He put his head on my stomach and was silent.
I stroked his long hair, holding the glass to my mouth. Water had never tasted so good.

Antonio came in with a pitcher of black coffee and some bread. "Let's feed that baby now."
"Coffee, is this really coffee?" I smelled the cup he had filled.
Antonio smiled. "As much to eat and drink as you want, that priest brings us the best food; we all gained weight here in the last week."

The hot liquid filled my mouth with a taste of heaven. "My god," I said, "I will never forget this sip of coffee."
"Try the bread." Antonio handed me a piece. "The priest brings it every morning fresh from the bakery."
I breathed in the aroma and closed my eyes, and chewed the bread slowly, savoring every mouthful.

TAMBOURINE

"Gisele?" I asked.
"Talking like there is no tomorrow." Pablo raised his head from my stomach. "She made friends with the Jewish girls; she looks better than before."
I sighed in relief. "How long was I out?" I asked.
"Seven days." Pablo rubbed his face. "We thought you were dying. You were burning with fever, screaming, crying, and clawing your face. Only yesterday you quieted down; the medicines started working."

"The priest brought a doctor; he said the baby is doing fine," said Antonio.
"Local French doctor?" I asked.
"Yes, Anna, you think I would let anybody touch you without checking who he is first?" Antonio narrowed his eyes at me.

"Who bathed me?" I asked and blushed.
"We took turns," Pablo laughed.
"I am so embarrassed."
They looked at each other and laughed. "You have nothing to be shy about; you are beautiful," Pablo said.
I slapped him lightly. "You two stripped me naked. I know it, I remember."
"Can you give a bath to a dressed up person?" Pablo tried to escape my hand that was going after him, laughing.

All this noise woke up Gisele and Paco who crawled to both sides of my mattress, pushing Pablo and Antonio away.
I hugged them both, smelling them like a mother smelling her cubs. I kissed them again and again, until

they both started giggling. Paco was blushing and trying to push me away.
"You think you are so grown up your aunty can't kiss you anymore?" I kept going after him laughing and kissing his cheeks again and again, and then going after Gisele's face.

"He is in love with Gita," she giggled.
"Who is Gita?" I asked, narrowing my eyes at him.
"Stop," he pushed Gisele.
I looked from one to the other and smiled.
"You are in love, Pacito?" I asked.
He blushed and got up. "You are all stupid."
We were laughing. I had not realized how much the boy had grown.

Paco was sixteen. He had the shadow of a moustache already, and his chest had grown hair. He had become a man so quickly in the last year; I had no idea when it happened.
"The parents are not too happy," said Pablo. "They disappear upstairs at night for hours."
"Where do they go?" I asked.
"I guess they go to some corner in the church to have privacy."

Pablo smiled. "Those parents don't want her to have a relationship with a Gypsy, and the priest warned them not to ever go upstairs."
"That's not good," I said to Paco, "You are putting us all in danger."
Paco gave me the familiar family stubborn look.
"I know what I am doing! I am not an idiot!"

TAMBOURINE

"Paco these people are very religious Jews. They will never let their daughter be with you. Don't ask for trouble."
"So how come you married my brother?" he asked. "You are Jewish."
"It was different," I said.
"How is it different? He asked angrily. "The girl is in love with me. She is two years older than I am. If she wants to be with me, nobody can stop her. She is an adult now."
"So she is eighteen?" I smiled. "Pacito, isn't she a bit big on you?"
"She is just my size!" he yelled out frustrated, and exited the room.

I looked at Pablo and Antonio and we burst out laughing. We were laughing so hard my stomach hurt. It was good to laugh after all that we had gone through. I could not stop. I would look at Antonio raising a brow, and then at Pablo making his faces, and explode with laughter again. Gisele would laugh and laugh with me, throwing her arms around and stamping her feet. I started clapping my hands. I felt weak again, sitting up like this, and dug into my blanket.

"Dance for me, Gisele," I said.
She started hitting her tambourine and moving her fingers, raising her arms. She started stepping around Antonio who immediately woke up to life and began stamping his feet, barefoot as he was. He was clapping his hands, dancing along with Gisele.

Pablo got up now and started moving his

incredible body, throwing his hair backwards, clapping his hands and stamping his feet. The people started pouring into the room, staring at the three of them in disbelief.

Paco and his girl were standing there hand in hand. I smiled to them. She was pretty, with a stubborn chin and blond hair. Two of the older men began clapping together with Pablo and Antonio. The beat of the dance took over them. I started singing,

"Ale' ale' ho,
Ale' ale' ho,
Ale' ale' ho,
Ley ley ley,
Ley ley lo,"

"Ale' ale' ho,
Ale' ale' ho,
Ley ley le,
Ley ley lo…"

The people started singing along as if they had known the melody all their lives. Paco was moving to the music, stamping his feet and clapping around his girl. I smiled, hearing Andres saying to me, "When a Gypsy hears music he automatically starts dancing; otherwise he is not a real Gypsy."

They were all dancing and standing around my mattress. It was a strange party, huddled in the little room singing and dancing. The older men shook their heads, swinging their ear locks, moving their bodies with their hands up like the men used to dance in my synagogue, singing,

"Ale' ale 'ho,
A ya ya ya yay,
Ale' ale ho,
Aya aya yay,"

"Ley ley lo li li lo,
Lay lay lo li li lo..."

     I closed my eyes to the incredible combination of the Gypsy and the Jewish music. I wished Andres could be there to listen to it. He would dance like no Gypsy had ever danced before. I could feel Pablo's warm breath on my face. I opened my eyes; his dark eyes were looking at me, switching to Andres' eyes. I reached for his face. "Andres," I whispered. The people around me were still dancing and singing. I smiled feeling Andres lips on my lips. "Andres," I mumbled, and dived into deep sleep again.

You will be the father of my child!

     After about two weeks, I could stand up. Having been in the teeth of death, I knew it was Pablo and Antonio to whom I owed my life. I could smell the food cooking, and realized how hungry I was. In the main room people were sitting around the table; the girls were serving food to everyone. Gisele saw me

and jumped up, "Tia Anna!" and came to help me get to the table. Antonio brought me a chair and helped me sit down. Pablo came with a glass of water and handed it to me.
"I am starved, I said."

One of the women brought me a bowl of soup and a piece of bread. "You should be hungry. You did not eat a decent meal for two weeks."
"Thank you," I said, and looked at the people around me.

Paco was smiling to me from across the table. "This is Gita" he said.
The girl came near me and smiled, "I am glad you are better, we were so worried," and sat by me.
"You are a pretty girl," I said "No wonder our Paco fell in love with you."
She glanced at him. "My parents are giving me a hard time; my brothers call me names," she said quietly.
I ate my bread and my soup slowly. "Is it because he is too young for you?" I asked.

"That and because he is a Gypsy," she said.
I looked at Paco and smiled. War brings us to the most ridiculous of situations, I thought.
"What shall I do? You are Jewish and you married a man out of your faith." She wiped a tear.

"Gita," I said, "love does not have a religion, and we don't even know if we will be alive tomorrow. As long as our Paco doesn't get hurt, you just go with your heart."

TAMBOURINE

"I wish you could say this to my parents," she said, and went to sit with Paco. I could see the disapproval on her family's faces.

I looked at my empty plate, and then looked at Antonio; he got up right away and brought me more bread and soup.
"I don't want to take more if there is not enough," I said.
"There is enough," he said, "Eat as much as you want."
Pablo was sitting by me handing me more water.

"From where did we get all this food?" I asked.
"The priest brings it." He shrugged his shoulders, and then looked at me.
"What's wrong, Anna?"
I shook my head. "I am always bringing you worries," I said.
"What's wrong, Anna?" he asked again.
"I don't know, maybe it's me."
Pablo took my hand. "It's too easy?"
"It is," I said.

"Antonio says we got hurt so much, we can't be at peace with a good situation," he said.
"He might be right," I said, "Where are your rifles?"
"We have them nearby all the time."
"And the knives?"
"In the pocket. We are Gypsies."

"Pablo," I said.
He squeezed my hand.

"You will be the father of my child, Pablo."
I could hear him sighing, his fingers linked to my fingers.
"Andres would like that," I said. I then looked into his dark eyes, the glint of passion there, a tear coming down his face. "You will sleep with me from now on," I said clearly.
He closed his eyes, that single tear going down his cheek slowly.

Antonio looked at me surprised. I could see the pain in his eyes. I shook my head slowly, licking my lips, looking right into his soul.
"That is what Andres would want," I said again out loud. Antonio covered his face with his hands. My heart was in agony. The decision had been made by Andres this time.

Part Two: Nadine

TAMBOURINE

(Tarbes – France – 1943)

Flocks of May birds were overhead, noisily seeking places to build their nests. I was walking hand in hand with Jacob, breathing in the freshness of the new leaves. He took me in his arms. "Promise me you will be mine forever."
"Forever is a long time," I giggled.
"Promise," he insisted.

"I am a Gypsy; your parents will never agree," I said.
"I don't think I have any parents left," Jacob's eyes clouded.
"Jacob, they are fine; don't say that." I touched his face.
"Well if they are, they will fall in love with you just like I did." He picked me up in the air and started swinging me round and round. He put me on my feet and our lips met.

Jacob had brought me so much happiness. I would almost feel guilty, with my family scattered all over the country on the run, the horror of the rapes, the murders, and my poor sister's ordeal. Rachelle was always sad and angry, but I just had a new burst of energy. I had never felt so much hope and strength in my life.

"Jacob," I said, "I want to go on missions."
Jacob looked at me surprised. "Forget it!"
"I need to go, I can do this."

"You need to be behind in the woods, so that I can come back from missions to your warm body," he said, and kissed me.

"Jacob, I must go on missions to feel that I am doing something. I need a sense of revenge for what those animals did to my family and to me and my people. I have to close the circle, or I won't be able to continue living."

Jacob shook his head. "It is very dangerous; you never know if you are coming back. I think you deserve to live after what you went through."

"I already talked to Louis; he agreed to send me on missions from now on."

"What will your sister think? What will your cousins say?" he asked.

"It does not matter. They are all going on missions, all except Rachelle. I have the right to do it too."

Jacob smiled. "You are my stubborn Gypsy; I gave up arguing with you a long time ago."

"I am going on a mission with you tonight to bomb the bridges in town, and then we move north. Louis told me that we have to prepare for the British and Americans' arrival. They will be here in two months."

"You'll stay near me all the time?" he asked.

"Kiss me again, and I will," I smiled.

Jacob sighed and pulled me into his arms. "Come here, my little Gypsy."

We could hear the tambourines in the distance, the fresh smell of meat cooking. Of the four cousins that remained with us in the camp, Henri was the oldest; he was 27 and had the French girls eating out of his hand. Chico was 24 and was the best looking of all the males in my family. My brother Pablo looked like him, but Chico was different somehow; he was quiet and reserved. Things always went his way, but he never had to work hard to get them. Then there was George who was eighteen, and Jean who was sixteen.

Chico was jealous as hell of Jacob. He had promised my father to personally watch Rachelle and me, and now I was with Jacob, Rachelle with Allen and things were out of his hands.

"*Gitana* supposed to be with a *Gitan*o," he would say.
Rachelle would get angry. "Anybody disturbing you, going every day with a different girl partisan? I don't see you hanging out with no *Gitanas*!"
Chico would mumble something and turn his back on her angrily. "If your father would see you two like this, he would kill you!"
And Rachelle would blast at him "Go mind your own business!"

When we arrived back at the camp we sat by the fire getting our instructions from Louis. Rachelle and the other girls were serving each one his portion of food. We had very little, and ate only once a day except for some coffee or tea in the morning. The supplies came more and more rarely. The other partisans who would take care of our needs had trouble making it to our location, since the Germans were everywhere now looking desperately for resistance fighters.

The Germans knew that all intelligence information was coming from us, and that we were the ones who kept bombing the bridges and roads so they would not be able to move north. We were low on food and ammunition, and some people got sick and could not fight. We were constantly moving to various forest encampments to avoid getting caught.

Louis wanted to get closer to Pointe-du-Hoc, where there was significant German naval activity. Our top commander George Mercader, who was chief of the Bayeux resistance, had been a professional cyclist and had a permit to go into the forbidden zones that the Germans had created along the Normandy coast. He created a map of the German defenses and through coded broadcasts would communicate to us our bombing targets and the routes that we should take when we went on a mission.

We were moving toward Normandy slowly, usually at night, causing as much destruction as possible along the way. The Allied invasion was supposed to begin in June. We had hardly one month to get to Normandy, and since we could move only at night, progress was difficult.

We did have the wagons and plenty of horses, but they would shy at traveling through the forests at night. The horses would stick their feet in the ground and would refuse to move. Six of them were my family's horses. Louis used to call them Gypsies. "Those Gypsy horses of yours," he used to laugh, "they are the ones that are ruining our good natured horses."

That night I was sitting listening to the instructions from Louis, when Chico got up.
"What is she doing here?" he asked, narrowing his Gypsy eyes.
"None of your business!" I blasted out.
He turned his back on me.
"My cousin is not going with us on missions; her father made me swear that I will keep her alive."

"She is my responsibility," said Louis.
Chico shook his head and turned to Rachelle. "What do you have to say about this?" he asked angrily.
"It's her call," Rachelle said. "Chico, enough! Let her be."
I placed the grenades around me, and pushed the gun in my belt.
"Extra bullets," Jacob handed me a handful, "use them wisely."
I nodded my head. I was so excited I could hardly stop myself from jumping up and down from happiness.

"Chico," I put my arm on his shoulder, "don't be angry, cousin. I have to do this. I can't stay behind anymore. It's the only way for me to close the matter of the rapes in my heart"
His face was covered with a painful expression. He hugged me. "Sorry, Nadine, I had no right. I am just worried about you."

I kissed him on his forehead. "You know you are my favorite gorgeous looking cousin. I don't want anger between us."

He looked at Jacob and then at me. "Nadine, you are not serious about this guy are you?"
"What do you think?" I pinched his cheek.

Chico shook his head. "Be careful Nadine; he will break your heart. He is not a *Gitano*."
"You are a *Gitano* and you breaking hearts ever since I knew you, dear cousin, I replied.
"It's not the same" he muttered.

I looked at his dark eyes; Chico was the best looking man I had ever seen in my life. I touched his lips. "If you were not my cousin I would choose you a long time ago," I said gazing at him, "not because of your good looks or the amount of hearts you have broken, but merely for the way you care about me."
He smiled. "Lots of *Gitanos* marry their cousins; your own parents are cousins."

I smiled and started clapping my hands, and turned around him singing,

"Why do you ignore me so?
Come and live your life with me,
We'll live like the lovers in the love stories."

"The guitar is brand new,
My father taught me the tune,
The violin is fixed now,

TAMBOURINE

My mother taught me the dance."

*"I dug a hole in the ground,
And there I buried my thoughts,
Then I cry myself to sleep,
So my heart will not shatter to bits."*

At this point Chico began turning around me too, dancing and stamping his feet, and soon all the rest were dancing around the fire. Henri started strumming the guitar and George took out his violin.

We were all dancing around each other while Rachelle and I were singing. Louis once told us that thanks to our music and dance his people did not feel the hunger as much. And now after eating the tiny piece of meat and thin slice of bread that did not fill me up at all, I realized the man was right.

"A Gypsy would choose flamenco over diamonds," father used to say. We kept on singing, our eyes gazing at each other; I could guess Chico's thoughts.
*"I will dig a hole in the ground,
And there I will bury my thoughts,
Then I will cry myself to sleep,
So my heart will not shatter to pieces.*

Chico was circling around me moving his thighs and stamping his feet. Chico was the most sensual of men. I could see the burning looks of the girls around me, and shook my head tossing my hair backwards. Chico too threw his long hair back and brushed against me.

I was thinking about Anna and my brother Pablo who was so much in love with her, and wondered if he had found a cure for his tormented soul. I was thinking too about Michel, my favorite of all of them. Michel would sit and talk to me for hours back home. I was the only one he trusted other then cousin Antonio. When Cousin Antonio would get tired of Michel's questions he would tell him "Go to Nadine, she is smarter then me."

I missed my family so much my head started spinning.
I stopped dancing and sat by Jacob. He put his arm around me. I breathed the forest air deep and put my head on his shoulder, looking at the young partisans dancing and wondering how many of them would come back alive tonight.

On the 23rd of March and then again on the 26th we had had significant losses to our people after air raids and shelling. The Germans took the offensive; we were fighting for days until there was no alternative but to retreat. We lost 200 men and women, some of whom were taken prisoner and tortured to death. We knew well that going to seek intelligence or just bombing a bridge could lead to a very bloody battle.

During the month of April just minor operations lost us twenty of our best fighters. Rachelle and I and a few other girls were always left behind to wash the laundry and cook and sew. It had taken begging and tears to make Louis let me join the fighters; he had made promises to father and felt like a traitor breaking them. But in the end he could not take my bugging him and said yes.

The Bridge

Louis divided us into two groups. There were two bridges that had to be destroyed. One of them we had blown up some time ago, but the Germans had rebuilt it because it was a connection to important supply corridors for their trucks. Henri and Chico were with my group and Jacob was in the other, in spite of all our begging. Louis said "Leave your romance in camp. I will not have you take it on a mission."

Henri would hold my hand from time to time to reassure me, and Chico tagged behind me like a shadow. We were moving parallel to the road that led to the bridge. There was no activity there; only from time to time would a car or a man on a bicycle pass by. When we got to the bridge we were hiding in the ditch nearby. Chico was getting ready to set up the bombs with Henri and the others.

"Stay here," Chico whispered. "Don't move."
I squeezed his hand.
"Come back, *Chico,* come back to me or I will die." An indefinable wave of emotion flooded me; I looked into his eyes and started tearing. He started walking away and then turned around and said,
"If you wait for me I will be back; just for you I will be back."
 I could feel the lump in my throat, watching his figure receding.

There were only a few of us left behind for cover. I pointed my rifle toward the bridge; the men were under it now setting up the cables. Jean crawled closer to me and pushed his elbow in my thigh.
 "So how does it feel to be a fighter?"
I smiled. "Better than to cook; that's for sure."
George sighed, "Remember mother's *fiesta* dish? That was cooking."
"With fresh baked white bread," Jean added.
"And my mother's lentil soups, remember?" I sighed too.
"When all this is over let's make a big *fiesta* and cook all our favorite food.
 George collected our hands together. "It's a promise." We shook hands.

We could see bright lights in the distance; the boys were running back to the ditch. There were two SS supply trucks on the road coming to cross the bridge. I looked around. Henri had just made it to the ditch.
 "Where is Chico," I asked.

TAMBOURINE

"He is tying the last cable; he'll make it," said Henri.

I could see Chico still hanging under the bridge with two more of our men. The trucks were almost there.
"They will never make it," I said. "Those are supply trucks. Louis, let me stall them. We could kill the drivers, get their ammunition and blow the bridge."

Louis rubbed his face. "You go with Sara; she looks very French. I will give the boys the instructions. Don't do anything stupid."
I tied my coat over my grenades, and walked out of the ditch with Sara. She took off her shawl and spread her long blond hair on her back.
"Come on Nadine," she smiled, let's show the bastards what we're made of."

We started walking in the middle of the road, moving our thighs from side to side, laughing carelessly. "Whatever you do," I said, "we must give Chico enough time to finish the job and run. If something happens to my cousin I will die."
Sara looked at me and smiled. "If something happened to your cousin, I would die first."

I giggled, "You too?"
"Show me one girl that is not ready to die for that Gypsy," she said, glancing at his image, hanging under our feet.

We were strolling along the bridge as the trucks were getting on behind us. There were three trucks driving one behind the other. I touched the revolver in my pocket and the knife in my bra. This time I will slit their throats long before we exchange two words, I was thinking to myself.

One of the drivers stuck his head out and shouted in German,
"You are in the middle of the road, *Frauleines*!"
Sara looked back and waved her hand to him, as if she didn't understand what he was saying.

The truck stopped right by us; the driver was all alone. He stopped the engine and jumped out. He was a short guy. I measured with my eyes the distance from my hand to his throat; I could kill him in an instant.
"Heimlich," he gave his hand to Sara. She shook his hand as the others stopped their trucks and came closer.

"You have found "*gute zeiten*" (good time) Heimlich?" one of them asked. There were four of them. Their rifles were hanging loose on their shoulders; they were relaxed.
I gave them one of my most seductive smiles.
"Marie," I extended my hand.

"My god, Heimlich, you did find some good times," muttered one of them looking at my figure.
"We both will have this dark one. You and Felix take the blond one, and then we will change, ha?" he said.
"And the trucks?" asked his friend.
"We made it early. They won't expect us until an hour from now."

TAMBOURINE

    I could see from the corner of my eye Chico and the others running to the ditch. I put my hand on one of the soldier's arms and started walking him off the bridge. The other one was tagging along behind us. I stopped and put my other arm around him too. We were walking off the bridge onto the road laughing.

    One of them took out a bottle of alcohol from his pocket and they passed it from one to other offering me a drink. "*Gekommen lassen sie mich ihnen ein gules deutsches bumsen ziegen.* (Come we will show you a good German love making).
I took the bottle, pretending to take a drink.

    I stopped behind a bush; one of them threw his coat on the ground and dropped his rifle. The other one was laughing, starting to take of his pants.
"Wait. Behave now, fellows," I said, "Warteziet, enzein"
(Wait, one at a time).

    He nodded his head laughing again. I had one lie on the ground, saying to him "ssh" as he burst out laughing again. Then I drew my knife in the fastest movement and slashed his throat; he snorted his last breath and died on the spot.
The other one was standing with his back to us, still laughing and drinking from his bottle. I got up and sneaked behind him and slashed his throat in one fast strong wave of an arm. He rocked a bit, not even screaming from the shock, and then collapsed like a sack of potatoes.

Nily Naiman

I looked at my watch. If these trucks were expected to arrive an hour from now, we had to rush and empty them out. I could hear a couple of gunshots from the bridge. I ran back; Sara was still there, looking at the bodies of the two Germans, calmly smoking a cigarette.

"Very nice," I said, "let me know when you finish your cigarette so we can move forward with our plan."

She laughed. "The bastards have rifles in there; I heard them talking. Let's go get the guys."

We got off the bridge. "Cigarette?" She offered me a pack.

"How many packs did you get out of their pockets?" I asked.

"Three," she laughed. "You and I are a good team, and from now on we will stick together. The other women in the team piss in their pants when they have to do missions like this."

I nodded my head.

"And in return for the pleasure of my company you make those good-looking cousins of yours aware of me." She added

I smiled as we went to the ditch. "We have half an hour, boss; go get those rifles."

Louis slapped our shoulders. "Good job girls," he said, and gave a sign to the men to go and empty out the trucks.

"I take back what I said." Chico put his arms around me. "You are a very brave woman."

The adrenalin was rushing to my brain now.

TAMBOURINE

"Hold me, Chico, I am not brave; I am shaking, I just killed two people in cold blood," I said putting my face in his chest.
Chico held me. I could release my tears now, feeling the bloody knife in my pocket. I was crying quietly in his arms. He raised my chin, wiping my tears with his sleeves.
"Nadine," he said, "you know you saved my life now."
"I will die for you if I have to, I said.

We kept holding each other; my heart was still pounding from fear. He kissed my face. I could feel the electric shock going through my body. I was in a fog; my head was spinning. It is not right, I said to myself, not letting go of Chico's arms. It is not right, repeating it to myself. I raised my head, looking right at Chico's eyes, and our lips met.

I could taste the sweet taste of his mouth in mine; I never kissed a man like I kissed Chico now. Our bodies were burning, our tongues tangling in each other. I was moaning for him, tightening my grip around his neck. His lips on my lips were the most wonderful thing I had ever experienced.
"Chico!" Louis' voice brought us back to reality. "Go help the men; we have to blow up the bridge in two minutes."

We separated ourselves from each other, and stood there breathing heavily, both of us flushed.
"This never happened," I said.
Chico turned around and left.
I was standing there perplexed.

Louis touched my hair. "You did well for a first mission."
I looked at him in confusion.
"The strangest things happen in wartime, daughter. Let your heart lead you."
I looked down at the ground.

In different times our families would prepare a wedding for us immediately. A *Gitano* never touched a *Gitana* who was family member unless it was very serious. What came over me? My body was still shaking with desire. What have I done?

I put my fingers in my ears against the sound of the blast. "Run," Louis yelled, "run fast to the woods and then get ready to move on."
We started running; we had gotten a lot of rifles off the trucks. Each one of us had to carry at least four rifles, along with grenades around our bodies. The Germans would have heard the blast and would be searching for us now. One of the men had already sent a message in Morse code to the people in the camp to pack up and have everything ready to move. They would throw garbage in the opposite direction so the Germans would search the other way.

Chico's footsteps were behind me, catching up with me.
"I am sorry, Nadine," he said, running by my side.
"It never happened," I repeated.
"But it did," he said, breathing heavily beside me.
"Leave me alone, Chico, it never ever happened."

TAMBOURINE

Jacob's arms were waiting for me in the camp and I ran straight to them. He hugged me. "Thank God you are back," he said.
I sobbed in his arms, feeling confused and miserable.
"I will never let Louis separate us again." He kissed me.

I got onto the wagon and curled up in the hay by Rachelle.
"What happened," she asked, letting me cry in her arms. "Was it scary?"
"It was fine," I sobbed.
Rachelle held on to me. "Why are you crying?"
"Chico," I said.
"Something happened to him?" She shook me. "What about Chico?"
"I kissed him," I said.

Rachelle was quiet for a while. "I thought you were in love with Jacob."
"I thought so too," I cried.
"Chico has loved you since he was a little boy. I am not surprised," she giggled.
"I had no idea," I said. "He was always running around with plenty of girls; how could I ever know?"

"He was promised to you when you were a baby by Uncle George, but mother convinced father to cancel the promise. She wanted us to choose our husbands for ourselves. Do you know I was almost promised to Henri?"
I started giggling. "He is much better looking than

Alain."
"Nobody is better looking than Alain." Rachel was angry.

"Sorry" I said," I am only telling the truth. When Alain grows older he will look just like his father."
"What's wrong with his father?" she asked, as the wagon started moving.
"Well, he is kind of round," I giggled again.

Rachelle smiled now. "I love him, and he is just my size. He brought me out of my misery. I was seriously thinking about killing myself after the rape. I hated myself so much that I did not want to live any more. He brought me back to life; he brought me back my happiness. I will stay with him as long as he wants me."

I sighed, "What do I do, Rachelle?"
"Choose first who you are in love with, Chico or Jacob. Start from there," she said. "Then you will know what to do."
"My body is on fire, Rachel, help me. I never felt like this before. My soul is on fire."
"You are in love with Chico," she said softly, "Come to terms with it."

I closed my eyes feeling his strong arms around me, his lips on my lips burning me. I shivered. When he held me tightly I could feel his heart beat against mine. My body was crying for him. "It will never be," I said. "I will not let it happen again."
Rachelle shook her head slowly. "You are both mad."

TAMBOURINE

Why do you hate me so?

"Why do you hate me so?
Look at me crying..."

"I dug a hole in the ground,
And there I buried my thoughts,
And then I cried myself to sleep,
So my heart wouldn't shatter……."

I would sing by the campfire, feeling Chico's eyes burning me. I had been ignoring him for almost a month. I stayed away from Jacob too. He would try to talk to me, but I could not face him. I would look at his tormented expression and walk away. We would move from camp to camp, and I just stayed by myself most of the time.

"You ignore me because, I'm poor,
And I say nothing,
I'm the one, who loves you,
And you're driving me mad."

"As the Gypsies on the corner of the road,
Waved to me and smiled,

Nily Naiman

There I stood in my apron, crying;
Please don't leave me."

"No end to my tears,
I go to the fountain and drink,
All I do is cry some more,
To make the water taste like salt."

    I would sing and sway my hips brushing against Chico's broken heart. He would grab one of the girls, and turn his back on me and disappear with her in the woods. I would dance and sing, the tears spilling from my swollen eyes, looking at the empty spot by the campfire, and then look at poor Jacob who was sitting there desperate and confused. It was Chico I desired; I had to admit it to myself. It was a desire I had never experienced before. It was a painful, burning love.

    Ever since he kissed me I could not find peace for my body or my soul. I was yearning for Chico. He was like fire for me. If I were to touch him I would burn to ashes. I was frightened that I would lose my mind. I would toss and turn at night, "Chico," curling my body under the blanket, crying for him.

"Amor mio amor mio,
Amor mio mi amor."

"Amor mio amor mio,
Lo li lo li lo li lo,
La la lo lo,
Lo la lo li li lo li lo,
Lai lai lai Lola…"

TAMBOURINE

We were sitting in camp, hardly going on missions now. The Germans were everywhere, searching for us "bandits" in all the woods. We would dress up as peasants and move through the villages, pretending to buy and sell vegetables, while trying to pick up information. The lack of the mission's adrenalin did not help me much in my situation with Jacob and Chico. In the end I told Jacob I would not be with him anymore.

"Why, what happened? I thought you loved me!" He was heartbroken.
"You must move on with your life," I said, being as cruel as I could.
Jacob never talked to me again, and Chico hated me. I was in bad shape. Sometimes I would sit on my own and sing for hours and cry. Jean and George would sit by me with their violin and guitar.

We would mourn our miserable fate together, wailing our Gypsy sorrow into the night. We had never created such good music before. The partisans would come and stand around us listening and crying, sometimes clapping. Rachelle and Henri would stamp their feet and turn around each other, their fingers becoming birds, their hearts a wail of blood.

"I have no money,
I have no name,
I have no home,
I have no shame.

Nily Naiman

"I have no money
I have no home,
I have no love,
I have no shame."

"With my hips I sway to you,
I start your body on fire,
My heart,
Can make you love me.
We were born for each other,
I've always known that.,
We were born to love each other,
I know that for sure."

On May 2, 1944, there was a meeting of the chiefs of the resistance groups of Auvergne, chaired by Henri Ingrand, chief of the M.U.R (United Movements of Resistance). It was decided to join the maquis and organize in preparation for the Allied Forces.

By foot, automobile, bus, and train more than 4,000 volunteers converged on the area. They were divided into 15 companies, all well armed now because previous parachute drops had provided over 55 tons of weapons. These included thousands of individual weapons and grenades, and six of the companies were able to be equipped with light machine guns and bazookas.

Loaded as we were with weapons and ready for the final confrontation, this was an exciting time for our little group. People were pouring into our camp, asking to join us; there were Jews and Frenchmen and even

TAMBOURINE

German deserters. Louis was happy. "Victory is close," he said. "The Americans will land in two weeks according to British intelligence."

We had plenty of food. The villagers would share their last piece of bread with us now, sensing that the war was going to be over and all collaborators would be judged harshly. It seemed that everyone was excited, everyone but me.

Rachelle begged me to go talk to Chico. "You are love sick; you are killing yourself."
"It will never happen," I said, and glanced at his tall distant figure, surrounded as usual with young women.
"You are a fool," Rachelle said, and he is an idiot."
I fell in her arms crying again. "What shall I do, Rachelle? Tell me what to do."
"What I have to say, you don't want to hear. How can I help you? Go tell him you love him and stop this nonsense."

On June 10 and 11 the Germans attacked with everything they had, machine guns, light mortars, artillery and aviation. Losses overall were relatively light, but I had my hands full now caring for the sick and the wounded that were coming to us from other partisan divisions. The girls were not often taken to combat anymore. We would stay behind to care for the fighters; Louis did not want to take chances. In a matter of days the Americans would come and they would need our help.

I would watch nervously for the arrival of our

fighters, and then start to breathe more easily at the sight of my cousins coming back tired, their rifles rocking on their shoulders. Rachelle and I would run to them and take their shoes off, and wash their feet with warm water. The other men would smirk at the sight of us bending down caring for our cousins. "Why do only Gypsies get the royal treatment?"

I would kneel in front of Chico, washing his feet slowly. I could feel his warm breath on my hair as I would pass the sponge slowly on his toes, as if wiping the pain from my heart.
I would then raise my eyes and look at him painfully, and wash his face and shave him carefully, touching his face lightly, washing and brushing his long hair, as if I were worshiping a god, knowing I was preparing him for another girl to come and make love to him.

I would put my face in his chest, weeping. He would pet my hair and sigh without saying a word. Sometimes he would put his arms around me as I was crying, and let me hear his heart beating. He was no longer angry; he would just wait for me, wait for all the pain to dissolve out of my tormented soul.

On June 5 at 10:15 local time, the BBC transmitted the second line of a Paul Verlaine poem to the underground resistance indicating that the invasion of Europe was about to begin. On June 6, 155,000 allied troops landed on the beaches of Normandy. The fighting was ferocious and the casualties massive, but the combined American, British and Canadian forces were able to push through and eventually overcome the

TAMBOURINE

powerful German defenses.

As the soldiers moved inland from the beaches, we were running to them, hugging and kissing them. Louis was drawing maps for the commanders. The soldiers were so young. I was wondering how many of them would live. They would share their cigarettes and their food with us. The sound of the English language was as music to our ears. On June 7 Bayeux was liberated by British forces.

We started moving south. The Americans did not need us in the north any more. They were due to land in St. Maxim on August 15. We would have to gather all the information they needed by then, and bomb as many bridges and railways as we could, to interrupt German ground attacks. We started our running in the woods again, now with ample supplies of ammunition. We were angry enough to attack any German troops along our way after hearing about the massacre in Oradour sur Glane where 642 men, women and children were killed.

It was the hottest summer I had ever been through. We had to abandon the wagons, and we now walked and used the horses. The Germans were desperate now for revenge. Every time we acted against them they would attack a whole village, destroying it and killing hundreds of innocent civilians.

On the 18th of June we entered Saint Marcel and fought to the death. With 2500 men of the French resistance against more than 5000 German soldiers, we were able to release the village from the German grip. The Germans withdrew, but we suffered heavy losses and many of our fighters were taken prisoner.

The way *Gitana* loves *Gitano*

The night we went to sabotage the railway at Saint Marcel was the night my pain finally dissolved. We were lying in the ditch when our men went to put the cables on the tracks. I could see Chico's and Henri's backs in the distance until they disappeared from my sight. I pointed my rifle, ready for anything. I had gotten quite accurate with my shooting, and in training I rarely missed the targets.

Louis now put me with the first row of gunners on all our missions. We were 35 left in Louis' mobile group. Many partisans had remained in the north to fight and guide the Americans. Jacob was among them. He was heartbroken because of me, and I was uncomfortable around him. When he asked Louis for a transfer, Louis granted it immediately.

TAMBOURINE

My friends Sara and Charlotte remained with the Americans. The laughter was gone from my life. Those two were determined to find American husbands and go after them to live the good life. Rachelle was married to Alain two weeks before we left for the south, in a simple ceremony in Normandy by an American priest. She was four months pregnant and Louis insisted they do the right thing.

Jean was crouched down near me in the ditch. The boy was growing fast. He was my brother Paco's age, but he was a different personality. Where Paco was stubborn and rough, Jean was gentle, sensitive, and imaginative. He was a great guitar and violin player and had a beautiful voice. When the partisans wanted to party, they would call Jean to play for them.

Louis hardly ever took him on missions. Jean was too young to get killed; that's what Henri told him. But Louis was short on manpower now, and he agreed to take Jean along.
I touched his shoulder. "You okay?" I asked.
"Fine," he nodded, and gripped his rifle.
"I will tell the all family after this is over what a brave young man you were," I whispered.

"You think they're all still alive, Nadine?"
"I am sure. Your father and my father are very smart; they will cross the border fine."
"Something is wrong," I heard Louis saying. They were supposed to be back already. The train is due here in one minute."

Nily Naiman

My heart froze; "I am going," I said, and started running, not listening to Louis calling me to stay. My heart was beating so fast I felt sharp pains in my chest. Chico, Chico that was all I was thinking, I have to get Chico.

I went close to the railway and found the men.
"Get going," I said, "The train will be here in a minute."
"He is tangled," Henri pointed to Chico. "We just finished with the bomb, and we found out he was stuck. We were starting to help him out of the cables."

"I will take care of it; you go." I said.
The men ran off. I came close to Chico; he was tangled in the cable.
"I will get you out; don't move," I said.
I looked nervously at my watch. I had less than a minute before the train would arrive and we would be blasted. Chico was composed; he was on his knees, his heel wedged between the railway and the cable. I bent down in front of him and carefully untied his shoe.

"We might die together now," he said.
"Like Romeo and Juliet," I smiled.
"I love you" he said, his breath on my face.
"Pull your leg slowly out of your shoe," I said, surprised at how calm I was.
"I love you," he said again quietly.

"Sit! I will get you out!" I said.
He sat down, I held the shoe firmly, and he got out in a second.

TAMBOURINE

"Run" he held my hand dragging me, "run fast!"
We could hear the train coming; we ran as fast as we could and then rolled on the ground as the blast came. Chico's body was covering me, his hands pushing my head to the ground.

The noise of the blast was so loud and the force of the fire reached so far, I said to myself we were going to die. I was not able to move there, under Chico's body, feeling his weight on me as the heat of the fire burned me. I closed my eyes. It was the end; we were both going to die.

I smiled to myself; I will hold his hand as we go to heaven. We will love each other in heaven, just the way *Gitana s*hould love *Gitano*.
"Chico, hold my hand!" I cried out to him, but I could not hear my own voice, and then there was the darkness, the blessed comfortable darkness.

Chico

I woke up in Rachelle's arms back in camp.
"Chico," I said
"He is fine," Rachelle smiled, "You just fainted, and then you fell asleep." She handed me a glass of water. "Drink slowly. You have to get on your feet. We must get away from here before the Germans come looking for us."
I sat up and rubbed my eyes. "Where is Chico," I

asked.

"He carried you all the way here from the railroad. You were fainting on and off in his arms all the way."
"His arms," I mumbled and closed my eyes.
"You are a hero, sister, you saved Chico's life."
"Is he burnt at all?"
"Minor burns on his back; we took care of him."
"He was covering me with his body. That's why he got burned and I did not." The tears came to my eyes.

Rachelle handed me a piece of bread, "Eat fast, we have to go. Louis gave Chico a horse. He can't walk with his injuries; you will ride with him," she smiled.

"Rachelle." I heard Chico's voice, "we are moving."
"She is ready," Rachelle called to him, and got up and left.
Chico stood in front of me looking at my eyes piercingly. "You feel better?" he asked.
I nodded my head, and walked behind him and lifted up his shirt.

"Is it very painful?" I asked.
"Not as painful as my love for you," he answered.
I came close to him and touched his face. "Chico."
He took me in his arms and his lips searched for mine, and again I tasted heaven.
"Don't cry, Nadine, we will live our lives for each other from now on."

TAMBOURINE

"I was an idiot," I said, "all this wasted time, the unnecessary pain I caused you."

I was holding him, determined not to let go ever again, until we heard Louis calling for us.
"Come Nadine," Chico pulled me in his arms, "we will not part from now on."

In July all ANVIL preparations intensified. We got word that D-Day in the south would be during the night of 14-15 August, and the air raids were to start on August 5. We were supposed to destroy all communications sites and paralyze German movements behind the battle area. In return the Germans would take out their anger on the local villages, raping, killing and causing as much turmoil as they could.

As we were riding from village to village we found devastating scenes of misery and destruction, burnt homes, dead bodies, and hungry children. We would stand in front of huge piles of corpses with tormented looks on their frozen faces. We came across mass graves sometimes holding more than 200 bodies. There were mothers still holding their babies, and couples still holding each other. I would demand of Chico, "Why? Tell me why?" He would caress me gently and cover my eyes with his kisses. "We will live! This will be our revenge! We must live!

Chico had become the world for me. Sometimes I would look at him sleeping next to me, in the short breaks we had, and say to myself it's still a dream. He would rest in my arms. "Like a *Gitano* loves a *Gitana* that is how you love me," I would say. He would kiss me and sigh, "Like no *Gitano* ever loved a *Gitana*, I love you.'

We were heading to Marseille and Toulon, to get the area ready for the Allies. We had managed to take over a few Jeeps and trucks from the Germans. This helped us to carry our artillery and equipment; the sick and the wounded could now be transported from place to place.

As we progressed further south there was less and less of a German presence, but more scenes of destruction. I was ready to adopt two hundred hungry orphans on the way. There were crying babies and children everywhere, looking for their parents. There were mass graves on top of mass graves. The Nazis left behind destruction and horror. Our food supplies were low, but we would give whatever we could to the desperate, crying villagers on the way.

The last mission

On August 5, the Allies began an air raid attack against the southern French coastline and the

TAMBOURINE

immediate interior. Targets all along the coastline were struck, and there were attacks on the bridges of the Rhone River that were the main movement routes for the Germans. We were to focus on smaller water crossings.

From time to time we would hook up with the American paratroopers and soldiers who came from small fleets of patrol craft to coordinate attacks with them. Then at night in the woods they would sit with us sharing their cigarettes and army food packages, and we would call Jean to start a fiesta.

Rachelle and I would sing and the men would dance until their feet hurt. I would lean on Chico, his arms wrapped around me, looking at the fire, wondering if mother and father were still alive, thinking about Anna, the smartest, bravest woman I had ever met, and my brother Andres who loved her so much. Would she have delivered her baby yet? I was thinking about Pablo and Paco, and most of all I missed my little Gisele, my poor, wounded, beautiful little Gisele. I could see her in my mind, in Anna's arms shaking like an animal, her little hands holding her tambourine to her heart.

Our final mission before D-Day was to take place tonight. I better let Chico sleep, I thought; who knows when we'll be able to close our eyes again.

When night fell we prepared our ammunition and the camp was ready to move. Rachelle hugged me. She looked big now; it would not be long before I would become an aunt. She and some of the wounded partisans were to stay behind in the woods, to wait for us to finish our mission and then join us on our final departure to Marseille.

"Take care of yourselves," she kissed Chico and me, "and take care of my Alain; this will be your last mission before we can smell freedom."

We got on the horse. Chico wrapped his arms around me. "When it's all over I am going to get you into bed, a real bed, and never come out again, *Chiquita.*"
"You promise?" I asked.
He kissed me and kicked the horse. "I swear to you."

The wind was hitting my face lightly. It was a clear night. I closed my eyes for a moment; I could ride like this in his arms forever. We crossed the field behind the other horses and Jeeps. "We will take a side route," Chico said, "just to make sure the bastards did not leave mines on the open fields."

We parted from the group, Jean and George following us. We could see Henri and some others taking a second alternative route. We were heading toward the railway, the last railway that had still not been sabotaged by us. Suddenly we heard the gunshots and then explosions.

"It's an ambush," I said, and Chico stopped the horse.
"Our wagons, our Jeeps," said David.

TAMBOURINE

Henri came riding his horse from nowhere. "Get deep into the woods, they have found us."
"Everybody?" asked Chico.
Henri nodded his head, and rode off.
"Rachelle," I cried, "what are we going to tell Rachelle?"
Chico lifted me up on the horse. "We must get out of here."

    We rode into the woods where we had left the wagons. "Chico," I cried, "Alain and Louis were in the leading jeep."
Chico was silent. Henri was riding in front of us. We had only six horses. My god, I thought as the horrible knowledge was hitting me, they are all dead. Louis, our commander who had become like a father to us, Alain, my sweet, gentle brother in law, and twenty-three of our best men and women were gone. Henri tried to use the radio, calling for them again and again, but here was no answer. The other side was dead.

    The tears were flowing out of my eyes now like a river. I could feel Chico's tears on my neck as we arrived in the woods.
We got off the horses; I ran and hugged George and Jean. At least they had been spared, I thought, as Rachelle got down from the wagon.
"What happened?" she asked, "What were those blast sounds?"

    "Get in the wagon," Henri said, "we have to go."
We could hear the German vehicles moving now on the

field. Henri signaled to us to be quiet.
"Alain, where is Alain?" Rachelle was crying.
Henri put his palm on her mouth. "Be quiet, Rachelle," he said holding her in his arms from behind, not letting her move.
I could see her struggling in his arms crying into his palm.
I looked at Chico; he was holding his mouth shut watching her crying. I counted fifteen horses left and thirteen people, some of them wounded.

    The forest was silent now; the Germans had left. Henri removed his palm from Rachelle's face and I caught her in my arms.
"I want to go there," she said.
"It's too dangerous. We have to go," I said quietly.
"I am not leaving with out him," she raised her voice.
"Yes you are," Henri raised his voice too. "How are you going to help him? By killing all of us and yourself and his baby? Get in the wagon. We are leaving."
"No," she was struggling, "I am staying here."
Henri grabbed her from me and picked her up.
"Rachelle, you stupid *Gitana*, get in now!"

    Rachelle stopped fighting at this point. She was lying on the hay in the wagon, crying. I climbed up and sat by her. "He might have survived; we will find him," I said. "Alain is smart. He might have found a way to escape. Be strong, sister!"

    Rachelle wept. The wagon had started to move. Chico and Jean were sitting in the front. I was still in shock. We had been going through seven months with

TAMBOURINE

the partisans. Our original group had managed to survive all this time and now when it was almost over this had to happen. I hugged my crying sister and tried to comfort her, the tears flooding my face.

"Soon we will see mother and father. Little Gisele and Nicola and Michel must be all grown up by now. Anna and Andres had their baby; think about it Rachelle. We will make a big fiesta and cook your favorite foods and sing and dance for your baby."

Rachelle kept sobbing, shaking her head, not saying a word. *"Ven Rachelle, canta para mi"* (come Rachelle sing for me) I said. I started singing to her; the rest of the wounded in the wagons were lying there quietly, crying.

"I slept so deeply,
My dearest mother
Has been taken away.
I slept so deeply,
That I heard nothing.

"Now let me fall on bended knee,
For the return of Saint Sara.

"So she may receive
 My dearest mother,
Let us all kneel down,
For the receiving of the Saints."

"I pray to the moon,

High up in the sky,
To grant my father rest,
For I love him dearly."

      Rachelle sat up now; the song caught her attention. She was touching her stomach and joined me singing.
"A Gypsy without song and dance is a dead Gypsy", my father used to say. I hit the tambourine that was lying on the wagon and Rachelle sang, tears running across her cheeks.

"I fell asleep.
My dearest love
Has been shot and killed.
I fell asleep
And did not even hear a thing.

Now let me pray and cry
For the mercy of the Lord.

Maybe he will comfort
My aching soul.
Pray with my sister
For the mercy of the Lord.

I pray to the soul
Of my love to forgive me.
I loved him more than life."

TAMBOURINE

To be a Gypsy again

The Allies launched their sea and air assault in the south on August 15. We were in radio contact with the other partisan groups, and joined with them in the woods near Marseille. It was strange. The Germans put up hardly any resistance against the paratroopers. They seemed to have lost their will to fight, knowing that it was all over. With our help the British and American paratroopers quickly seized all of the Germans' important facilities.

On the next day French troops landed and headed west, successfully taking control of the ports of Toulon and Marseilles. The Germans were retreating, with our resistance fighters harassing them every step of the way.

Our numbers had grown tremendously. I later learned that at that point we were some 70,000 armed Frenchman along with thousands of others who were unarmed, keeping after the Germans, chasing them out. We liberated a major piece of the country south of the Loire River and west of the Rhone.

In Toulon and Marseilles the Germans did put up a fight. Even though French troops had seized the two ports by August 28, the fighting in those cities was fierce. In the first two weeks of fighting after the Allied invasion in the south, tens of thousands of German soldiers and officers had been taken prisoner and all posts had been captured, but the cost was high. The casualties numbered 4,000 Frenchmen and 2,700

Nily Naiman

Americans.

On August 25 the German garrison in Paris surrendered to General Lecher, whose French first division had rushed into the city. Early in September, the Allies approached the fortified Siegfried line along Germany's western border. France was free.

It was still warm in the woods when we got the news that it was all over, that we were suddenly free. We found ourselves all alone, confused and overwhelmed with mixed emotions. After the parties and the singing the dancing, the feeling of freedom hit us Gypsies in a strange way.

While others were drinking and shouting for joy, we were left empty and wandering like neglected little children, not knowing where to turn next. The six of us would sit together silently in front of the suddenly enormous amounts of food that the people in town would prepare for us every day, not being able to eat more than a bite. We would toss and turn on the comfortable beds that the villagers would make available to us. The soft pillows and blankets were as thorns.

All our lives we had wished to live like human beings, in regular homes with real beds, real toilets, real roofs above our heads, and real showers; but now when people would fight over us to have us in their homes, and we had those luxuries every day, it all seemed insignificant and foreign.

TAMBOURINE

I woke up in Chico's arms, in a stranger's home on a soft bed, to meet his eyes. I smiled to him, cuddling in his arms. "Why don't you sleep, Chico?" He held me, "I want to be on the hay in the wagon again. I miss the smell of the horses, the laughter of the children, the smell of the cooked food in the street. I miss being a Gypsy!"

Far away in Andalucía, our Gypsy fate was waiting for us. France would never be our land again.

Part Three: Michel

Nily Naiman

(Toulouse –France – 1943)

Father Philippe took me to plant vegetables in the small inner garden near the dormitories now that the warmth of spring had softened the ground. We planted the seeds and watered them, and father Philippe made the sign of the cross over the little rows. "By the time those tomatoes grow the war will be over," he said.

There was not much food to spare in the monastery. Some of the nuns were nasty; they would beat you up if you would steal from the holy bread. But there were nights that my stomach growled from hunger; I had to take my chances.

Nicola was with the other small kids and they were getting enough food from their nuns. But I was used as a cleaning boy, and I was allowed only one meal a day.

There were other children my age, all of them Jewish. They were treated differently at the monastery; the nuns gave them respect and sometimes even spoiled them. They did not have to do housework. They were allowed to practice their religion and got enough food. We were the only Gypsy family, and we were clearly second class citizens here, just like everywhere we had ever been.

TAMBOURINE

Our women and girls were used right from the start for kitchen help and cleaning, and I was made a general janitor. Some of the nuns would call me for every little chore. If they would drop something on the floor it was,
"Where is that Gypsy boy? Call him to clean this mess up!"

I had to carry things all the time and shine some of the nuns' shoes. Back home we boys were treated differently. We were not allowed to do any housework. That's why I had no idea how to do what they wanted me to do. The nasty nuns would loose their patience with me if I did something wrong in my chores, and would beat me mercilessly.

It was Jesuit father Pierre Chaillet, who was a hero of the French resistance and the publisher of the underground newspaper, who used to haunt the streets of Lyons and the countryside looking for abandoned children. He would house hundreds of other refugees and rescued many Jewish children from French police stations where they were being held for questioning. Some of those children would be brought to our monastery, and that meant a lot more work for me.

Clearly not all the nuns were happy about these activities, but Jean-Gerard Saliege, the Archbishop of Toulouse, had given Georges Garel of the OSE a personal letter of introduction and encouraged him to place Jewish children in the church's boarding schools, orphanages, hospitals and youth hostels.

Some of the nuns disapproved of the sheltering of the children because it added to their work and meant less food. Since the order only specified hiding Jewish and resistance members' children, there was a reason for them to complain about us, the Gypsies.

Sometimes I got lucky and they would send me to peel potatoes in the kitchen where Aunt Claire and Aunt Carlita were working. They would sneak me a bite under the table. Aunt Claire would call me, "*Vengo Michel*," in Spanish so the nuns would not understand. I would brush against her and would pretend to stumble and fall. Aunt Claire would quickly throw me something to eat and I would stuff it in my pocket.

If I were caught I would not get a meal for two whole days. Sister Nanette was an especially mean one. She would always follow me with her eyes, trying to find something wrong.
"You are dirty; Jesus doesn't like dirty Gypsies," she used to say. "You are a lazy Gypsy pig," she would tell me. "You should pray harder and ask forgiveness for your people's sins. You are a cursed breed."

"My people never sinned against God or anyone else," I would answer.
 She would turn around, her eyes spitting fire, and slap me across my face.
"You talk only when you are asked to talk!"

I would run into my little corner in the church. Father Philippe would look at me and ask, "What's

TAMBOURINE

wrong, Michel?"
"Nothing," I would answer. All I needed was trouble, and they would throw us all to the Nazi dogs. Sister Nanette and other nuns made sure to tell me that the first day we arrived there, and reminded me of it every day.

Mother died two weeks after the nuns took us in. My cousin Lorain passed away three days later, and my little cousin José died three weeks after her. I was as sick as they were, but somehow, as Sister Brigitte told me, Jesus decided he wanted me to live.

Sister Brigitte was my favorite nun. She was very young and pretty, kind and generous, and I never heard her raising her voice. Sometimes she would sneak me an extra piece of bread or a rare bit of chocolate.
"You stay away from Sister Nanette and Sister Charlotte and the others as best you can and you will be safe," she used to whisper to me.

She would take me to her room for a while every day to teach me how to read. I looked forward to these brief moments alone with her; these were the only times I felt that there was actually a reason for me to live.

"You must get some education or you will not be able to survive out there." She gave me a notebook and pencils. "Study hard, Michel, it will pay off," she would pat my head.

Nily Naiman

Sister Charlotte sneered at her.
"You are wasting your time; Gypsies are born stupid. All they are good for is to steal and kill."
Sister Brigitte smiled, trying to calm her down.
"The Lord loves everybody and he would love to see this boy happy. Don't you think so sister?"
Sister Charlotte gave her a nasty look and turned her back and left.

Sister Brigitte smiled a sad smile at me.
"Don't pay attention to them, Michel; you are the smartest boy I have ever met."
"Why do they hate me so?" I asked her.
She hugged me and said, "They don't hate you; they hate themselves."

I missed Mother; I missed her hugging me and kissing me and telling me a secret in my ear, "You are my favorite, but don't tell." Even though I knew she would tell this secret to each one of us, it was still always the best secret I ever heard. I missed the family warmth, the laughter, the sense of belonging, the music, the perfect harmony of clapping and stamping, my sister Nadine's laughing and kissing me until my cheeks would hurt and telling me I was her favorite brother in the whole wide world.

I missed my father and my brothers and my cousins, especially Andres and Antonio. Andres was the best person on earth; he always listened to me and sang to me. He was the one that taught me how to dance flamenco properly. Everyone was always jealous

TAMBOURINE

of me for having Andres as my brother and Antonio as my cousin. He was the one to whom I would go to tell all my secrets.

I always wanted to be Antonio when I grew up. He was good looking, composed, assertive, smart, and strong. Antonio would walk around as if he owned the world. He had lighter features than the rest of us, and the French girls would try to get his attention without any shame.

Antonio could have all the girls he wanted; all he needed to do was snap his fingers. People would tip their hats to him, "*Bon jour,*" (good day) as if he were the master of the ground that he was walking on, and in our camp everybody tried to be on his good side.

When I first fell for Janet, I went to Antonio to tell him about it and to ask his advice. Janet was a wild Gypsy. She was living in our camp in Paris and I had known her ever since I was a baby. She was three years older than I was. I used to play ball with her brother, and when we had fiestas she would always choose me as her dance partner.

Among the children I was the best dancer; it was Gisele and I who were always drawing attention. Janet was a good dancer too, and she would whirl around me, swaying her thighs, making me feel all kinds of strange things in my body.

Antonio told me that it was natural for a growing boy to feel like this. "When you feel very strange, you can rub yourself under the blanket at night until you calm down."

"It's a sin," I responded.

Antonio burst out laughing, "*Mackito, echo*, it's a sin to breathe in this camp."

The girls went crazy for Antonio, Some *Gitanas* used to give me notes to deliver to him. "Go give it to your cousin," they would whisper to me, and would put a coin or a candy in my pocket.

There was one girl, Louise, who would look for me every day and send me to Antonio with fresh flowers.

"Tell him I will drown myself in the river if he doesn't answer," she would say, pushing some coins in my hands. Antonio would give me a bored look, stretching his body slowly and lazily like a tiger,

. "Give it to your mother tell her I said she is my favorite aunt.

"Antonio! She said she will kill herself if you don't talk to her!" I would say.

"Tell the stupid *Gitana* to get off my back already," he yawned.

"She will do it!" I warned him, watching him staring at Anna's blond hair, shaking her behind from side to side while running to Andres' wagon.

"Your brother is lucky, so lucky" he sighed.

"She is prettier then Louise," I admitted.

Antonio laughed painfully. "She is prettier than any girl I have ever seen, smart, beautiful, gorgeous! And it's all Andres'! Lucky devil!"

TAMBOURINE

"You can't find any girl like this for yourself?" I asked. "There are no other girls like this in this world. There is only one, and that one belongs to your brother."

Louise did make good on her promise. After following Antonio one day, crying her love to him, he told her in no uncertain terms that he was not interested. "Stop sending me presents and following me around; nothing will ever happen between us. I don't like you. I am not attracted to you."
She disappeared one day. Her brothers found her body washed up on the riverbank.

The taste of heaven

During the spring of 1944 we received more than two hundred children in our monastery. It was mainly a lot of work for me. Sister Nanette would send me to wash the little boys and clean their clothes and shoes. A lot of the little ones were wetting the bed at night; the sisters would put it on me to wash the sheets. I would get beaten with a belt if I would miss a detail.

My Aunts Claire and Carlita would take care of my wounds and sigh, "Those nuns have no God in them. They are not human; they are monsters. Is this a way to treat an orphan? Not only do they work you to death, they beat you up like this? You should go tell father Philippe." But I would rather die than risk our shelter and cause any of my family to be thrown out in the street.

The day Father Regis de Perceval came to visit our monastery I was working all day cleaning and preparing for him, inside and outside. The nuns were nervous. Everything had to look clean and in order. If something were amiss it would mean trouble for them and less food. The mother superior would then punish the others by various means including beating.

Nobody called me to eat that day. I kept looking nervously in the direction of the kitchen. I could see clearly the smoke coming out of the stoves. My aunts were called early in the morning to help cook the big meal for the guests, and I knew that a lot of dishes were being prepared in there. My stomach was growling. I was so hungry I thought I was going to die.

By six o'clock in the evening I could not see straight anymore. My head was spinning; I had to have some food. My body felt weak. I knew everybody would be getting ready for dinner and the evening prayers.

The smell of the food in the kitchen was irresistible. When important guests were expected the nuns would open the special food storage bins and let the cooks do wonders. If I did not have a bite I would die; that is all that was in my mind.

I sneaked into the main building. It was quiet. It seemed that people were getting ready in their rooms.

TAMBOURINE

I went into the kitchen; the dishes were ready to be served. All those trays full of food were lined up on the table. My head was spinning from the aroma of baked chicken and fresh bread, the soups and the cakes. I held on to the table, the saliva leaking out of my mouth.

Seeing no one I grabbed a spoon and started eating, going from bowl to bowl and shoving handfuls into my mouth.
Food had never tasted so good before. I broke off a piece of chicken and walked around taking handfuls of rice and beans and potatoes. I ate until I felt I was going to explode.

"Nice job, Gypsy, you ruined the dinner!"
Sister Charlotte and Sister Nanette were standing at the door.
They are going to kill me, I thought. I stepped backwards.
Sister Nanette had a stick in her hand and Sister Charlotte was holding her thick belt, turning it round and round in the air so I would hear its vicious sound.

"Take off your pants and bend down," said sister Nanette threateningly.
I let my pants fall and stood in front of her.
"The underwear too," she said, her voice becoming hoarse as it always did when she would make me strip.
I took off my underpants; my penis was sticking out hard from fear.

"Look, sister," she giggled, her eyes fixated on my genitals, "Look at this filth!" She came close to me and then grabbed me in her hand, rubbing me curiously as if examining an object that had fallen from outer space.

The sisters looked at each other smiling, and Sister Charlotte also came close to me. They had the smell of rotten eggs. Sister Nanette brought her face close to mine. I could see her mustache above her upper lip.

Sister Charlotte took off her underwear beneath her habit and lay down on the floor. "Stick it in her," commanded Sister Nannette, and pushed me to the floor. I could see the layers of flab of Sister Charlotte's fat stomach spilling to her sides. "Stick it in, Gypsy," sister Nanette pushed me again.
Sister Charlotte was snorting, pulling me to herself. I felt I was drowning in fat; I was choking and nauseated. "Harder!"

Sister Charlotte breathed heavily in my face, her breath stinking like a toilet. She started moving her fat body. I felt I was being swallowed by a huge monster. "Mother," I mumbled, "Mother, help me! Send me the Black Madonna to rescue me."

I could not hold it anymore; I started heaving. All the food that I had shoved into my body came out now in a river of goo, right on Sister Charlotte's face. The vomit was covering her face and her neck, and leaking to all sides. I could feel the stick on my behind, the burning sensation of the blows, not able to stop throwing up.

TAMBOURINE

Sister Charlotte was trying to push me away, blinded by the foul liquid that covered her eyes; and Sister Nannette was hitting me with her stick as hard as she could from above, screaming, "Filth, get off her, filth! Curse you and your all filthy Gypsy ancestors that brought you to this world!"

She was completely hysterical, yelling and hitting me while the other fat blob was trying to get the mess off her face. I started laughing, unable to stop the flood of laughter welling up in me. I was laughing and laughing while the stick tore my back and my behind to the point were I felt that my body was burning in the fires of hell.

"Stop!" It was Father Philippe's commanding voice.
The beating stopped. Father Philippe was standing there shocked. The honorable Archbishop of Toulouse, Jean-Gerard Saliege, was standing by his side watching us in horror.

Father Philippe approached sister Nannette and grabbed the stick from her hand, hitting her across her face with it as hard as he could. She gave a wild, sharp howl that echoed through the entire monastery, and backed off shaking.

Then he pulled me off of Sister Charlotte, who was still struggling to get up. "Go wash, and get some clean clothes on yourself," he said to me.
I looked at the priests, trying to cover my naked

genitals with my hands. The archbishop was staring at the fresh bright red lines the stick had left on me and all the other scars and black and blue bruises that I had been collecting over the year in the monastery. He signaled to father Philippe, showing him my body in horror.

"Get up!" Father Philippe shouted at the nun, who was trying desperately to get her fat body off the floor. The archbishop grabbed the belt and started hitting her all over while father Daniel was helping him with the stick. Every time the belt would come up from a hit the stick would come down. The two kept on in perfect rhythm while the nun was screaming like an animal rolling on the floor in the puddle of vomit.

I left the kitchen pulling my pants on, and ran to the bathroom where I stood under the water for a long time. My head was hurting; I was sobbing under the water, scrubbing my skin with the sponge as hard as I could. The nausea was still choking me; the burning scratches on my back felt raw and deep.

Father Philippe came into the bathroom and said quietly, "Turn off the water, boy."
He handed me a towel. I wrapped myself in it slowly and said, "Now you will throw me out to the Nazi dogs."
Father Philippe shook his head. "Is this what those nuns told you would happen?"
I nodded my head and the tears started flowing against my will.
"How long is this abuse has been going on?"

TAMBOURINE

He asked, putting cream on my wounds.
"Ever since we got here," I said. "They told me I was a filthy Gypsy and beat me up and made me go without food for days. They said Gypsies don't deserve human treatment."

Father Philippe was panting. I had never seen him so angry. His face turned bright red. "For God's sake, boy, you have been suffering this hell and nobody knew? You should have come to tell me."
"My aunts knew. They told me to tell you, but I was afraid we would all be thrown out," I was sobbing.

After I got dressed Father Philippe said, "Go get your aunts and your brother and cousins, and come to the dining room with them."
"But father," I said, "This is a dinner for the nuns and the guests only."
"You are my honorary guests tonight," he answered and left.

That night we were seated on both sides of the Archbishop of Toulouse. Father Regis de Perceval and the nuns were seated in front of us surprised at the honor that we had been given. We could hear Sisters Charlotte and Nannette crying from the prison cages above us. Father Philippe would not kick them out of the monastery, for fear that they would tell the Germans about the refugees that he was hiding.

"The sisters are going on a serious diet," my cousin Dina giggled in my ear.
Father Philippe got up and put his arm around me.

"Today was the last day of our Gypsy refugees suffering abuse. From now on they will be our honorary guests, and the ladies will be referred to as Madame and the young ladies as Mademoiselle. They will get their reading and writing lessons like all the others. They will have lessons in French, English, math and bible. These people will eat with the nuns, and will get exactly the same portions as they do. If I hear that any of them were insulted or abused, I will personally punish the abuser severely."
Sister Brigitte was smiling to me, raising her two fingers in the victory sign.

Archbishop Jean-Gerard Saliege got up and said, "I have personally written to all the convents and monasteries. From now on our main focus will be to save as many Jews and other refugees as possible. Millions have been murdered by the Nazis in Europe already. We have to do what we can, to save whoever is left."

The nuns nodded their heads. I smiled to Sister Brigitte and started eating. "Who cooked?" I whispered to Dina.
"My mother and Aunt Carlita," she answered. "The nuns can't cook for their lives. Watch the archbishop licking his fingers," she giggled. "Only Gypsies know how to cook."

TAMBOURINE

Father Philippe

By the end of May I was reading books very well. I would go to the monastery's dusty shelves and find old books that nobody had touched for years and read them one by one. Other than my daily classes I did not have to work anymore. Sometimes I would go to the garden to clean up the wild bushes, just to breathe some fresh air. I would take Nicola and my guitar and teach him how to strum and dance.

"A man who can't dance the flamenco or play the instruments is not a real Gypsy," I would tell him. "You better do your best to learn so we can go to Spain after the war like proud Gypsies."
Nicola would strum the guitar with his little hands. "Mackito, I miss Mommy," his eyes would fill with tears.

"Mother is watching you from heaven all the time," I patted his head. "Soon we will meet with Rachelle and Nadine and Gisele, and father will buy you your own guitar."
I stood up stamping my feet, moving my hands fast around my waist and then froze. Sister Brigitte was watching me with a group of Jewish girls.

"Don't stop, Michel, it is so beautiful," she said.

Nily Naiman

"I never saw such beautiful dancing in my all life."
"It's flamenco; only Gypsies can do flamenco," said Nicola.
Sister Brigitte sat down with the girls and clapped her hands, "Sing for us Michel; teach us the Gypsy dance."

    I smiled and clapped my hands, going toward one of the girls who looked to be my age. She got up and turned around me, trying to follow my steps and clapping her hands. I looked right in her eyes; she was about my height. She was a blond girl with sky blue eyes, and she smiled and stretched her back, swaying her hips around me.

    She caught on fast. Everybody was clapping. Nicola was playing the guitar and I was dancing, stamping my feet hard on the ground and singing.

"We travel, we travel,
Nobody wants us.
We were born to flee,
They all hate us.

"Why did you leave me?
You would not listen.
They made a fool out of me
And you didn't even care.

"Give me a heel
So I can stamp my feet.
As I dance,
You will change your mind."

TAMBOURINE

The Jewish girl was sweating now; she had caught the tune and the step. She was brushing against me, clapping her hands. I was thinking of Janet at that moment, Janet who would pass her fingers over my hair, and sway her hips toward mine while dancing, Janet who would whisper things to me that even the horses would blush to hear, Janet who would shake her long black curls, her big hoop earrings rocking from side to side on her ears.

Janet now disappeared from my heart for the first time since I had left Paris. Here was this blue-eyed pretty girl, licking her lips slowly, looking at me as if in a dream, her hips, her legs, her beautiful figure turning around me, lighting me on fire. Her bright blue eyes shone in the sun and her golden hair was flying with the wind against her fair skinned, beautiful face.

Sister Brigitte got up and put her hand on the girl's shoulder. "Calm down, Miriam," she said, sensing the dangerous passion between us. I stopped dancing and held on to Nicola. "We will go in now," I said, and went inside holding his hand. I would dream from now on in yellow and bright blue colors.

Father Philippe told me that the resistance was getting stronger and the Germans were becoming more and more nervous. Freedom was near but the danger was greater than before. The Germans had burnt villages and murdered people by the hundreds. There were stories of torture and rape.
"We have to be extra careful now," he said.

"Abbe Rene de Naurios has fled the country, Bishop Pierre-Marie Thetas from Montauban was arrested by the Gestapo and it is doubtful that he is still alive, and Father Favre of St. Francis was betrayed and was executed."

"Why do you take the risk?" I asked.
"Why am I a priest?" answered Father Philippe.
Many times we were given the coded warning that the Germans were in the monastery searching or asking questions. The nuns would offer them a drink (that was when the alcohol bottles were opened) and we would take cover in our assigned hiding places.

"When it's all over I want to become a teacher," I said to him. "I will go to study education in Spain."
"What kind of teacher do you want to become?" Father Philippe smiled.
"I will teach history; I will make sure to teach the truth about all the atrocities against Gypsies all over the world for so many years," I answered, my eyes filling with tears.

"Why Spain? Your homeland is France."
"I will never live in France again. The French people hated us long before the war and destroyed us during the war and will hate us again after the war ends. I will never live among them again."

Father Philippe nodded his head. He knew that we had never been allowed in the regular schools in France. To be born a Gypsy in France meant being born cursed. We were never allowed to live among the

TAMBOURINE

rest of the French citizens; we were abused and kicked around wherever we went.

I would sit for hours in the library of the monastery, sorting through anything that had to do with my people. The nuns got used to me being there all the time. Anyone who wanted to find me knew that I would be in the library.

Sister Brigitte had opened up a whole new world for me by teaching me to read. I would wake up in the morning and run to the library, forgetting to even eat breakfast. I found newspaper articles and history books that had to do with Gypsy laws. I was in shock to find that the hate for us had been going on forever.

In 1890 there was a conference in Swabia that was called "The Gypsy Filth." In 1899 in Munich the Central Office of Fighting the Gypsy Nuisance was created. Then I learned that all over Europe there had been abuses against us. In Switzerland in the beginning of the nineteen hundreds we had to be registered as "different citizens". Hungarian Gypsies had to be branded for identification. In France in 1912 Gypsies were forced to carry identity cards and could be arrested without them. In Germany Gypsies were banned from holiday resorts and had to return trading licenses. In Prussia in November of 1927 there were armed raids on Gypsy communities. And in 1933 when the Nazi party was voted into power they activated laws against Gypsies that had been on the books since the Middle Ages.

Nily Naiman

In 1935 Robert Ritter in Germany determined that Gypsies and Negroes were sub-humans. His supposed findings would have been amusing if not for the implications. He collected Gypsies everywhere for testing, and came to this conclusion: "We have been able to establish that more than 90% of so-called native Gypsies are of mixed blood. They are people of entirely primitive ethnological origins, whose mental backwardness makes them incapable of real social adaptation."
He said that the Gypsy problem could only be solved when the main body of Gypsy individuals would be collected together in large camps and kept working there, and their breeding stopped once and for all.

To my horror I read that in the last four years since the war had begun the Germans and the Vichy police had killed and incinerated thousands of Gypsies in France. In 1933 a large population of Gypsies disappeared into concentration camps where they were sterilized and killed. The children were used as guinea pigs for testing Zyklon-B cyanide gas crystals.

In June of 1941 there were reports that three hundred Gypsy boys between the ages of fourteen and nineteen years of age were sent to Mauthausen in Austria, where they were tested for the effectiveness of the gas chambers. None survived.

I read articles that were written by partisans in the resistance papers, saying that more then 3000 prisoners in the French camps had died from lack of medical attention and starvation. The operation "Vent

TAMBOURINE

Printanier" (spring wind), was the worst of all. More then 12,800 men, women, and children aged between two and twelve were transported to the stadium in Paris, the Velodrome d'Hivre. The children were kept there for five miserable days without any food or medical care, and then they were transferred to Drancy.

I remembered Drancy very well; our boys and men were the ones who had built it. I could remember the vicious abuse and the shouted insults of the Vichy policemen, the little boys crying from pain, being raped and beaten by them.

In Drancy the children were separated from their parents, who were transported to Auschwitz and gassed. The children stayed in Drancy for weeks, and many died from lack of care and the brutality of the French guards. Finally those that survived were all transferred to Auschwitz and sent to the gas chambers upon their arrival.

Tears of anger would boil up out of my eyes as I would sit there swallowing the information. I would go up to the punishment cages and kick the metal bars that enclosed Sister Nannette and Sister Charlotte and scream and curse them until my feet hurt and my voice was gone. They would squeeze to the wall frightened, and silently sob. I would spit in their faces, thinking how miserable these women of authority had become. How quickly one can go from power to absolutely nothing!

Flamenco

The sun was strong. Summer would be coming soon to Toulouse. I was sitting outside strumming my guitar and thinking I would cross the border to Spain and would fight for the right to go to school. I was going to become a great man and that's how I would avenge all the sub-humans of the world. I had passed my sixteenth birthday two months before, but I felt old, as if having experienced so much evil I had seen everything I needed to see and there was not much left to discover.

"Teach me to dance," I heard her sweet voice, and stopped strumming my guitar. She was standing there behind me, her hair shining golden in the sunlight. She was licking her beautiful red lips slowly. I came to her face and started clapping my hands, looking right at her eyes. She began to clap her hands too, a little hesitant.

"Hold your skirt in one hand and lift it up when you turn," I said, "Listen to the clapping and tap your feet to the beat."
Miriam was stamping her feet as hard as she could, clapping her hands. She had good rhythm. "Now imagine your hands are birds, your fingers are wings," I said, moving as close as I could to her body. "Let your birds fly like this," I showed her the movement of my fingers.

Miriam was moving her fingers, trying to do

what I was doing. We were brushing against each other, our faces almost touching. I could see the drops of sweat on her upper lip, She was wrapped up in the beat of my clapping, swaying her hips, looking at me as if she were bewitched. I stopped and put my lips on hers. I could feel her hesitating, but then she moaned and kissed me with all her soul.

    I closed my eyes. Janet's kisses were never as sweet as this. I held her head, looking at her closed eyes, touching her golden hair, thinking God has sent me an angel. I remembered Andres coming back from the river the first time, smiling to me. At the time he had said the same thing about Anna, "God sent me an angel."
"What does an angel look like?" I asked.
"Angels have golden hair and blue eyes and they are Jewish," he said, his eyes all lit up.
"The Jews killed Jesus," I said. "They are no angels."
"Your head is filled with ghost stories. Drop the Gitano legends," Andres pinched my nose.

    Miriam opened her eyes and a flood of blue water washed over my heart.
"You are so pretty" I said.
"I never kissed a boy before," she said blushing.
"I never kissed a girl as pretty as you before," I said.
"Hold me tight," she said and put her arms around my neck.
"They will catch us, we will be punished," I said and held her as strongly as I could, feeling my whole body awakening to her.

"I know a place," she said, and grabbed my hand and dragged me behind the building to a broken, abandoned shack. I peered around nervously. We could see the front of the monastery from here. If the nuns would find me violating the girl it would be the end for me and all my family.

Miriam found a torn blanket and threw it on the floor. "Come," she said, and we lay down together. "This will be our hiding place from now on," she whispered
"How did you get here?" I asked.
She sat down, straightening her shirt. "What do you mean?"
Miriam was silent for a long time and started sobbing. I held her in my arms and stroked her hair,
"Don't cry, Miriam."

"They shot Mama and Papa in front of my face," she cried out suddenly.
I felt her tears wetting my heart.
"Mama pushed me under the bed. 'Stay there; don't move!' she said and covered the bed so that the bedspread hung all the way to the floor. The Nazis tore open the door and yelled at Papa, '*Raus, Juden!*' Papa asked, 'Where are you taking me?' The Nazi hit him on the head with his rifle; I could hear his skull cracking and put my palm on my mouth to choke a scream.

"They were shouting, '*Raus! Juden Raus*!' pushing Mama to the door. I saw Mama running to Papa trying to help him get up. One of the Nazis

TAMBOURINE

slapped her face. 'Get up *Juden Shmutz'* (filth) he screamed, '*Raus Schnell'!* (Out! Fast!).
Mama held on to Papa. I could see her face from the crack in the blanket looking at my direction. Papa was gripping the rug, refusing to get up. Mama was kicking the Nazi with her knee.

"I could hear the shots above me. My parents' faces and heads were riddled with holes and covered with blood. They stiffened, dead, holding each other. It was quiet for a second. Then I heard one of the Nazis spit on their bodies, and then I heard a pants zipper opening and one of them was urinating on the two bodies.

"'Kommen, Ludwig,' one of them said.
'Eine minute,' I heard the other one saying. The refrigerator was open. '*Es gibt nahrung hier!*' (There is food here!).
The Nazis were eating, emptying out the refrigerator. I could hear them chewing, stuffing their faces. Mama had just finished cooking Shabbat dinner and putting it away, in order to serve it after we got back from the synagogue.

"Then one of the Nazis said. '*Gehen sie suchen geld und nach schmucksachen,*' (go look for jewelry and money). I heard them emptying out boxes and filling up their pockets. I squeezed to the floor when one of them bent down and checked Papa's pockets. His face lit up. There was a package of bills in it. He shoved the money in his pocket and wiped his hands on Papa's clothes. Then they finally left.

"I crawled out from under the bed; my Mama and Papa were lying there covered with blood and urine. My Mama and Papa, the greatest, the nicest, the most beautiful people I have ever known. The most life loving, generous, sensual people were now lying there like two pieces of garbage.

"Mama was a great singer. She used to sing all the Edith Piaf songs by heart, and Papa danced just like a professional dancer. He could do the tango so well the ladies always fought over who would dance with him.

"How can people be so lively one minute and then the next minute lie like sacks of garbage on the floor, dead?"
She sobbed in my arms. My heart was breaking for her. Tears flooded my eyes, and anger was overwhelming me.

She continued talking. "I ran outside. Luckily there were no SS men there. I went to the park and curled up on the bench thinking, let somebody come and murder me. I don't want to live anyway. I don't know how long I was there until Bishop Pierre-Marie Theas came and brought me here."

She was crying in my arms. I kissed her and said, "We will be here for each other now." I wiped her tears with my fingers. "You know my brother Andres married a Jewish girl who looks just like you. Her name is Anna; you would like her very much."

TAMBOURINE

"You will take me with you after the war?" She wiped her tears.
"I will if you want me to. I will go to Spain," I said.
She held me. "I will go with you. If you'll take me I will go with you anywhere; there is nobody left for me in this world."

We heard trucks. I looked outside. "Germans," I said, "They are going into the monastery."
"The nuns will be hysterical not finding us," she said.
I piled up broken chairs and other broken furniture in front of us, until we could not see the door any more.
"Lie down quietly; it will be over soon." I pulled her to the floor.

The nuns would butter up the pigs with some alcohol and sausages and show them the basements again, so they would see that there were no hidden treasures and would leave. Usually the whole thing did not take more than an hour. We all had our assigned hiding places. The little ones would be taken to the secret attics; some of the older children would hide in the huge laundry bins. Others would jump into the big pots in the kitchen.

Father Philippe had constructed hidden doorways to back rooms all over the monastery. There were plenty of places to stay out of sight.
Miriam held my face to hers. "I am glad we have each other," she whispered

Suddenly we heard shouting and screaming outside. I hissed at her, "Something's gone wrong. Be

quiet!"
We could hear the Nazis yelling, "*Anordnung!*" (Line up).
I could see through a crack some of the nuns lining up with a group of Jewish girls from Miriam's group. Father Philippe was walking beside a Nazi soldier, a gun to his head. He was trying to say something but the SS slapped him across his face and screamed, "*Halt die schnauzer*" (shut up).

    The girls were crying; I could see Sister Brigitte trying to keep them quiet. *"Steigen sie ail lkwas ein!"* (Get in the truck) the SS were shouting.
They were all going into the truck. One of the soldiers pushed Sister Brigitte aside, tearing off her head covering. I could see him bending down to her. He pushed her to the floor, "Take it in your mouth if you want to live!"
I could see Sister Brigitte bending down bringing her mouth to his genitals. Miriam was stunned, watching the horror unfold.

    We crouched down behind the furniture and the blanket. She was weeping in my arms, and then we heard the boot steps. I put my palm on her mouth to silence her. The door was opened roughly. I could hear the heavy breath of the Nazi right above us, and then he said *"Niemand heir"* (no one here).
The trucks then moved off and it was quiet.

TAMBOURINE

Time to go

"Nicola," I said, and started pulling apart the pile of furniture. My heart was pounding. "Nicola," I kept saying. Miriam got up shaking and helped me pass. I opened the door and ran out, Miriam hurrying after me.

Nicola, my head was pounding. I ran and found Sister Brigitte on the floor still lying there quietly. I stepped toward her slowly. "She is dead," Miriam said.

I bent down and shook her, "Sister Brigitte," I said, "It's me, Michel." She opened her eyes and looked at me dazed. "Help me," I said to Miriam. We managed to lift her up; I had never seen Sister Brigitte so lost, so lifeless. The anger was choking me. I would go to the forests now and join the partisans. I made up my mind; I would fight the Germans to the death.

We brought Sister Brigitte to the monastery. The sisters were frantic. I left Miriam and Sister Brigitte with them and ran to the secret room. "Nicola," I was sobbing. I barged in and the life came back to me. Nicola was being held by Aunt Claire. Ninet, Dina, and Jean Paul were huddled together at the edge of the room. My family was alive.

Nicola ran into my arms; I picked him up and hugged him. "My God, thank the Lord," I sobbed, "You are alive, thank God."
I could hear his little heart beating hard. "Mackito," he cried,

"I want *Papi*." (Father) I held him to my heart. "I promise you *hermano (brother)*, I will bring you to *Papi*!"

All the little kids were frightened. They had been trained in hiding just like Nicola, but they all sensed that something had gone wrong this time. "It's quiet now," I told the nuns, "the Germans left."

"What happened out there," asked Sister Paulette.
"They took all the Jewish girls from the teenage group and at least seven nuns."
"Father Philippe?" she asked
"Arrested," I answered.
She sighed and gathered the kids. "I will take them to the play area now," she said to my aunts. "You start on lunch for them."

We walked to the kitchen. I sat down with Nicola still in my arms.
"They arrested father Philippe," I said.
Aunt Carlita looked at me silently and sighed.
"I want to go to the woods and join the partisans," I said.
"You are not leaving anywhere," said Aunt Claire.
"It's my decision," I answered.
"You are not old enough to make any decisions here!" she lashed at me.
"I will not sit here doing nothing and wait for them to come and kill us," I raised my voice.

Dina started crying and Nicola pushed his face

TAMBOURINE

in my chest. Aunt Claire touched me.

"Hijo," (son) she said, *"Ven hijo, antes que muriera tu madre, le prometimos a ella, cuidarlos como nuestro hijos.* (Before your mother died, we promised her you and Nicola will be like our own). We promised your mother that as long as we will be alive we will never let any harm come to you, and that we will never let you part from us."

"Then you come with me, all of you," I looked at their doubtful faces. "The Nazis know now that this monastery is hiding refugees. They will come again, and anyway who knows what the nuns will say under torture. We have to get out of here."
Aunt Carlita sat down looking at Aunt Claire. "The boy has a point," she said.

"What is your plan, *Hijo*?" she asked.
"We will go south and try to cross the border to Spain," I said. "If we are lucky we will find partisans on the way that will help us."
"And if we are not lucky?" asked Ninet.
"Then we'll die together; at least we'll know we tried," I answered impatiently.

They all looked at each other. "Mother, we should listen to him," Dina said. "The Nazis will be back after they interrogate the nuns and father Philippe. We will be shot on the spot with the Jews. "
Aunt Claire pinched my cheek "When did you become so grown up, Mackito?" she sighed.

"I will go pack up," I said. I took Nicola by the

hand and packed up his bundle and then mine. After that I went to Father Philippe's room. I knew where he hid his most important things. I pulled the wooden case from under his bed and shoved the two handguns and bullets into my pocket. I put the knife and money in my bag. Father Philippe will forgive me, I thought.

Miriam was sitting in her room staring at the empty beds of her friends. "They have gone," she sobbed, "They are all gone."
"Pack up fast," I said, "we are leaving."
She got up. "Michel," she said, "Are you sure you want to take me with you?"
"I am," I said. "Make a bundle and let's go! My family is waiting."

She smiled at Nicola and pushed some clothes in a backpack. I handed her a gun. "Shove it in your skirt belt. If we are in trouble I trust you to use it."
Miriam looked at the gun. "I never used one before."
"When you have to shoot, just pull the trigger," I said.

We went downstairs and said goodbye to the nuns. They were hugging us, wishing us a safe trip. We walked over to my family.
"What's she doing here?" Dina asked, looking at Miriam.
"She is coming with us," I said.
My cousin looked at her aunts, waiting for them to protest. Aunt Carlita hugged Miriam. "You will be one of us from now on, daughter."

Dina got angrier. "She is not family, she is just a

TAMBOURINE

spoiled Jew!"
"*Callate, Dina,*" (shut up Dina) I said.
"*Por que' tenemos que andar con tu estupida novia*"?
(Why do we have to drag your stupid girlfriend with us)
Dina was so angry she started hitting me.
"*Callate estupida Gitana. Ella es mi seleccion*" (shut up stupid Gypsy she is my choice) I said pushing her off me.
"Calm down Dina" Aunt Claire said, "You behave like a stupid jealous cow. The girl looks Christian. She will be beneficial to us."

Dina was Aunt Claire's daughter. She was about my age. Her sister Ninet was eighteen. There was Sara who had remained with her father, and she was nineteen by now. She was her mother's favorite; Aunt Claire would cry at night for her. They were Antonio's sisters; they had two other brothers who had remained with my father and my uncles.

Aunt Carlita's little ones, Lorain and Jose, had died a short time after mother died. All she had left was Jean Paul. For a long time we had kept watch on her; she did not want to live after her children died.

Mother once told me that the three were Aunt Carlita's world. She could not have anymore children. She had almost died delivering each those three. Her husband, my Uncle Gerard, had run off with a wild young *Gitana* far away to Brazil, and we never heard from him again.

My mother was her best friend. They were

sisters and very close in age. Aunt Carlita told everything to my mother, and after mother died my aunt was howling like an animal. "Pilar, Pilar, come back!" The nuns could not calm her down for days. I think she mourned my mother much more than her kids.

The only thing that brought her back to life was her love for the kitchen. The nuns would let her plan and cook the meals from time to time. She would light up and attack the kitchen, letting her imagination come up with the best of the food. We had never had ovens and stoves back in our old camp in Paris. We always cooked on an open fire; that was all we knew. Here Aunt Carlita discovered the seven miracles of the universe, and swore that if she would ever marry another Gitano again, first he would have to buy her a stove and an oven to prove his love for her.

Sister Brigitte was half asleep in her room, two of the nuns sitting by her. I took her lifeless hand and said, "Sister Brigitte, it's me, Michel."
"Michel," she mumbled.
"I am leaving," I said. "I will never forget you, sister."

She squeezed my hand. "Michel, my dear boy."
"I will come looking for you after the war," I said.
"Sing for me" she begged, "Just one more time."
I looked at the nuns; they nodded their heads, "Go on Michel, it will make her feel better."
I started strumming my guitar; I could see her look getting livelier.

TAMBOURINE

*"I can dance,
I can sing,
I can feel,
I am not worthless.*

*"Nobody can make
Music and lyrics
Like a Gypsy.*

*"Give me bright
Colored cloth to wear
And ringing bracelets to place
On my hands and feet,
And I will make you
The happiest woman in the world.*

*"It's you I love,
It's you I choose.
I can dance,
I can sing,
I can feel,
I am not worthless."*

Sister Brigitte was crying now, "You will be a great musician one day, Michel."
I kissed her hand, "I will pray for you sister."
She took her gold cross necklace off her neck and put it on mine. "This will remind you of me."
I left her room heavy hearted; she had been the world for me ever since I got to the monastery. I swore to myself never to forget her as long as I lived.

Eighty

A beautiful May evening had fallen on the Toulouse area; we were walking without any interruptions into the night, until we reached the woods. "We will walk all night toward the southeast," I said to my aunts. "The Germans are not active during the night; we'll have to hide during the day."

We entered the forest holding our flashlights; Nicola's hand was in mine. Miriam was on the other side of him. We were walking for a long time; I could see the little ones and my aunts getting tired. I looked at my watch; it was four o'clock in the morning. I sat down on a tree stump. "Let's rest."

Aunt Claire sat down and pulled sandwiches out of her bag. She gave each of us one and sighed, "We will have to go buy food soon. Every day we have to send Miriam to the villages; she looks like an average French girl."
"I can go," said Dina.
"You cannot, you look like a Gypsy," I said.
She gave me an angry glare. "*Callate* !" (Shut up)
"Dina you are getting on my nerves," I said, grabbing Miriam's hand intentionally.
"To madre me prometio, cuando era nina, que nos casariamos cuando crezcas." (Your mother told me,

TAMBOURINE

when I was a small girl that you will marry me).
"*No te amo, la amo a ella*" (I don't love you, I love her)
I pointed at Miriam, "*Para! Me estas volviendo loco*
"(Stop driving me crazy)

    Dina started crying. She had always been a whiner ever since we were little kids. She always ran after me wherever we went, and demanded attention. I never really thought that she had taken my mother seriously. My mother loved Dina. She used to do her hair and teach her the secrets of fortune telling.

    As a little girl Dina was always dirty; her hair was rarely washed and would fall on her shoulders like rags. She was always getting into trouble, hitting the girls and bothering the boys. Antonio used to tell me that one day somebody would hunt her down like a wild animal. "She is the most irritating person I have ever met," I would say angrily.

    Antonio would smile and say, "Calm down, Gitano, that crazy girl will be your wife one day."
"First I will die!" I would answer.
Antonio would laugh loudly, his hands thrown to all sides. Nobody would make Antonio marry a girl ever. Antonio was a free spirit; he would marry only the girl of his choice.

    Dina had grown in the monastery in the last year. Her breasts were protruding firmly, and her hair was Gypsy shiny black. She had become a beautiful *Gitana*. I had no idea she was serious about my mother's promise; I always treated her just as a nuisance for a cousin, and now I was confused. I

finished my sandwich and looked at Aunt Claire and smiled, shaking my head.
"Don't mind her Mackito," she said "she'll get over it."

Miriam squeezed my hand. "Why is she crying?"
"She is a pain in the neck, that's why," I said, and pulled her away from everybody. "Let's get some sleep," I said, and threw a blanket on the floor. We lay down on the ground beneath the bushes. "You are not sorry you came with me?" I asked.
"I am so grateful to you," she said. "I have nowhere to go, no family left, no friends, and no home. I will never forget you letting me come with you and giving me some hope for a future."
She put her head on my chest and closed her eyes. I held her t in my arms and prayed to the Black Madonna to grant me my wish and bring us all to Spain in one piece.

I woke up. Nicola's little face was above me and he was shaking me, "Get up, Mackito."
"What happened," I asked.
"Trucks, lots of trucks coming"
I jumped up and shook Miriam. "Run deep into the woods," I said. "Tell my aunts to hide until I find you."
"I am coming with you," she said.
"No, go with them," I insisted.

The noise of the trucks was tearing up the silence of the forest. Ninet was running toward me. "Go hide," I said.
"I am staying with you" she said, "no sense in you

TAMBOURINE

staying alone."
"No hysterical *Gitana's* outbursts?"
"No," she shook her head. "Little cousin Mackito, do I look like a hysterical *Gitana* to you? Whenever did you become such a big shot? Anyway I have a gun." She showed me.
"Who gave it to you?"
"I stole it from mother superior before we left," she smiled, "You think I cleaned up her stinking room for a whole year for nothing?"

We made our way silently toward the edge of the forest. It was noon; the sun was lingering beneath the treetops. Now we could hear dogs barking and people screaming. I stopped Ninet. "Dogs, be careful!" We looked between the bushes, ducking down; there must have been thirty trucks in front of us.

The SS were holding the dogs on a short leash. There must have been four hundred people there, men, women, children, and screaming babies in their mother's arms. They were hustled out of the trucks, scared to death.
The SS handed shovels to all the men.
"*Grabung!*" (Dig)
They were yelling. The men were digging fast; the SS would come behind them with the growling dogs and kick them hard "*Grabung!*" They were screaming again and again; the children were crying, clinging to their mothers.

One woman was running to a guard with a baby in her arms crying;

Nily Naiman

"*Ich bin keine Juden*" (I am not Jewish).
The guard pushed her away from him, as if she were a dirty dog. She fell on the ground with the baby in her arms, wailing.

The guard held his forehead,
"Shut up, bitch! Make this scum shut up!"
He kicked her hard with his boot.
"My migraine is getting worse!" The woman was struggling to get up and then the guard sprayed her and the baby with bullets.

Ninet squeezed my hand. I could feel my knees getting weak; my whole body was shaking. I held to Ninet thanking God she was there with me. I looked at her as she was watching it, a fascinated look on her face as if she were watching a movie or something unreal.

At this point the guards pulled the men out of the deep ditches that they had dug and stood them with their backs to them in a row. There were five ditches there. I started calculating in my feverish mind how many people each ditch would store.

"Eighty," I whispered to Ninet.
"Eighty what?" She asked surprised.
I did not answer; the guard was arranging the people in perfect rows in front of the ditches; not one stood out of line. They were quiet now. Even the little children and the babies were silent, as if there had been a sign from God to shut up.

One of the commanders went to each line, like a

TAMBOURINE

engineer measuring his blocks, to measure if they were all lining up straight. I could see him closing one eye, standing there at the edge of the row, narrowing his eye again and again, measuring carefully how straight the lines were.

There were four hundred of them, I was thinking, and there are only thirty SS soldiers. They could take them in a minute even without any weapons if they wanted to. I was looking in shock at how four hundred people were standing there silently, like rows of sheep waiting silently to be slaughtered, and no one even tried to raise a brow.

Then the commandant gave the command, screaming,
"Feuer" (fire).
The machine guns were spraying the people's backs systematically. They fell one by one into the ditches like long rows of cards, and in one minute it was all over.

It was quiet now; the SS were wiping their sweat. One of them was passing a bottle of alcohol. They were exchanging conversation as if they just had finished spraying some vegetables. They were filling in the ditches with the dirt, leveling the area to look as if there had never been any digging.

The truck drivers turned on their engines; the soldiers climbed up and left. It was completely silent in the forest. I could hear the birds cheeping above our heads. Ninet pulled my sleeve; we walked over to the murder sight and looked around.

"Nothing," she said, "it's like nothing ever happened."
I started sobbing. "Eighty," I kept saying.
Ninet touched my shoulder." Mackito, what Eighty?"
"In each ditch, eighty people."

She put her arms around me; I was crying and crying like I had never cried before. I was crying for all I had seen in my short life, for my dead mother and siblings, for human cruelty, for the youth that had lost. I was crying for all the Gitanos in the world, for all the unfortunates. I was unable to stop. Ninet held me silently letting me get it all out.

"Let's take a vow," she said. "You and I, we are going to make it big in Spain," .
I nodded my head.
"We will go to university and go as high as we can go," she said.
"Don't ever forget what you saw now," I said, wiping my tears. "Don't tell the family anything, but don't ever forget."
Ninet put her arm around me, "Let's go Mackito, I will never forget, I promise!"

TAMBOURINE

Partisans

    We kept moving for three nights. On the way Miriam would go into the villages to buy us bread and milk. We would collect berries and drink from streams in the woods. One time I shot a deer and we cooked it on an open fire.

    On our fourth night it was raining; the paths through the forest became muddy. Nicola and Jean Paul were whining all the way. They were wet and uncomfortable. Aunt Claire stopped and said, "We have to find shelter."

    "Ninet," I said, "we have to find a place to hide until the rain passes."
She looked toward the lights coming from the road at the edge of the forest. "I will go with Miriam," she said. "We will try to find a church, or a villager who will take money for a room for the night."

The two got up to go; I held Miriam in my arms and kissed her.
"Don't worry about me," she smiled, "I am getting good at this."
"You are an exceptional girl!"
"You are flattering me!"
"We will come out of this war as big as giants, you'll see! I said, feeling the knot in my throat.

Nily Naiman

They were entering the darkness when we heard the sound of horses galloping; somebody was yelling, "*Qui est-il"?* (Who is it?) Flashlights blinded my eyes. Miriam and Ninet drew their guns and were running back toward us. Aunt Claire was on her knees already in the mud praying to the saints. Ninet took her gun out of her pocket, pointing toward the voice.

"Don't shoot!" we heard a voice. "*Nous ne sommes pas des Allemands, que nous sommes des Partisans"* (We are not Germans, we are Partisans). The four men dismounted. My heart was beating so hard I could hardly stand it. I walked closer to the men. "Partisans," I asked in disbelief, "real partisans?" I touched one of the men's faces. "The Black Madonna sent you."

The man smiled and looked at us. "Gypsies?" I nodded my head.
"And her?" He pointed at Miriam,
"Jewish," I said.

"We are in luck; we found a bunch of Gypsies," he smiled to his friends. "We could use some entertainment," he slapped my shoulder.

"You come with us to our camp; we will take care of you."
I fell on my shaky knees, I could not believe my luck, I kissed the ground at my feet. Saint Sara had mercy on us.

TAMBOURINE

They had us walk behind them, further into the woods. They had hid themselves cleverly. Behind a very thick growth of pines they had built ditches and tunnels for hiding and for storing weapons. There were tents spread out all over the area.

"Get in here," the man said, and pointed to a big tent in the center. "We will get you something to eat." We entered the tent. There was a row of benches set up around a folding table. "Jaclyn," the man said, "Coffee!" Some of the men were sitting together, smoking and drinking coffee.
"What did you bring us this time Daniel?" one of the men asked, examining us.

"Gypsies," Daniel smiled, "real Gypsies; this one almost killed us!" he pointed at Ninet smiling.
The man slapped his shoulder,
"Gypsies, ha?" He got up and looked at us. "We fought along some Gypsies from another one of our units, and they were great fighters."

Aunt Claire came close to him,
"Who were those Gypsies? You remember names?"
"Sure I do," he smiled, "How could I forget? They were singing and dancing for us; we were all in love with their pretty girls. We were trying to convince them to move to our unit but they would not leave Louis."

"Louis," Aunt Claire was rocking, putting her hand on her mouth to choke a scream.
I took her by the arm and sat her down. "Tell us the

names of the Gypsies you met," I said to the man.
He looked at his friends. "You remember the guy that was good with the explosives?"

The man said, "Yes, that was Chico; he was the best bomb maker I have ever met. And there was his brother Henri," the man continued, scratching his head, trying to come up with the names. "There were Jean and George, who played the guitar and the violin very well. And there were the beautiful sisters Rachelle and Nadine."
We all started sobbing, "They are alive." We were huddling in each other's arms. A wave of happiness flooded us; we hugged the young men crying and laughing at the same time. It was the happiest day of my life.

We stayed with the partisans. It was the month of June. The Americans would be landing soon in Normandy. My aunts were cooking for the men. There were no women in that particular unit; they had all been taken to help with the wounded partisans. They were happy for our girls and women. Now all the work of housekeeping cooking fell on them.

After a few weeks of being left behind again and again when the men went on their missions, Ninet was laughing, "We are some partisan fighters, cooking and cleaning and dancing flamenco."
"I will talk to Daniel tonight; I have to start going out on missions."
"I talked to him already," she giggled.
"When?" I asked.

TAMBOURINE

"In between kisses," she smiled.
"I did not notice," I smiled back.
"You were too busy with your blond," she laughed.
"Have you ever noticed anything since the day you met her?"

    I walked over to Daniel; he was cleaning his rifle.
"Daniel," I said, "it's time I start earning my living here."
"It's time," he nodded his head.
"I will do whatever you tell me to do," I said.
He put his rifle down.

    "You *Gitanos* have fast and strong hands, don't you?"
"That's why we are good with musical instruments; that's why they call us pickpockets," I smiled.
"You will learn the art of explosives. From now on you will be Enrique's shadow. Everything he tells you to do you will do."
He picked up his rifle and continued cleaning it.

    Enrique was standing behind me, brushing a horse. He smiled and waved to me, aware that we were talking about him.
"When do I start?" I asked.
"Don't get too excited. Explosives are a complicated business." "We lost three guys because the bombs exploded too early in their hands," said Daniel.
I was quiet. If Pablo and Henri could do it, I would be able to do it.
"Tonight we are bombing a bridge; you will shadow

Enrique and watch what he is doing."

"And the girls?" I asked. "They are sick of cooking."
"The girls," he sighed. "Ho, your cousin Ninet is quite a girl; she boils my blood that *Gitana*!" He looked at Ninet swaying her hips walking by.
"She is quite a girl," I agreed. "She has no fear. It's a shame to waste her in the kitchen."
"If she can shoot as well as she can dance the flamenco and as well as she can make love to me, I will bring her on missions."

"And Miriam"? I asked.
"She is too young; not possible!" he said.
"I saw her under pressure. She is tough," I said. "Please give her a chance."
"If I let her come, I have to let your other cousin Dina come. It's getting to be too much; I will not do it." He was firm; I knew I would not be able to change his mind. "Keep that pretty blond back here. She will keep you warm when you come back shaking from the missions," he laughed.

"What did he say," asked Ninet when I got back to our tent. "We going out with them tonight on a mission," I said.
She smiled. "He is crazy about me."
"Your father will not like it much; he always said you should marry my brother Pablito," I said.
"Pablito never loved me. All these *Gitano* arrangements are so stupid. It's like you were supposed to marry Dina. You don't love her, so why should you

do that?"

      Inside the tent Miriam was curled up under the blanket. She did look like an angel, her golden hair falling on her face. I lay down by her and touched her hair, moving it away from her eyes. I kissed her lightly on her lips; she opened her blue eyes and smiled.

      I smiled back and moved my finger slowly on her face, "You are the most beautiful creature I have ever seen," I said.
She reached for me, "Hold me, Michel."
I held her close against me; I could feel her hands passing over my hair. She reached for me, kissing my lips. I closed my eyes. There was a rainbow around me with ten thousands colors, the most beautiful colors I had ever seen. And then it all came together, the knowledge that there would be a better world for us.

Miriam

      By the middle of June I was blowing bridges and railways all by myself. The explosives were an art; Daniel was right. It fascinated me; you could be in the teeth of the angel of death in an instant with the slightest mistake.

      There was a black angel standing on one side of me, waiting to grab me when I would tie the bombs on the bridges, hanging halfway in the air, and on the other side was the Black Madonna watching me with her sad smile, her hands over my hands like two black doves.

It was a constant war between the angel of death and the Madonna. Enrique taught me how to make a bomb from the most common materials. I learned quickly all there was to learn about the various combinations of liquids. There was always the danger that I would mix the wrong portions of the materials that I had, and the whole thing would blow up in my face.

Germany received much of its oil from Romania. After the bombing of the Danube, Austria opened its oil fields. Germany had gotten 12 million barrels from them by 1944 and even this was not enough. We were mixing special explosives to blow up the shipments of oil that were coming into France from Germany by trains and trucks. The less oil they would have, the less would be their ability to fight.

I also had to learn how to calculate precisely the time interval between detonations. I had to know how to determine the appropriate nerve centers of the electric systems.
Enrique was proud of me.
"I had to go to college for four years to study mathematics and chemistry in order to understand what I am doing here, and you come along never having even been in school in your life and you get all this in few days. If you survive this war, you will go places, my Gypsy!"

TAMBOURINE

In the two weeks that we were working together we sabotaged two major railways and three important bridges. The Germans started to move forces to the north after the Allies landed there; we were going further south to assist with the upcoming landing of the Allies on the southern coast.
We would move from camp to camp, sometimes being housed by people who just wanted to be part of the resistance.
It was during this time that Miriam became sick. At first it was a high fever, and she would be vomiting nonstop. We brought a doctor from one of the villages. "It's a stomach virus; just give her boiled water and she will get over it," he said.

She was in pain for days. My aunts would go into the woods to pick berries and certain plants, and they would mix various potions and try them on her, but Miriam got worse. My cousins Ninet and Dina would sit by her and cover her body with cool wet rags to try and get the fever down.

Dina especially would not leave her sight for a minute. She felt terrible for having treated Miriam so badly ever since we left the monastery, calling her names and making her feel unwanted. Now she wanted to make it up to the poor gentle soul, to release her guilt feelings. She would kneel in front of Miriam crying and praying to the Saint Sara for her recovery.

I would lie by my Miriam watching her wasting away. She would open her eyes from time to time, gazing at me as if she did not know me. We would move from camp to camp, and everywhere we went we would find a different doctor with a different opinion.

At last we got to Montpellier; we had no choice but to put her in the hospital. I would not be allowed to sit by her bed for fear that the Germans would recognize me as a Gypsy. But Daniel went every day to see her and get reports from the doctors. Miriam was suffering from a severe and unidentified bacterial infection. The doctors were helpless; they tried everything. At the beginning of July Daniel and Ninet came to me with grim faces.

"She is dead," I said.
Daniel put his arm on my shoulder. "They will bury her in a Jewish cemetery."
I walked to the hill overlooking the road to Marseille; I could still taste her lips on my lips, her legs around my waist opening the gates to heaven for me. The chills were rocking my body. I spread my arms to her image, her gold hair her sea blue eyes. "Miriam" and the tears came flowing hot from my eyes, "Miriam."

A few days later we came to Marseille. It was obvious that the German presence was becoming reduced. Many of their troops had left. The locals had become very defiant and many had joined the resistance. Over one third of the old quarter of the city had been destroyed in a massive clearance project aimed at reducing opportunities for resistance members to hide and operate out of the densely populated old buildings.

TAMBOURINE

I would go to my missions ready to die; I could not get over Miriam's death. If not for little Nicola and my responsibility to my aunts I would already be dead. I had so much despair and anger in me I did not know what to do with it. Sometimes in my sleep I would see Miriam coming toward me naked, her golden hair covering her shoulders down to her legs. A bubble of some kind would be covering her from head to toe, and she would be trying to get out of it. I could see her mouth open trying to breathe, trying to scream, but the covering would not let her be heard.

She would step back and forth trying to tear the bubble with her fingers, but it wouldn't tear. She would look at me desperately, "Help me!" I could hear her screaming silently, but my feet would freeze to the ground, not being able to move.
I would wake up screaming, full of sweat. Dina and Ninet would wash my shaking body with cold towels. *"Tranquil Michel, tout tre' bien"* (calm down Michel, everything is fine).

I would look at the blue sea, thinking that in a matter of minutes I could be crossing the border to Spain. I would look from there to the French side and be happy. I would never come back here. But I was the only explosives expert now. Enrique had been taken to another unit. I could set up the bombs now in a matter of minutes. The big packages of wires looked like snakes tangled in each other. Daniel used to sigh, "How the hell can you make sense out of all this?" I would separate the wires in minutes and know exactly which one went where.

My hair grew long. I collected it in a pony tail. The women would wash my hair with soap and sea water. It always tasted like salt. I became very dark from the hot sun, and grew tall and muscular. Daniel warned me again and again not to be seen. "You look like you invented the Gypsies."

"They are not looking for Gypsies any more. All of our people are dead," I would answer bitterly, "No more Jews either!"
I would walk among the abandoned half-destroyed homes. Nobody would pay attention to me or notice me at all. People were walking around like ghosts, and the Germans were making their last plans for retreat.

Dina

My aunts had become depressed and did not talk much. Dina would be silent most of the time. She felt responsible for Miriam's death since she had been so jealous of her and used to come up with any idea she could to make her suffer. She was not even able to look in my eyes any more, being so ashamed and angry at herself. I kept telling myself I should talk to her, calm her down, but could not bring myself to do it.

I would take my guitar and strum with Nicola

TAMBOURINE

by the fire, the hand clapping bringing some life back to my sour heart.

*"I can hear the wagon
Of my childhood
Moving along slowly.
It brings me to my family.*

*"They took me away
From my beloved souls.
My mother is crying,
My father is sore,
My brothers and sisters
Running barefoot in the fields
Singing and dancing
Crying for mother.*

*"I was cursed,
I was torn away from my family,
My mother is crying,
My father is sore,
I will take the wagon
And go look for them.*

*"Nobody can stop me
From being so stubborn,
I so want to go
Back to my loved ones
And sleep on the hay
To the sound of the guitars."*

    My aunts would cry and move their bodies to the melody, letting their fingers move and twist, crying

their cry. Dina and Ninet would sway their hips slowly, stamping their feet as hard as they could, turning around the men, brushing against them.
The men would get up and start dancing.

Dina would sneak a look at me and give a sad smile as if apologizing to me. I would strum the guitar and sing, pretending I did not see her, a wave of anger coming upon me.

I missed my father, my mother, my talks with Antonio, my strong wonderful brother Andres. I missed Paco my cousin, with whom I had grown up as with a twin brother, the laughter, the secrets we shared. The big fiestas by the open fire, the huge pots boiling over, the simple wagons, the smell of the hay, these were all I wanted, all I was longing for.

I was weeping. Nicola touched me.
"Mackito, don't cry, we soon will see *Papi*."
I stopped playing and put the guitar aside, and took him in my arms.
"Remember the story Anna told you and Gisele about the little Gypsy girl?"
Nicola nodded his head, "Rosa! The girl's name was Rosa! *Como abuella*!"
"*Como abuella*!" I agreed.
"You know the story? Anna told you?" Nicola's eyes shone.
"I know the end of the story," I said.
"Tell me," Nicola opened his big dark eyes, the joy gleaming from them.

TAMBOURINE

"It was a very bad time for the Gypsies; there was not enough food. 'Go to the palace,' Rosa's mother said, 'At least you will have enough food to eat'.
'But mother,' she said, 'I don't want to leave you.'
'You go and the Black Madonna will watch over us until we meet again,' said her mother.

"Sadly Rosa left her house and went to the palace. She walked up to the palace gates. The guards stopped her, 'Where are you going, *Gitana*?'
'The prince told me to come to the palace to dance for him,' she said.
The guards looked at each other, and started laughing, 'Why would the prince invite a dirty *Gitana* like you to the palace?'

"Rosa started crying, but the guards would not let her in. She sat down on the ground and waited. The prince's head servant passed by and saw Rosa sitting and crying. He recognized her right away and asked, 'Why are you crying?'
'The guards will not let me in,' she said.
The head servant commanded the guards to open the gates, and he took Rosa into the palace.

"The palace was huge; everything was made out of marble and gold. Rosa looked around with her mouth wide open. How could a place like this exist while her family was living in an old wagon and sleeping on old hay? Her heart was beating fast and her head was spinning. She held on to the head servant to steady herself. He saw that she was weak, and he brought her to the kitchen. He sat her down and served her chicken and soup and fresh baked bread. Rosa had never seen so much food in her life.

"She took few bites and then asked, 'May I take the rest for my family?'
The servant laughed, 'You are not going back to your family; you will stay here from now on.'
They were trying to make her eat some more, but Rosa just could not eat; all she was thinking about was her hungry family.

"Some of the servants washed her and gave her a nice new dress to wear. Rosa was taken to the prince's chamber. The prince was waiting for her on his golden chair.
'I have been waiting for you Rosa.'
'Why do you look sad, my prince?' asked Rosa.
'My mother the queen is very sick. The doctors say they cannot find the reason why. I am afraid my mother will die if we don't find a cure for her.'

"'Take me to the queen,' said Rosa.
The prince took her to the queen's room. She was lying in her bed, pale and weak, her eyes closed.
'Madre,' said the prince, 'I brought you the little *Gitana* I told you about.'

"The queen opened her eyes and looked at little Rosa.
'Baila para mi' (dance for me) she whispered to her.
Rosa started clapping her little hands and stamping her feet. The prince handed her a tambourine and said,

TAMBOURINE

'This is yours.'
Little Rosa started tapping the tambourine against her thighs and raised her other hand, letting her fingers fly like birds.

"The queen smiled now, and sat up watching Rosa dancing. Rosa started swaying her hips and wiggling her body in the most beautiful flamenco dance she had ever performed. Everyone was mesmerized; a smile came upon the faces of all the servants. The king started dancing too, moving around little Rosa with his huge stomach, clapping his hands to the rhythm. The queen started laughing, until she had tears of joy coming out of her eyes. Rosa started singing now.

"'Eh' le' le' le' le'
Le' le' la
I love you so
I love you so

"Eh' le' le' le' le'
Le' le' le' le' la
Give me your hand
Merry my soul
I sing to my Gitano
I dance for my love,

"E' le' le' le' le'
Le' le' le' le' la
Le' le' le' le' le'
Le' le' le' le' la'"

"Everybody was clapping and dancing with little Rosa now. The queen got out of her bed. She was cured.
The prince was so happy, he asked Rosa, 'What can I do for you, to make you happy? My only wish now is that you will be happy.'
Rosa answered him *'No puedo estar feliz sin mi familia'* (I cannot be happy without my family).

"The prince brought all Rosa's family to the palace. They had plenty to eat from then on, and the queen issued a new command to her people, to respect and take care of all the Gypsies, to make sure they all had plenty to eat and nice warm homes to live in.

"'Gypsies are as valuable as the finest doctors because they bring joy and cure for the heart with their music and dance. The Gypsies are the rarest of the treasures of Spain,' said the queen.
Rosa was playing her tambourine and dancing and singing happily forever after."

"Did she marry the prince?" Asked Dina.
I started laughing; it was the first time I had laughed since Miriam died.
"That's not the point, you stupid cow," said Ninet.
"Yes, but did she?" Dina asked again, her eyes all dreamy.
I laughed so hard my stomach hurt. Daniel and the rest started laughing too. There was no limit to Dina's strange mind. Dina got angry and left upset and Ninet kept laughing, imitating her angry walk.

TAMBOURINE

I went to Dina's tent. She was sitting on a stone, sobbing. I touched her shoulder, "Stop crying, Gitana," I said.
"They always laugh at me!"
"Well you can be very ridiculous sometimes; you must admit it," I smiled.
"It's been nothing but misery ever since we left the monastery," she said in anger.

"That's because you chose to be miserable," I said.
"You think I did not see you and Miriam together? You have any idea how much it hurt me?"
I was silent.
"And then she died after I prayed and begged the Black Madonna for her death. I am the one who killed her." She was crying hard now.

"You did not kill her; nobody killed her. She got sick, very sick. It was nobody's fault. The doctors in the hospital told Daniel that the bacteria were in her body long before we left the monastery," I said.
She wiped her tears. "So you don't hate me, Mackito?"
"How can I hate a silly Gitana like you?" I smiled.

She smiled now too, wiping her tears with her sleeve. "I was behaving like a stupid baby," she said.
"That is your special beauty," I said.
"You are a beautiful girl. When you get to Spain you will find yourself a nice *Gitano* who will love you to death."
"It will never be you, *Mackito*?"

"No," I said, "take me out of your heart. I will never bring you happiness. I don't love you like that, but I will always be there for you. I am your cousin." She nodded her head silently. Dina was stubborn, but she understood now. I could see it in her eyes; she would start thinking differently from now on.

Soy un Gitano

When August came the heat was unbearable. On August 15 the Americans landed. General O'Daniel's 3rd division put ashore on the southernmost beaches on the St. Tropez peninsula. Dahlquist's 36th Division headed for the Frejus Gulf on the eastern portion of the landing area, and the Eagles' 45th division employed a series of small stands in between, near the town of Ste. Maxim.

The Germans hardly fought back. We were blowing up their bridges and they did not have much artillery or gasoline left. They had lost most of their lines of communication. On the morning of the 15th the armor-supported American infantry eliminated almost all the resistance of the Germans.

TAMBOURINE

Between the 17th and 19th of August the two American divisions pushed west and the German leadership finally ordered a general withdrawal from France. Instructions came from Berlin. All units had to withdraw except for one unit on the border with Italy. On August 19 the American army seized and freed Marseille and Toulon.

We were dancing with the locals, drinking and singing for four nights. We ate so much our stomachs nearly exploded. We were hugging each other; the seven of us had survived. I would put Nicola on my shoulders and run around with him shouting joyfully our freedom. Jean Paul would climb into my arms and I would whirl him around as fast as I could, dancing and singing.

We were drunk from happiness.
"Now it's time to cross the border," I said to my family. "We made a promise to meet all the family in Andalucía; we should not waste any time."

We started to say our goodbyes. Most of the young partisans went back inland to look for their families and reunite with them. We would sit outside watching the endless lines of German prisoners being marched along by the Americans. We were not even able to feel any anger, just emptiness and disgust.

Some of the locals would throw stones and spit on them and some would attack them physically or yell and scream their frustrations at them. But for us it was just rows and rows of human scum, a useless stream of insignificant stupidity. There was absolutely no anger left in me, no will to take revenge or to even look at them.

On the boat crossing the border we were looking everywhere to see if could find any of our family. Aunt Claire kept saying, "They are here, I can feel it in my bones." It was a chaotic atmosphere; there were thousands of people streaming back and forth across the border.

We learned that many Jews and other refugees who had fled to Spain at the beginning of the war were now coming back to France in the thousands to search for their families.
Other thousands were going from France to Spain to look for relatives.

Nicola was squeezing my hand nervously at the sight of so many people around him on the ferry. I gazed at the blue water with a knot in my throat, not knowing what to feel any more.

All my anger was gone; I was tired of rage. I held Nicola in my arms kissing him from time to time; he is going to grow up to be a tough man, I thought, with all he has seen in his short life.

We walked into the bus station and went to buy tickets.
"Aqui esta el autobus para ir a Andalucía"? I asked

(where is the bus to Andalucía?).
The man handed me seven tickets and pointed to the bus.
"Soy un Gitano," I said (I am a Gypsy).
The man looked at me puzzled.
"Soy un Gitano, estoy orgulloso de ser Gitano" (I am a proud Gypsy).
The man gave me a look and shook his head; he had no idea what it meant for me to say it out loud.

Stop the bus!

By September we had our own apartments. Aunt Carlita started working in a bakery, and we were all enrolled in schools. The little ones started talking Spanish like natives. The community helped a lot. People brought us furniture and pots and pans.

Daniel came from France and joined us; Ninet was to be his wife. He came with some money and bought a little house for Ninet and himself, not far from us. We posted messages everywhere looking for our family, and Ninet swore that she would not get married until we found them.

The morning of September 18 was a sunny one. We were boarding the bus as usual to go to school. As the bus drove into town Nicola pulled my arm and

pointed at the window. "Anna," he said.
It was Anna. It was Anna in the flesh! I had difficulty breathing suddenly. I held on to Nicola. My chest hurt. I stared out the window in disbelief.

Anna was wheeling a stroller. Her blond curls were rocking from side to side. My eyes widened. Right behind her was my sister Rachelle, my own beloved sister Rachelle, pushing another stroller. I jumped up and screamed, "Stop the bus!"
The driver slammed the brakes in surprise. We ran to the door, Nicola, Dina, Jean Paul and me, and then we ran toward them. We were running to heaven.

Part Four: Lucia

(Madrid – 2005)

TAMBOURINE

The suit I was wearing was sitting a bit loose on me. It was too hot anyway for this time of year to be wearing a suit. I was walking into my office. *"Teresa, Café"* I said to my secretary. I took my jacket off and sat on my chair, looking down from the twentieth floor of my office building over Madrid.

Things had gone well for us; the movie industry in Spain was booming. I had nothing to complain about. Bruno came in with a bunch of papers, *"Como esta usted, Lucia?"* (How are you Lucia). I stretched on my chair enjoying his hungry look at the sight of my breasts pushing out of my shirt. "Too early in the morning, Bruno," I smiled.

"You going away this weekend?" he asked, his eyes still lingering on my breasts.
"Andalucía," I said, my grandmother's birthday."
"Oh, oh," said Teresa coming in with coffee, "they are going to drive you crazy there. Another whole year passed and you still did not get married."

I had to smile. Being thirty-two and not married yet, I was definitely considered a problem within my family. My two younger sisters had been married already for six years now, and had had three babies between the two of them. "You are married to your job. Your work will not be there for you when you grow old and need a companion," my mother would say to me. "Find a nice man and get married, Lucia, the clock is ticking."

Nily Naiman

I liked my little apartment on the top floor of a high rise building. Everything was simple there. I could see the entire city from my balcony. My neighbors were pleasant but reserved. My lovers would come and then leave as I pleased. Marriage was not for me. I liked to be my own master; whenever a man started being too possessive, I would end the relationship right then and there.

Newspapers were spread everywhere, and I could relax with my music and my books. Mama would come every once in a while to bring me something "normal" to eat, and would make a show of "I am going to die" at the sight of the mess.

Sometimes my cousin Norine would come to share a bite with me. Norine was the best cook; she was the youngest child of my Aunt Pilar, who was great aunt Nadine's daughter. She would make her incredible rice dishes and would come with them to eat. "Only here can I eat in peace," she used to sigh. "The kids are driving me crazy at home." I was very close to Norine; she was the only real female friend I had.

We used to sit and discuss our strange family together, trying to figure out all the aunts, uncles, and cousins, and who belonged where. We would get so mixed up after a while that we would start giggling and drop our efforts. Nadine, my great aunt, was married to my great uncle Chico. They were still alive and living in their little apartment in Andalucía. They were still very much in love and would not take their hands off each other.

TAMBOURINE

My whole family was tangled among cousins. Nadine and Chico were cousins, my late great aunt Rachelle had been married to my late great uncle Henri, and my great uncle Paco had been married to my late great aunt Dina. We used to joke that the people in our family were so suspicious of strangers that they wouldn't even fall in love with them. Everything stayed within the family. Anybody else was called an outsider.

My great uncle Michel was now retired in Granada. He had been married to French professor whom he had met at the university where he was teaching. He told me on the day of her funeral that until the day she died the family members called her The French Woman, and never by her name. She always stayed away from family gatherings, feeling that she could never connect with them no matter how hard she tried.

My grandmother Anna was going to have her 81st birthday. Her second husband Pablo had died ten years earlier, which finally provided the opportunity for great uncle Antonio to marry her. He had been married to a Gypsy woman whom he had met after the war, and had had four children with her.

Everybody always knew that he loved my grandmother. His wife died just before Pablo did, and as soon as the mourning period was over, the two got married, looking like a young couple in love.

Nily Naiman

My father Andres was a mix of his late father Andres and my grandmother's light features. Then he got married to my mother, who was a Polish girl and as light as light could be. The result was that all of us came out a mix of a *Gitano* blood in blond and blue eyed bodies.

I never really thought about having *Gitano* blood until I would get into the music. Music transformed me; my body would react to the *Gitano* music as if it had a life of its own. All my childhood my mother would insist that I take ballet and flamenco dance classes. But when I was fourteen I refused to go anymore. I hated the sweaty stuffed studios, packed with ambitious, eager, pushy youngsters who would do anything to be noticed.

In my line of work in the entertainment industry I met a lot of musicians and dancers and would go out with them frequently. I always wound up in the flamenco fiestas where I could wrap the shawl around my hips and let my body fly with the music.

The flamenco was in my *Gitano* blood. My feet would stamp to the music, my hands would start going up, my fingers would wiggle like birds, and I would be in seventh heaven.

Now I was stretching my body on my chair. My office was sitting in a high rise building right in the heart of Madrid; I had become the manager of our entertainment business just a year before. More and

TAMBOURINE

more *Gitanos* were becoming successful. Their lives and music were now one of the most fascinating factors in Spanish entertainment, in movies, shows, and clubs.

Thanks to my work I myself became very interested in my family's history. All of a sudden I found myself telling people that I was part *Gitana,* as if it were some wonder of the world, unlike when I was a little girl. Then I was ashamed of my grandfather Pablo. When my friends used to come the house I would introduce them to my grandmother Anna and try to skip my grandfather since he looked so much like a *Gitano* and I was afraid they would think less of me knowing that had some Gypsy blood in me.

I used to visit with my parents in Andalucía, and could not wait to get back home, always staying away from my cousins and struggling out of my aunts and uncles hugs and kisses.
"They smell," I used to say to my mother. "They are dark and ugly." My mother used to yell at me,
"They are beautiful people; they are your family. How dare you?"

The whole place there in Andalucía looked like a ghetto to me, those ugly apartment buildings that all looked the same, the incredible amount of people squeezed in there, the stink of the cooking, the people hanging around in the streets aimlessly.

The sharp looks of the teenagers at my figure, the couples making out in the streets almost riding on each other genitals, made me say to my grandmother,

"They are shameless, like animals."
"*No hija,*" she would answer, "They are sensual; they are fascinating."

Now since the movie industry had discovered world wide that the life of the *Gitanos* fascinated audiences, to be a *Gitano* had become something special. When my father would say to me,
"*soy Un Gitano estoy orgulloso de ser Gitano*" (I am a gypsy, I am proud to be a gypsy) I would no longer get angry; I would understand what he meant.

"What are you thinking about, boss?" asked Bruno
I shook my head, "*Nada*, I was thinking about my strange family."
"Let me come with you; I've never been to a real authentic Gypsy *fiesta,*" he said.
"If I were not your boss or were ten years younger, Bruno, I would take you with me," I smiled. "But no! You stay in Madrid and mind the phone calls."

Andalucía

When I got to Andalucía it seemed that most of the family members had already arrived. There was an

TAMBOURINE

endless line of cars parked by grandmother's apartment. For the life of me I never understood how all these people could stream into that little apartment every year and find space to even stand up.

There were so many cousins and nieces and nephews I had lost count a long time ago. We would squeeze in every year to drink to grandmother's long life and then go on to great aunt Gisele's and her husband great uncle George's house, which had a very large back yard, and have our fiesta.

I climbed the stairs to the apartment shaking my head, not understanding how grandmother and great uncle Antonio could negotiate those stairs every day at their age. I could hear the noise and the singing flowing out of the apartment.

I was about to enter when a young man who was hurrying up the stairs two at a time stopped by me. "Excuse me; are you going to Anna and Antonio's house?" He asked.
"Yes I am, they live right here."

He was about my age; I was wondering if he was another one of my thousands of cousins. He was dark, his long pony tail gathered on his back with a rubber band. He looked like a typical Gypsy. He was breathing hard from the run.
"Are you family?" he asked.
"I am," I smiled "and you?"
"I am; my father is Nicola. He is Antonio's cousin. And you? Who are you?"

"I am Lucia, Andres' daughter, and Anna is my grandmother."

He shook my hand smiling. "Nice to meet you, cousin. I am Tomas."
"Where have you been all my life?" I asked.
"I live in England. I am a doctor. I went to study medicine in London and stayed there."
"And your wife?" I asked.
"Divorced," he smiled, "didn't work out."

Thank God, I thought to myself. Who would have thought I had such a treasure for a cousin as this one anywhere in the world?

We entered the apartment and my mother gave me an angry look. "You are late, Lucia," she said.
"It's my fault," said Tomas, "I kept her from coming in."
Uncle Nicola came to greet us. "You have grown, Lucia," he said.
"Grown old," I said.
"You look beautiful and young," he kissed me on my cheeks.
"I see you met my young *Hijo*."
"I did," I smiled. "Uncle Nicola, who else did you hide from me?"
"He is a doctor, busy like you. We hardly ever see him. You youngsters are always busy with work," he sighed.

I went to my grandmother and kissed her. I found myself wishing that I would be looking like her at her age. "You look beautiful grandmother."

TAMBOURINE

"You too," she smiled. "You know, I am thankful to you, for coming all the way from Madrid.
"I am honored, *Abuela,*" (grandmother) I said.

I kissed Antonio. "You look younger every time I see you, Tio *Antonio.*" (Uncle Antonio).
"Your grandmother is keeping me young," he smiled, giving his wife a lively look. "I wish for you to find a man who will love you like I love your grandmother," he said, his eyes getting watery.

My grandmother Anna was about the only non-Gypsy in the family, who was not called "damn outsider." She had earned her status fair and square during the war. I had heard many times how she had saved the family again and again from becoming part of the unknown numbers of Gypsies who were murdered in the "*Parrajmos*", (the Gypsy great devouring).

Grandmother Anna was a Gypsy soul in the body of a Jew, they used to say. She danced like a Gypsy, talked like a Gypsy, loved like a Gypsy, and was brave like a Gypsy. That brings you the honorary title of Gypsy.

The best stories I heard from my aunt Gisele, who was the closest one to my grandmother. They were so close that there was never too much talking between the two of them. They would sign to each other, or even just look at each other and guess one another's thoughts.

Nily Naiman

"One time," Gisele told me, "as pregnant as she was, she slit four Nazis' throats in five seconds when we were hiding in the church. The pigs came at the end of the war to look for art treasures to steal from the church. Anna ambushed the bustards and slit their throats. Then Antonio and Pablo shot the rest of them dead. All the Jews that were hiding with us got killed by the bastards, but we were saved thanks to Anna."

For hours she would sit and tell the stories about my grandmother, holding close to her heart the old tambourine that grandmother had given her when she was a little girl. Then my grandmother would smile and say,
"Para de hablar tanto." (Stop talking so much), and Gisele would start tapping her tambourine and everybody would dance.

The relatives kept pouring in, and my cheeks were hurting from kisses. We all raised our cups and wished happy birthday to grandmother. We were to move now to Gisele's house for the fiesta.
"Come with us," my cousin Norine was pulling my hand.
"She is coming with me," I heard Tomas voice behind me. He had the most pleasant voice; you could not mistake it for another.

Norine looked at him smiling. "And you are?"
He smiled back and shook her hand, "Your cousin Tomas, I am Nicola's son."
Norine raised her hand. "My god, you are the British doctor, aren't you? You look just like a *Gitano* from

TAMBOURINE

next door."
"I am just a *Gitano* from next door" he laughed. Norine backed up. "She is all yours, cousin," and pushed her elbow in my side. "You are on to the cousins thing, aren't you!" she whispered to me.

We went together to his car; I could feel the looks of the family on my back. I laughed to myself. Now the gossip and the anticipation as to what would happen between the two of us would be at its peak. The heads turned and the eyes were following us. Their eyes were narrowed in interest. The old maid might yet be saved, they thought.

Tomas asked, "Know the way to Aunt Gisele?" He turned on the engine.
"Follow the rest of them," I said, "Andalucía is small enough."

"I used to come here with my parents all the time when I was a kid. My father, being in the army, was hardly ever home. My mother used to send me here for all my school vacations. I hated it," he said.
"Me too," I smiled, "I hated coming here; I always felt that it smelled bad and it that it was a miserable place. I missed out on a lot, I was such a brat."

"And I felt that the boys were so strong. I was always scared I would get beat up," he laughed. "One time, when I was twelve, my cousins took me to a girl. They told her, "You make a man out of this brat and we will buy you dinner."
"Did she?" I asked.

"She did," he laughed, "She had to work very hard, the poor *Gitana,* for her meal. I was scared to death; it was a real trauma for me, my first sexual experience."

We walked together to Aunt Gisele's back yard. As every year, the place was full of tables and benches. The trays of food kept coming out of the kitchen. I started walking away but Tomas held my arm.
"You're not to leave me!"
"You scared?" I asked.
"Scared that you are going to abandon me!"
"I will be back," I smiled.
He let go of my arm and looked at me right in the eyes.
"Promise, cousin!"
"I promise," I smiled, and walked away.

Norine was pulling my shoulder waving her finger at my nose,
"Be careful, Lucia."
"Of what, Norine?"
"*No soy un Idiota* (I am not an idiot) Lucia."
"I don't know what you're talking about."

"Remember this," she said, "He is your cousin and he is Uncle Nicola's son and he is a Gypsy."
"So?"
"So be careful. He cannot be just one of your lovers. You are going to have the whole family on your back."
I smiled going into the kitchen.
"You like him, don't you," she said.
"He is fine," I said, blushing.

My mother handed me a tray.

TAMBOURINE

"That man, Nicola's son, anything you want to tell me?"
"Nothing to tell; he is a nice guy."
My mother sighed and looked at Norine. "You think everybody here is blind? We all saw how you two were looking at each other."
"You always exaggerate things. He is just a nice guy. Besides, we are cousins."
"Since when are you interested in your cousins?" my mother snapped at me.

I brought the tray out to the yard; the place was packed with people and there were already the sounds of guitars and violins. I came to my uncle Michel and hugged him. "I missed you, *Tio.*"

He kissed my cheeks "You are my favorite niece, you know."
"I bet you tell this to everyone," I smiled.
"You are going to let me dance at your wedding before I die?"
"Ho god, *Tio,* not you too."

"An old Jewish saying is that it is not good for a person to be on his own."
"*Tio* Michel, there is an old Gypsy saying that if you are not living with someone you truly love, you are as good as dead."

Tomas appeared out of nowhere.
"I saw that you met my little nephew," Uncle Michel smiled.

Nily Naiman

I looked at Tomas. "Is this your favorite *Tio* too?"
"I knew we had a lot in common," he answered.

Tio Michel was pleased and passed his eyes to *Tio* Nicola. "We will have a reason to dance soon," he slapped his shoulder.

I lowered my head blushing. It seemed my fate was sealed. I might not be coming home to my empty apartment to enjoy my privacy much longer.

Tomas took my arm. "May I bring you something to eat?"
I could see the looks all around the yard. Necks were stretching and heads turning after us. I smiled leaning on him. "I will go with you," I said.
We walked over to the buffet table. "We are making news here today in Andalucía," he whispered in my ear.

"How come I never met you?" I asked. "This is so unfair, passing all these years not ever seeing you."
"We probably met hundreds of times as kids but did not notice each other, being so wrapped up in ourselves," he said. "You are right, it is a shame, but we can make up for it now."

Gisele started tapping her tambourine. Everyone stopped talking right away as usual. Gisele's tambourine was very old; she had gotten it as a present from my grandmother in 1942. My family members believed that it had magical powers. There were legends told of how again and again, thanks to the tambourine, people were saved from murder, diseases

TAMBOURINE

and sadness. The men and women started clapping their hands and were soon joined by the guitars and violins.

"My love is finally here,
I am so happy,
Strange how much
I am ready to forget.
I was in misery until now,
But you are finally here.
I am so happy
le le le le le le le la
Le le ele le le le le le la"

Tio Antonio was stamping his feet and approached grandmother, who now got up from her seat and held the edge of her skirt. Her hands rose and her fingers began moving like birds flying in heaven.

My flamenco teacher used to yell at us to move our fingers properly, "*como paloma* "(like a dove) she used to say. Watching my grandmother I had never seen more beautiful finger movements. "*Como paloma,*" I mumbled.

Tomas was standing by me, his eyes fixated on the two, and then he also said, "*como paloma.*" I looked at him and started moving my hips; I raised my hand, moving my fingers, turning my body around him. He was staring at me, and then in a sudden decision began to stamp his heels.

He could dance very well, the *Gitano* doctor. He

was sensual and sexy, the way he was brushing around my body. I had never felt so attracted to a man in my life as I was attracted to him. The faces all turned to me; I caught a glimpse of my mother's worried face and of *Tio* Nicola and *Tio* Michel whispering to each other. Norine was shaking her finger toward me, but then I did not see anybody anymore.

We were alone there, Tomas and me, Gisele hitting her magic tambourine, the music, the clapping, the foot stamping, and our eyes looking into each other's souls.

His face came close to my face; we were dancing the flamenco around each other shoulder to shoulder now, his hands clapping to the side of his head.
"Holy saints," I whispered against my will, to my surprise. It was not me. It's somebody else, it's the damn magic tambourine, I was thinking. It's the music; it's the *Gitano* spell that came always with flamenco.

I stopped dancing. Thank God he had not heard me, I was thinking. "I am going outside for some air," I said.
Everybody was dancing now. My head spun. I felt stupid and ridiculous. I walked out of the gate and stood leaning on the wall of the house, breathing in deeply.

The gate opened. I closed my eyes. If it's Tomas coming after me I will be his forever, I thought. If it's not him, I will forget about this whole stupid thing and go back to my old cozy life.

"Lucia," I heard his beautiful voice; I kept my eyes closed. I could feel his warm breath on my face. "Lucia," he said again, and then our lips met.

Epilogue

The *Parrajmos* (the great devouring), the holocaust of the Romani people, the Gypsies, was rooted in hatreds that preceded the Second World War. For hundreds of years harsh measures had been taken against Gypsies in Europe. In Germany they were hunted for sport as animals, and huntsmen would return proudly displaying the severed heads that they had taken as souvenirs. Beginning in 1890 many European countries passed a variety of laws restricting "the Gypsy filth", placing limits on their interactions with the general population and prohibiting them from engaging in trades or owning land.

Upon coming to power the Nazis reinstituted anti-Gypsy laws that had been on the books since the Middle Ages. But with their racist ideology they soon moved beyond those statutes. The Nazis established the Racial Hygiene and Criminal Biology Research Unit. This institution concluded that Gypsies were sub-humans.

On June 11, 1941, three hundred teenage Gypsy boys were sent to a camp in Austria were they were used to test the effectiveness of the gas chambers. None survived

More then 3000 Gypsy prisoners died in French camps from disease and starvation, and almost 13.000 were sent just from Drancy in France to death camps such as Auschwitz where they were gassed upon arrival. Other transit camps in France from which Gypsies were sent to their deaths included Noe, Gurs, Recebedou, and others.

It is estimated that by the end of the war the Nazis and their minions had murdered seventy to eighty per cent of the Gypsy population of Europe.

TAMBOURINE

Approximately 675,000 of these deaths were registered, but many more went unrecorded.

At the Nuremberg trials no representatives of the Gypsies were called to bear witness. No war crimes reparations have been paid to the Roma as a people.

Nily Naiman

www.ingramcontent.com/pod-product-compliance
Ingram Content Group UK Ltd.
Pitfield, Milton Keynes, MK11 3LW, UK
UKHW041409180426
11947UKWH00007B/30